I0617742

Russian Uprising

S.R.Claridge

Global Publishing Group

Global Publishing Group

Copyright © 2011 by S.R.Claridge

Printed in the United States of America

First trade edition: November 2011

10 9 8 7 6 5 4 3 2 1

ISBN 978-0-9898467-2-1

Special thanks to God, Global Publishing Group, an
incredible team of editors, (Cash, Jerrye, Gary, Matt, and
Beth) and to my family and friends for their constant
love and support.

~

A complete list of books by S.R.Claridge is at the back of
this book.

For previews and information about the author, visit
AuthorSRClaridge.com or find her on Facebook.

CHAPTER 1

Kristen towel dried her blonde hair and wrapped herself in the complimentary, white cotton hotel robe. Stepping outside the bathroom, she felt his steely blue eyes drink her in from across the room. He reached for her as she passed by, uttering breathless desire in his native Russian tongue.

"Thomas Boglevich," she pushed his hands away, "is sex all you think about?" She gave a disgusted sigh, picked up her clothes from the bed and returned to the bathroom.

"When you walk around in only a towel what do you expect me to think about?" He ran his fingers over his square jaw line, lustfully eyeing her.

She poked her head outside the door, "I expect you to focus on more important things, like your meeting with Scotrovi." She flipped her hair back and forth to get rid of any excess water and combed it straight.

"Can't help it," he appeared behind her, his square, six foot stature filling the bathroom doorway. He wrapped his arms around her waist, pulling her against him. "I am unable to think of anything but your beauty. I have waited a long time to have you." Brushing her hair from one side of her neck, he kissed tenderly behind her ear. "I was patient while you played with Stefano."

5

His jaw tensed and a scowl formed on his thin lips. "Stefano," he seethed.

"Calm down," she turned to face him. "You know he was just part of the plan and meant nothing to me." She ran her fingers down the side of his face. "You are the man I have always wanted." He leaned down to kiss her, but she squirmed from his grasp.

"Дразните!" He grunted in Russian and frowned. "Why do you tease me? After all I have done for you, what more would you have me do?"

"For now, I'd have you hide your feelings for me as well as you hid your identity and accent from Giovanni all this time." He reached for her again but she spun on her heels and slapped his face. "Focus on the plan," she hissed, her eyes narrowing with anger. "I won't let my father's death be in vain because you have become distracted by desire. We will succeed at taking down Giovanni and Salvatore, and then," her voice softened and she kissed her index finger and ran it seductively across his bottom lip, "you and I will celebrate."

"And then I get to kill Stefano?"

Kristen's eyes lit with an evil smile. "Yes, you get to kill Stefano and I get to kill Angel."

Thomas grinned, pulling her close. "And then we celebrate."

When he left the room, Kristen flipped her head upside down and blew her hair dry with a handheld blower. She felt a small twinge of guilt, as it was obvious that

Boglevich had real feelings for her and she was merely using him. It wasn't her choice to string him along. He was her dad's pawn first. Her dad, Denarius, also known as Denny, was the one who strategically placed him inside Giovanni's organization where he could gain information and later help Kristen escape the Towers unnoticed. Her dad hand-selected Boglevich because he was one of the few Bratva members fluent in English and able to completely hide his Russian accent. He could also speak Italian and German. Then, by arranging the biggest FBI mob bust in New York history, her dad ensured the detainment of Giovanni's men by the Feds, leaving Giovanni short-handed. Simultaneously, he attacked the Maratinzano family in Chicago, kidnapping Giovanni's sister, Olga and Angel's mother, Sophia; forcing Giovanni to quickly hire new men, which was something he rarely did. As expected, Giovanni hired Thomas Boglevich and her dad's plan ran like clockwork; that is, until Angel got in the way. Ever since watching Angel gun down her father in Union Station, Kristen was obsessed with carrying out her dad's plan. Regardless of whom she had to string along or what she had to do, she would enact her father's revenge on Giovanni and Salvatore and then make Angel pay with her life.

Flipping her head upright, Kristen shrieked when she caught his enormous reflection in the mirror. He was dressed in black pants, black military style boots, a black t-shirt that clung tightly to his muscular arms and chest, and a solid black jacket with a silver zipper up the front. He was bald and his eyes glistened like onyx. She'd seen him several times before, but his presence always startled her. Maybe it was his sheer girth that frightened her or maybe the fact that she never heard him enter or leave a room. He just suddenly appeared, larger than life.

She turned to face him. "How did you get in here?" He didn't answer. "What do you want?" She snapped. "You already have your orders. Why did you come here?" He silently stared at her, his massive body filling the doorway. "Don't stand there like a big oaf, tell me what you want."

"Clarification," he uttered in his usual deep rasp. The Shark rarely spoke and when he did it was only to say what was absolutely necessary.

"Ha!" She squeezed by him and out of the bathroom. "We've gone over the plan a hundred times." She eyed him up and down. "Your brain obviously doesn't match your brawn," she sarcastically spewed. The words had no sooner left her lips then he grabbed her, pulled off her robe and threw her naked onto the bed. She tried to roll off the other side, but was no match for his strength. He held her down and climbed across her body. "Get off me," she yelled and he clamped his palm over her mouth.

Grabbing a .45 from the back of his waistband, he pressed the barrel to her forehead, instructing her to put her hands above her head and lay still while he duct

8

taped her wrists. He then taped her ankles together and her knees. "Unless you want a bullet in your brain, you'll lay still and answer my questions in a soft, normal tone."

"Why are you doing this? I thought you wanted revenge against Giovanni as much as my father did."

"What I want is clarification." When she was thoroughly taped, he climbed off the bed, sat in a chair and aimed the gun at her. "I came here for clarification and I'm not leaving until I get it."

"Clarification on what?" She struggled against the tape.

"The meeting with Scotrovi." His voice was low and gruff, and his dark eyes, intense.

"Why would I tell you that now? You're obviously not loyal to our plan." Despite being naked, taped and outstretched across the bed, Kristen's determination to follow-through on her father's revenge remained strong.

He calmly pulled a silencer from his jacket pocket and began to attach it to his gun. "You'll tell me because you want to live."

"You're too late," she seethed. "Boglevich has already left to meet Scotrovi."

The Shark let out a gritty chuckle. "If you believe Giovanni would let Thomas Boglevich betray him and get away with it, you are even more naïve than I thought." He shook his head.

"Giovanni doesn't know where to find us," she snipped. "He is concentrating all his efforts on the compound in Iowa. He won't think to look for us right here in Chicago, right under his nose." She squirmed against the tape. "Besides, by the time he knows what hit him, he'll be dead and the Bratva will have total control of the city."

"And you will fly off into the sunset with your millions," he gruffly mocked.

"With my billions," she grinned. "My father's deal with the Russians is worth more money than you or I could ever imagine in our wildest dreams." She looked at him, seduction oozing from her eyes and softening her expression. "You can be a part of all of this." She stared down at her own nakedness. "You can be a part of me."

The Shark chuckled low. "I thought Thomas Boglevich was a part of you?"

"No," she smiled and sensually bit her bottom lip. "He wanted to be but I wouldn't let him. I'll let you."

The Shark stood up and walked closer, pointing the gun at her forehead. "The only thing I want from you is information about the meeting with Scotrovi."

Kristen's eyes hardened. "I told you, you're too late. Boglevich already left to meet him."

"Boglevich isn't meeting anyone. He never made it off the elevator." Kristen's eyes widened and she kicked widely against the duct tape. "Now, I'll ask you one last time, where is the meeting with Scotrovi?"

CHAPTER 2

Angel carried a tray of dirty pint glasses back to the kitchen and set them in the stainless steel sink. "Do you mind putting these in the dish washer for me?" She asked Chase. "I need to get back out there. I can't believe how busy the Pub is tonight."

"Sure thing Boss lady," Chase grinned.

"Stop calling me that."

"Why? It's a two-fold title, you're the boss of Tetterbaum's Pub and you're the Boss of, well, you know. That makes it a cool-ass nickname." Angel rolled her eyes and walked back to the bar. There was no sense arguing with Chase. He was like a hyped up Chihuahua with his military style crew cut and bulgy eyes. His adrenaline was always pumping and it didn't take Angel long to learn that you didn't engage in a conversation with Chase unless you had energy to spare.

All of the bar stools, except for three, were now open and several of the restaurant tables were vacated. Angel wiped down the top of the bar, refilled two glasses with beer, and made small talk with some of the regulars. Mr. Kutis came to the Pub every weeknight around six o'clock and ordered two bourbon and cokes. He worked in some kind of sales, had a wife and six kids, and Angel guessed he probably needed the drinks just to

11

get through the rest of his evening at home. Mr. Malcoraine came in a couple nights a week and always on Sundays. He was an older gentleman, widowed last year, and Angel could see loneliness in his eyes. No matter how busy she was, she made it a point to talk with him whenever he came around. A stranger filled the third stool at the bar. He was in his mid-to-late thirties, had dark hair, brown eyes, olive skin and naturally pink, thin lips. He ordered chilled Vodka, no ice, and nodded a thank you as Angel served him; but he didn't look up or make any attempt at conversation. Some people were like that. They came to the pub just to have a drink and decompress.

Glancing around the restaurant, a sudden uneasiness gripped her. She scanned each table, noticing for the first time, two nicely dressed young men seated at a table near the door. There was nothing unusual about two men in suits sitting at a table alone. Tetterbaum's attracted all types from bikers passing through to bachelors celebrating their last night of freedom, to the boys from the bogatas. It was respected as a place of neutral territory and even considered, because of its quaint charm dating back to the early 1930's, a "unique family dining experience" by the Chicago Tribune. What made her uneasy about these men was the bulge under their coats. She was pretty sure they were armed. They looked to be in their mid-twenties, both wore dark suits, had dark short hair and no facial hair. Angel subtly studied them, ascertaining immediately that they weren't from any of the five Chicago families. She'd never seen them before.

She casually watched them for a few moments, and her uneasiness grew and she felt that all too familiar pit of fear forming in her stomach. They barely spoke to one another and took turns surveying the restaurant with their eyes. One glanced down as his watch and an alarm went off in Angel's head. Something wasn't right and if she'd learned anything the past several months, it was to trust her instincts. Rinsing her hands and wiping them on her apron, Angel excused herself from the small-talk at the bar and walked toward the kitchen to get Chase and her 9mm.

She had just reached the kitchen when she heard the sound of the back door opening and slam shut, followed by a shot. Instinctively she ducked and ran toward Chase as more gunfire filled the air.

"What the hell?" Chase yelled, slamming a clip into his .45 and tossing Angel her 9mm. "Who the hell is shooting?"

"I don't know," she was breathless. "I don't know them. It was two men in dark suits. They were sitting near the door."

All of a sudden a barrage of shots rang out as people screamed and tried to flee the building. "That ain't just two men," Chase quipped. "If it is, they're shooting Uzi's." Another round of bullets soared through the restaurant. "We've got to get out the back,"

Chase hollered. "You go first and I'll cover you down the hallway."

"We can't," she panted. "Someone just came in through the back."

Chase expelled obscenities. "Then we'll have to hold them off here. Help me tip over this table." They both grabbed an end of the stainless steel center table, normally used for food prep, and turned it on its side.

"Will this stop a bullet?" Angel asked, ducking behind the table.

"Hell, I dunno," Chase blurted. "I never shot at a steel table before."

Screams and shots continued to echo through the restaurant and Angel could hear police sirens off in the distance. "Someone called the police," she breathed heavily. "They'll be here soon."

"Listen Boss, unless they get here in the next thirty seconds, it ain't gonna be soon enough." Chase checked his clip again and slammed it shut.

She stared at the wild panic in Chase's eyes, knowing her face probably looked the same. Her heart was pounding so loudly in her ears, she could scarcely concentrate; and then the idea hit her. "Follow me," she blurted, no time to think the idea through. "Hurry!" Angel darted to the back of the kitchen, dove across the floor and reached beneath the stainless steel table in the corner. She felt around for the latch, popped it open and instructed Chase to help her lower the table to the floor. As the table lowered, the hatch to a secret room opened. It was the place Mr. Tetterbaum had hidden his infamous tapes.

Chase gasped. "What the...?"

Angel quickly climbed down into the opening. "Hurry," she said to Chase, who jumped in after her and they both lowered the table back into place. They were unable to lock it from the inside, but unless someone knew of the hiding spot, they would never think to tip over the table in the far back corner.

They ducked below the wall that divided the kitchen from the bar and climbed up into a narrow room between the back of the bar and the back of the kitchen. Angel's heart was beating rapidly in her chest and her throat was dry. Fear-driven adrenaline held all other emotions at bay, as she stood still with the 9mm pointed at the opening. If the hatch opened even the slightest bit, Angel was ready to fire.

Chase glanced around, taking in the room. "This is some cool-ass shit right here," he whispered, and Angel raised her fingers to her lips, motioning him to be quiet. "How'd you find this?"

"Long story," she whispered.

Moments later the screaming and gunshots stopped, which Angel knew probably meant everyone in the restaurant was dead; everyone except the two men in dark suits. She could hear footsteps and voices, though she couldn't make out what they were saying. Chase pressed his ear against the wall that backed up to the bar.

"Can you hear what they're saying?" Angel whispered.

He shook his head. "Even if I could, I don't think they're speaking English."

"What are they speaking?"

Chase shrugged. "Hard to tell through the wall. Sounds maybe German?" He shook his head, "no, maybe more Slavic, like Serbian..."

"Serbian and German?" Angel wrinkled her nose, "they don't have any kind of mob presence here."

"It could be Russian, maybe. I can't really hear what they're saying," Chase pressed his ear harder against the wall and raised his eyebrows.

"Russian?" Angel's mind tried to process. "Why would the Bratva attack us?"

"Hell if I know," his eyes bulged. "Maybe they're pissed about us killing Selovich."

Angel had forgotten about Selovich. He was the helicopter pilot Andrew took out on top the hospital during the rescue mission to save her mom. Selovich had been working for Kristen's dad, Denny, and was a key player in the revenge against her family. "How would anyone know we were the ones responsible for Selovich's death?"

"Dunno, but it sounds like there's a lot of them," Chase exhaled. "How many were out there?"

"I only noticed two, but there could have been more." Angel tried to remind herself to breathe and slow her heart rate down. Logic told her the police would arrive soon. All they had to do was sit tight until then.

"We sure do have some slow-ass cops in this city," Chase blurted in a hushed tone and Angel silently agreed. It did seem to be taking a long time for them to enter the building. "I don't hear the loud-ass sirens no more, so they gotta be right outside."

"If they're outside, why haven't they come in yet?" Angel held her gun steady with one hand and with the other she tucked strands of dark hair behind her ears. She nervously blew her bangs away from her forehead and took a deep breath. Her skin felt clammy.

"Remind me to voice a complaint to Andrew about his slow-ass response time," Chase quipped and then noticed the recording equipment in the corner and made a beeline for it. "What's all this?" Angel gave him a summed up version of the Tetterbaum tapes and his eyes lit up. "You mean you haven't dismantled the surveillance equipment yet?"

"I haven't exactly had time," Angel retorted, feeling a twinge of guilt because she had promised the other bosses it would be removed. "I mean, it's not recording anything. It's turned off."

"So if I turn it on, it will record what's happening out there?" Chase looked at Angel like a kid with a naughty idea.

"Yes," she quietly shrieked, excitement filling her chest. "It will record every room except the storage room." She inched her way closer to Chase and the equipment. "Do you think you can get it turned on?"

Chase grinned. "I've never met anything I can't turn on," he gave a wink. "If you know what I mean."

Angel rolled her eyes. *Even in the face of death the male ego prevails*, she thought.

Chase managed to turn the equipment on and at the very least, guarantee an audio recording. They both sat on the floor, leaning against the back of the bar wall with their guns facing the opening. If anyone lifted the table to come in, they would load him with lead. Even after they heard the police enter the restaurant, Angel and Chase agreed to sit in silence, uncertain as to who could be trusted. After all, Chicago's Finest also bore the dubious title of "most corrupt."

"We'll wait until Andrew arrives," Angel told Chase. "He's the only one who knows about this hiding place. He'll know to look for us here."

"I hope you're right," Chase muttered. "I guess this isn't the best time to tell you I sort-of hate small-ass places."

"What do you mean you sort of hate them?" Angel stared at the beads of sweat forming across Chase's forehead.

"I mean I kinda get claustrophobic and freak out in tight-ass places."

"You're joking, right?" Angel wanted to believe he was kidding, but she could tell he was not. Chase was sweating profusely and breathing heavily, and a hint of crazy had crept into his eyes. She squeezed his arm and spoke softly, "you've got to remain calm and relax and slow your breathing down before you make yourself hyperventilate." He shook his head up and down in acknowledgement, and Angel thought he looked like one of those bobble heads seen in the backs of car windows. "Just breathe," she whispered. "Andrew will be here soon. Just breathe."

Angel wasn't sure how long they'd been in there, but it felt like it was growing hotter and stuffier by the minute and she wasn't sure how much longer she'd be able to keep Chase from freaking out. She debated in her mind whether to crawl out or stay put. *Surely the cops that are here are the good guys; and by good guys I mean the ones working for us. The ones we're paying off.* She shook her head at how traditionally unethical her own ethics had become. *Of course, there's always the off-chance that one of the cops is being paid off by the bad guys and waiting for me to come out so he can finish the job.* She chewed on her left index fingernail and tried to think clearly.

Chase had flopped over on his left side, proclaiming there was more air on the floor. Angel didn't care what position he was in, as long as he stayed quiet and didn't flip out into a claustrophobic rage of insanity. She'd heard horror stories about people suffering claustrophobic attacks and doing crazy things like breaking though windows with their bare hands, and digging through wooden floorboards with their fingernails. She'd never witnessed the onset of Claustrophobia and was hoping to not see it tonight.

By the time the trap door opened and Andrew's voice cut through the silence, Angel and Chase were drenched in sweat. Chase emerged pale and made a beeline for the bathroom. Angel threw her arms around Andrew and buried her face in his chest.

"I knew you had to be in there, Sweetheart," he said, giving her a tight squeeze. "But I didn't feel safe about opening it until everyone else was gone."

Chase gimped back into the kitchen. "How'd you know we didn't escape out the back or something?"

"I didn't know for sure, but I figured you'd have contacted me if you had made it out of the building alive." Andrew ran his hand quickly through his dark brown hair. "When we didn't find you among the bodies, I knew you had to be hiding."

"How'd you know they didn't kidnap us?" Chase slid the .45 back into his waistband.

"Because YOU weren't among the dead," he said to Chase. "No offense."

Chase snorted. "You don't think I'm worth kidnapping?"

Andrew cleared his throat and smirked. "No comment." He turned his attention back to Angel. "Can you tell me what happened?"

Chase and Angel locked eyes as if to say, where do we begin. "Can we get out of here and talk about it?" Angel glanced around the kitchen, noticing the blood splattered on the walls, the tables and the floor. She swallowed hard and fought back the urge to gag.

"Wait," Chase blurted. "I almost forgot the tapes."

"Tapes?" Andrew's eyes widened.

Chase jumped back through the opening and disappeared between the walls, returning with a video and audio tape in his hands. "I'm pretty sure I got the audio to record but I'm not sure about the video," Chase explained. "That's some old-ass equipment."

CHAPTER 3

It was 10:00pm by the time they arrived at the Towers and everyone had convened in the family room to go over the surveillance tapes and try to make some sense out of what had happened. Giovanni sat in the white armed chair in front of the stone washed, white brick fireplace. Angel paced in the corner behind him, chewing on her fingernails. Her mother, Sophia, and grandfather, Salvatore, sat on the couch, while Aunt Olga, looking like Big Bird, in a fuzzy yellow fleece robe and matching fuzzy slippers, waddled back and forth between the kitchen and the family room serving homemade Cannoli and coffee.   Andrew and Chase hooked up the video to a computer screen and set it on the dining room table so everyone could see. Stefano sat on the floor by the fireplace and Tony, who had just arrived, stood next to Andrew and Chase, undoubtedly assessing assailant and motive.

When the equipment was ready to go, Andrew cleared his throat, "Giovanni, maybe it would be a good idea if I watched this first, before showing it to everyone."

"You are concerned about the content?" Giovanni raised his eyebrows.

"Yes sir, I'm concerned about the possible goriness."

Tony piped in, "I think we can all handle it, man."

Andrew licked his lips, as if feeling compelled to say something but not really wanting to say it. "With all due respect, what happened tonight was a massacre and I don't know that the ladies need to see what might be on..."

Angel interrupted him mid-sentence. "We can handle it."

Giovanni gave a nod to proceed and Chase pushed play. Nothing could have prepared Angel for what she was about to witness. By the time she and Chase had thought to turn on the surveillance equipment, all of the restaurant patrons were dead. Mr. Malcoraine took a bullet through the head and lay slumped over the bar. Mr. Kutis took several bullets to the chest and was sprawled on the floor. Her waitress, Valerie, lay face down, a couple feet from the bar. The shooters were walking through the dining area, finishing off anyone who twitched or moaned. Angel tried to force herself to focus on the men in dark suits and not to look at the bodies and the blood, but she couldn't help seeing some familiar faces. A mixture of anger and sadness rose within.

"Those are the two men I saw sitting at the table by the front door," Angel pointed to the screen.

"The shooters," Andrew clarified.

Tony inched closer to the screen. "I don't recognize those guys. They're not brotherhood."

"Not our brotherhood anyway," Andrew added.

Chase paused the tape and zoomed in until he had a clear picture of the gun held by one of the men. "See that," he pointed to the gun. "That's called a Pistol Makarova, or PM for short." Everyone stared at him, like deer in headlights, unsure of the relevance. He bounced up and down like an excited kid. "It's a Russian made semi-automatic pistol. It was made in the early 1950's and used to be the Soviet Union's standard military side arm, but production was discontinued in the early 1990's."

Salvatore stood and crept closer to the screen. "Let me take a good look at this."

"And?" Tony gawked at Chase.

"And," Chase emphasized. "The only person I know in this city who could get his hands on a mint condition PM is Selovich, and he's dead."

"So, maybe this guy bought the gun from Selovich before he died," Tony shrugged.

Chase shook his head and zoomed the video out to show both men. "Selovich was a low scale dealer. No way could he have gotten his hands on two PM's in mint-ass condition."

"How can you tell they're in mint condition?" Tony squint at the screen.

Chase zoomed back in on one of the guns. "Look closely. On an older pistol there are natural wear and tear marks, here on the grip and scuff marks here where the clip enters," Chase pointed. "These guns show no marks at all."

"So, your theory is that because the guns are Russian made, we are dealing with the Bratva?" Giovanni questioned.

"Non so," Salvatore interjected in Italian. "If these guns are brand new as he suspects, then it is not possible for them to be in the hands of the Bratva here."

"Exactly," Chase blurted. "He's tracking with me." Salvatore gave a nod to Chase and returned to the couch.

"I don't understand," Angel exhaled.

"The production of the PM's was stopped in the early 1990's. That means any PM in circulation is a used weapon and will undoubtedly show some form of wear and tear." Chase took a deep breath and continued. "A dealer can clean a gun up real nice, but he can't get every little-ass scuff off."

"What's this marking on the side?" Tony pointed to the screen.

"That's called a proof mark," Chase explained. "See, every Pistol Makarova bears a stamp on the side to show its country of origin. Every country has its own marking." Chase jumped up and dug into his black bag, pulling out a piece of paper and pen. "What you see here is the mark denoting Russian manufacturing." He scribbled it on the paper. "It's a circle with two triangles inside."

"So what does this mean?" Angel threw her hands up.

Salvatore exhaled loudly. "It means the Russian government produced these weapons and undoubtedly supplied them to these men for the purpose of this attack."

"Bah," Giovanni waved his hand in front of his face, "that is nonsense. The Bratva have never had a large presence here. Why would the Russian government want to support them?" Salvatore raised one eyebrow toward Giovanni, who muttered something in Italian that Angel suspected was not fit for a lady's ears.

"What would they have to gain by supporting the Bratva here in the States?" Angel asked.

"That's what we need to find out," Chase said.

They continued to watch the tape and Angel was astonished when she saw the Shark suddenly enter Tetterbaum's Pub through the back door. He carried a .45 and shot both men, and then he gathered up their guns and exited the same way he had come.

"That's the Shark!" She exclaimed when she saw him.

"He is one massive-ass dude," Chase blurted. "I mean that dude is ripped everywhere."

They all leaned in closer to the screen. "Why is he taking their guns?" Tony asked.

"That explains why no weapons were found at the scene," Andrew remarked. "We bag up sixteen bodies and not a single weapon among them."

"Sixteen bodies," Angel repeated it slowly, as the reality of that number hit her. Sixteen innocent people died in her restaurant, and she couldn't escape the feeling that it was somehow her fault.

Salvatore shook his head and looked at Giovanni. "What do we know of this Shark?"

"He's worked for me for many years as one of my most loyal men," Giovanni rubbed his hand over his jowls. "Up until last week I trusted him with my life. I know of no connection between him and the Russians; then again, he has not checked in with me since last week so his loyalty is in question."

"I know they have Russian guns, but before we assume these guys are Russian, do we have the audio tape?" Angel asked. "Maybe they say something on the tape that will tell us who they are or who they're working for."

Chase pressed play and the room filled with the eerie sound of people dying, moaning, whimpering, and crying out, footsteps of the men walking, scuffling chairs and their voices speaking one distinct language: Russian.

"I think we've seen and heard enough tonight," Andrew turned off the video and audio feed and leaned back against the dining room table. He crossed his arms over his chest and exhaled. "I'll take the tapes in and get them translated. Maybe that will give us a clue as to who we're dealing with."

"If these are Russian mob, backed by the Russian government and sent here to support fellow Bratva, we will have a bloody fight on our hands," Salvatore muttered.

"The timing of this attack is no coincidence. There is but one head to a snake," Giovanni gruffed. "We will find it and behead it."

27

Salvatore slammed his fist on the coffee table. "Bratva! Odio il Bratva!" He spewed; his face turning beet red. Angel didn't need a translation. She could tell there was a story behind Salvatore's deep hatred of the Russian mob and she made mental note to ask her mother about it later.

Sophia took Salvatore's hand, kissed the top of it and begged him to calm down. "E il padre giusto," she said softly and then turned her attention to Giovanni. "As you said, the timing of this attack seems coincidentally close to our dismantling of Denny's operation. Do you believe there is any connection between Denny and the Russians?"

"I do not know," Giovanni exhaled. "But we will find out."

"We know Denny was working with Selovich, but that's the only Russian connection thus far," Andrew interjected.

Angel exhaled, "I thought this whole thing would be over when we took out Denny and hit his Iowa compound."

"That was certainly the hope," Tony mumbled.

"It isn't that simple, Sweetheart," Andrew explained. "As far as we know, several key players weren't in the compound when we hit it."

Angel felt frustrated and tried to swallow the anger of injustice that gripped her. She had believed that with Denny gone and the Iowa compound destroyed, there would finally be peace. Well, maybe not total

28

peace, but an existence where she wouldn't have to worry about explosives and mass killings; a place where the only concern would be whether the Galantes had pissed off the Venturinis or the Cullatos had made threats against the Andriachinis. She longed for a place of Mafia pseudo-harmony, where they could all bicker over territory but not truly engage in battle. Most of all, she wanted the killing to stop. Ever since discovering her true identity, she had become obsessed with carrying out her father's proposal of peace between the bogatas. She wanted to make Mafia life a safe existence rather than the scary place she had come to know.

"Who wasn't there when we hit the compound?" Stefano asked.

"Everyone of importance," Tony remarked with a sarcasm directed at Andrew.

"There was no way for me to know who would be inside when we planned the attack," Andrew defended.

"Obviously your traitor mole was conveniently absent at the time." Tony was referring to the Shark, whom he still believed was a traitor. He glared at Andrew and everyone could feel the tension between them. Not only did Tony doubt the Shark's loyalty, but ever since the attack at the Towers, he had suspicions about Andrew's loyalty as well. Tempers had flared before and Angel wasn't sure what they might actually do to each other if it came to blows.

Andrew stood up straight and uncrossed his arms. "We went in to shut down the compound and that's exactly what we did. We took out everyone inside, except one, and confiscated all the weapons and equipment we could find."

"What do you mean 'except one'?" Angel asked.

Giovanni interjected, "I instructed them to take Vincent Carlachi alive."

"Uncle Vince is still alive," Stefano leapt to his feet. "Can I talk to him?"

"That is a matter for later discussion." Giovanni's eyes were set and Angel could tell that even Stefano knew not to bring up the topic again.

"So did you get any other key players?" Tony's question taunted Andrew and he tightened his lip. "Kristen, Thomas Boglevich and the Shark are still at large," Tony quipped. "Oh, wait, that's right, we know where the Shark is. He was at Tetterbaum's tonight, shooting up the place."

"He didn't shoot up the place," Andrew said through clenched teeth. "He shot the two Russians."

"That's right, just like he shot me," Tony's voice dripped disdain. "But he's one of the good guys right?" Andrew took a step closer to Tony and Giovanni raised his voice, instructing them both to sit down.

"Bickering amongst ourselves is not beneficial to our cause," Giovanni gruffed.

Salvatore piped in, "we must stay on task; find the serpent's head and chop it off." He made a slicing motion with his arm.

Angel mumbled under her breath. "I thought Denny was the head."

"I have a feeling he was only the head of a small part of this operation," Andrew commented.

"How do we find the main head?" Angel asked.

"I'll have the surveillance tapes analyzed and translated..." Andrew began and Chase cut him off.

"I'll find out if anyone in the city carries mint condition PM's," he said.

"I will check with my contacts back home and see what we can learn of any Russian plans here in the States," Salvatore said.

"My men will interrogate Carlachi," Giovanni added.

"I guess me and my boys will keep searching for Kristen, Thomas Boglevich and the Shark to finish the job for you, hot shot," Tony patted Andrew on the shoulder as he headed for the door.

"Regardless of the hour, you will all check in directly with me upon finding any new evidence," Giovanni ordered.

Stefano was escorted back to the spare bedroom by two of Giovanni's men, who were assigned to guard him day and night. Angel felt sorry for him because he was stuck somewhere between prisoner, death and a possible option to join the family if his loyalty could be proven. He could never again return home to his parents in Iowa, as it would most assuredly result in all of their deaths. The problem was Stefano had innocently gotten mixed up with his uncle, Vincent Carlachi, who was working for Denny.   His job was to guard Sophia after she was kidnapped and the only reason Stefano wasn't already wearing concrete boots at the bottom of Lake Michigan was that he had helped Sophia escape. Angel thought that, that act alone should prove his loyalty, but Giovanni was harder to convince. There had been too many traitors working closely among them and Giovanni wasn't taking any chances.

When everyone was gone, Angel sat down in Giovanni's chair, across from Sophia and Salvatore.

"Merciful Heavens," snorted Olga, waddling from the kitchen to the couch and plunking her round hips down next to Salvatore. "Those two are gonna come to blows over you."

"Who?" Angel asked.

"Tony and Andrew," Olga belted with a look that said "duh."

"They're not fighting over me," Angel sighed, which caused the other three to chuckle. "Why is that funny?"

Sophia grinned and gave her daughter a wink.

"Are you kidding? They're like two Alpha dogs trying to piss on the same tree," Olga snorted.

"My goodness, don't you paint a picture," Salvatore teased.

"She's always had an uncanny way with words," Sophia laughed.

Angel crossed her arms, defiantly. "There's tension between them because Tony doesn't trust Andrew."

"He doesn't trust Andrew to keep his paws off you," Olga blurted and Sophia and Salvatore giggled as they nibbled on Olga's Cannoli.

"That's not it," Angel stomped her foot and suddenly felt like she was a little girl again. "It's a lot more than that." Angel narrowed her brows. "That's not it!"

"Okay, okay," Olga appeased. "That's not it. Now why don't you come sit down and have some Cannoli?"

Angel rolled her eyes. There was no use talking to them. "I'm going to bed."

CHAPTER 4

It was four o'clock in the morning when Chase rapped loudly on her bedroom door. Angel sprung out of bed, leaping to her feet with that all impending sense of panic.

"Who is it?" She groggily blurted.

"It's me, Chase. Giovanni wants you in the family room, pronto."

This can't be good news, she thought. Good news can wait until a decent hour. Bad news is delivered regardless of the time. Angel pulled on her cream colored satin robe, tied it around her waist and hurried to the family room.

Giovanni was seated in the arm chair with two men, whom Angel didn't recognize, standing behind him. "Who are they?" She nodded her head toward the men behind him.

"This is my granddaughter, Michelangela," he introduced her and she extended her hand. "Michelangela, these are two of my most trusted men, Milo and Manuel. They flew in from New York late last night."

"I'm assuming you didn't wake me at four AM to have me meet Milo and Manuel."

"No, we have something you need to see." Giovanni nodded to Chase.

"I made a copy of the surveillance tapes from the pub because I knew Andrew was

34

going to take them to be analyzed and I wanted to get a closer look at the PM's." Chase explained in his usual excitedly animated fashion. "I mean, you have no idea how cool-ass these guns are."

"Remain on task," Giovanni gruffed.

"Right, anyway, I went home and pulled up the video and...," he paused. "Well, you better see for yourself."

He hit play and Angel watched closely. The Shark came in the back door, carrying a PM and shot the two men in suits, each in the chest. Chase paused the tape right there and Angel looked up. "That's the same thing we watched earlier," she shrugged. "I don't get it."

"I didn't either at first," Chase explained. "But remember when you and I were in the kitchen and we planned to escape through the back door?"

Angel nodded as the relevance hit her. "We heard the door open and slam shut and that was way before the surveillance tapes were running."

"Right," Chase agreed.

"Which means someone else either came in the door or went out the door before we ever went into hiding."

"Exactly," Chase said.

Angel started to pace and chew on her index fingernail. "The back door is always locked..."

Chase cut her off. "Then how did the Shark get in?"

Angel stopped pacing and stared at Chase. "Maybe he used a crowbar or something to break in?" She didn't remember hearing any noise from the door other than the usual sound it made when it opened and slammed shut, so the idea wasn't all that believable. Then again, her heart had been pounding so loudly in her ears that she could have missed the sound of the door being pried open.

"I asked myself these same questions, so I tapped into the satellite feed of local video surveillance and this is what I managed to pick up." He hit a few keys on the computer and when the image came up, Angel's heart leapt into her throat. It was Andrew unlocking the backdoor, pulling it open and a man dashing out from inside the pub. The door slammed shut and both men got into Andrew's SUV and drove off.

Angel's heart was pounding rapidly. "Andrew let that man out."

"And he left the door unlocked so the Shark could come in," Chase pointed out.

"Andrew let the man out and the Shark in?" Her breathing quickened. "Why would he do that?"

Chase started to speak but Angel pointed and glared at him. "Don't say anything. Just let me think. Just for a second, let me think." She bit her bottom lip and paced back and forth. "There's got to be a reason, a very good reason why he did this."

"There's no good reason," Chase blurted. "He knew we were under attack by freaking-ass Russians and he didn't do anything to help us!" Chase's voice grew high-pitched and he rose out of his chair. "He fed our asses to the wolves!"

Angel felt all the strength drain from her and she sank down onto the couch. "I don't understand," she shook her head.

"You don't want to understand," Chase said. "Because it means Tony is right and Andrew is a traitor."

"No, wait, go back," she jumped to her feet and came toward the computer screen. "Go back to the part where the man leaves the building. I want to see his face." Chase did as she asked and paused the frame, zooming in on a close up of the man's face.

"This is as close as I can get it without distorting the image," he said.

"I know this man. He was sitting on the left side of the bar and he ordered chilled Vodka, no ice." Angel stared at the screen as flashbacks of the shootings filled her mind. "It's impossible that he wasn't shot." She shook her head. "Mr. Kutis and Mr. Malcoraine were both sitting right there and they were killed. So was Valerie. It's not possible for the shooters to have missed him."

"Unless he was one of them," Chase said. "And they wanted to miss him."

"But if he was one of them, why wasn't he shooting anyone?" Angel asked.

"We don't know for sure that he didn't shoot anyone," Chase explained. "We only see him coming out of the building. We have no idea what he did while on the inside."

"Did he have a gun in his hand when he walked out?" Angel stared at the screen while Chase zoomed out on the image, revealing the man's two empty hands. "No gun," Angel sighed to herself. "This means he either didn't have a gun or didn't feel threatened by the men who were shooting."

"Shooting at us!" Chase yelled. "You're missing the point here."

"I understand your point," Angel hollered back.

"I don't think you do," Chase jumped up. "Andrew left us inside to be killed." Chase's eyes bugged out of his head and his mouth stood open wide. "I don't know about you, but that's not all fine-ass dandy with me."

Angel shook her head, fighting back a nauseating lump climbing into her throat. "No! I know him. There's got to be a good reason for what he did. He would never do anything to hurt me. Andrew is more loyal than anyone." She turned her gaze to Giovanni, "grandfather, there's got to be a reason he did this."

Giovanni rubbed his hand over his jowls and then rest his elbows on the arms of the chair and pushed his fingertips together. "There is always a reason for a man's actions, Michelangela," he exhaled. "But not always a good reason."

Angel's lip quivered and she tried to fight the tears filling her eyes. "I'll find out why," she sniveled. "He'll tell me the truth. I know he will, and then I'll prove to you that there is a good reason for this."

Giovanni moved to the couch and sat facing Angel. "Remember what I told you." He pointed at her chest and said, "Cuore." He then touched her forehead and said, "Astuto." Holding her face in his palms, Giovanni looked at her with eyes that were both powerful and tender. "Being a leader means balancing your heart, cuore, with your smarts, astuto. Capisce?"

Angel broke into sobs. Her mind couldn't deny that Giovanni's words were true, but her heart knew Andrew could not be a traitor.

"Sometimes believing a lie is more soothing to the soul," Giovanni wrapped his arm around her. "But a strong individual must face the truth as it reveals itself; and it always reveals itself."

Angel buried her face in Giovanni's shoulder and wept.

"I'm sorry, Angel," Chase mumbled as he packed up his laptop and quietly left.

CHAPTER 5

Angel dialed Andrew's cell phone at least fifty times between the time that Giovanni left and the time Olga tapped on her bedroom door. Each time his voicemail clicked on, she hung up; uncertain of what to say in a message. *Run! Hide! Giovanni knows you're a traitor and you're the next hit,* is what she wanted to say, but the words wouldn't form. She sent ten text messages asking him to call her; but he never responded.

Olga peeked her head in the door. "Merciful Heavens child, you look like you've been crying." She waddled in and plunked herself down on the bed. "You tell your old Aunt what's going on."

"It's nothing," she lied. "Just guy trouble."

Olga grinned. "Guy trouble is the best trouble to have, especially when it's two hot men fighting over you." She nudged her with her elbow and gave a wink. "Now, get your lazy bones up and come have some breakfast before the meeting."

Angel sat up in bed. "What meeting?"

"Your grandfather has called a meeting for ten o'clock sharp and he wants everyone in attendance, even me." She raised her eyebrows and made a silly face. "Aren't I something?" She teased and wiggled her hips,

40

"going to a big meeting." Olga moved toward the door. "I've got coffee brewing and some breakfast strudel in the oven."

Angel jumped out of bed, brushed her teeth, showered and threw on a pair of jeans, black converse tennis shoes and a black tank top. She towel dried her hair, dabbed on some blush, eyeliner, mascara and lip gloss and made a beeline to the kitchen; dialing Andrew once more on the way. No answer. She text him again. "Please call me ASAP."

She inhaled a piece of strudel and slammed her cup of coffee in one gulp, then headed for the door. "Merciful Heavens, you didn't even chew," Olga gasped.

"I'm in a hurry." Angel reached for the doorknob.

"Well, I should say so," Olga stood with both hands on her rounded hips. "Where are you hurrying off to?"

"I have some errands to run," she lied again. "I'll be back in time for the meeting."

"After the attack last night, I don't think you're supposed to be traipsing around the city alone?" Olga hollered, but Angel was already gone.

She took the emergency stairwell down the first several floors, to avoid bumping into any of Giovanni's men in the hallways. Then she rode the elevator down the rest of the way to the main lobby. She knew she'd encounter a guard at the front of the building, but felt confident she could use her clout to convince him to let her go out alone. After all, she was head of the Chicago Maratinzano family. By all rights people should be afraid to question her authority.

Standing guard at the door were Milo and Manuel. "May we escort you somewhere Ms. Maratinzano?" Milo asked. He was by far the better looking of the two. He stood six foot, had hazel eyes, sandy colored hair and muscles Angel was sure rippled like a washboard beneath his black t-shirt. Manuel was so-so looking. He was shorter than Milo, had darker hair, brown eyes and skin that looked like he lived in a tanning bed. There was something unmanly about picturing a bodyguard lying in a tanning bed.

"Nope," she answered flatly, "I'm running a couple of quick errands."

"We've been told not to let you leave without an escort," Milo explained.

Angel motioned them to lean in closer to her, as if to listen to a secret. Then she whispered. "You guys are new here so I don't want to embarrass you, but everyone knows my grandfather is overly protective. So my bodyguards and I have this unspoken arrangement that as long as I stay in our territory, I'm fine going out alone."

"Oh," Milo said and looked to Manuel, who raised his eyebrows and shrugged. "Well, I guess that makes sense if you're just staying on your turf."

"Absolutely," Angel smiled. "I'll be back before you know it."

Once she was behind the wheel of her black Town & Country, a.k.a. the Tank, Angel breathed a sigh of relief. Her mission was simple. Find Andrew. Confront him and get the truth. She feared what would happen if Milo and Manuel or some other of Giovanni's thugs got to him first.

She drove to the pub, sneaking in the back, despite the entrance being blocked by yellow crime scene tape. Then she drove to Andrew's house, the precinct where he worked and lastly, to the abandoned strip mall that housed what she playfully referred to as his bat cave. It was the place he had taken her the night she found out the truth about her family and her identity; and the place where he had taught her how to handle and shoot a gun. She returned to the Towers with just enough time to get to the meeting, which was held in the secret conference room designed by Giovanni himself. It was located two floors below the penthouse and the room itself, took up the entire floor. The windows were constructed of bullet proof glass and it was completely sound proof. There was no emergency stairwell access to and from the secret floor, and the elevator stopped on it only with the input of a special code. It was mysterious and Angel was impressed by the creative thought that went into its design.

Angel assumed Giovanni would be discussing Andrew's actions first thing and she needed to be there to defend him, even if her defense was weak.

Giovanni looked displeased as she rushed into the room thirty seconds late and took a seat near the end of the rectangular, mahogany table. Salvatore sat on one end and Giovanni on the other. Angel glanced around the table and noticed it was only her family and Chase present. None of the other bosses were there, neither was Tony, Andrew or Stefano. *Why didn't we just meet upstairs in the family room,* she wondered.

"Where's Stefano?" She asked.

"He will not be joining us today," Giovanni folded his hands on the table. "He has been granted permission to question his uncle on our behalf and will be returning this evening."

A test, Angel thought. *Giovanni probably bugged the room and is going to test Stefano by asking him questions later to see if he is truthful.* Angel was beginning to understand what made her grandfather tick and how he powerfully manipulated.

The door opened and Tony walked in, making a beeline for the table. "My apologies for being late," he said and then gave a quick nod to Giovanni. Angel saw the brief exchange between them and panic gripped her. She had seen this form of communication before. It happened when they found out Venito had been posing as her late father's Compare and one of Giovanni's men had been disloyal. With a simple nod of his head, Giovanni had instructed Tony to kill the traitor; and when Tony returned, the same nod assured Giovanni that the job had been done.

Angel's eyes darted from Giovanni to Tony and back to Giovanni. Her hands began to tremble and she rose to her feet. "Where were you?" She asked Tony, who looked to Giovanni and then lowered his eyes to table as he sat down across from her.

"I was running late, Babe." Tony rubbed his fingertips nervously across the edge of the table, as if to appear nonchalant; but Angel wasn't buying it.

"Tony!" She demanded. "Look at me." Tony raised his eyes to meet hers and she could see how difficult it was for him to hold her gaze. She could tell he wanted to look away and deep down she knew why. Tears filled her eyes and she narrowed her brows. "Tell me you didn't..."

Giovanni cut her off mid-sentence. "I sent Tony to finish a job and that is what he has done. End of discussion." Giovanni's voice was stern and his jaw tight, but Angel didn't care.

Tears streamed down her cheeks but she kept her eyes on Tony. She struggled to tighten her quivering lip as she spoke. "Did you..." she broke into sobs. "Where is he?" Her voice shook. "Did you...did you kill Andrew?" By the time she managed to say Andrew's name her voice was almost inaudible.

Olga gasped, "Merciful heavens!"

Tony leapt to his feet and slammed both palms onto the table. "Yes!" He screamed at Angel. "Yes! I killed him! You want to hear me say it, I'll say it. I killed Andrew because he was a traitor and because that's what I was ordered to do." Tony's face reddened and his nostrils flared as he sucked air in and out. "That's what I was ordered to do!"

Angel's body shook with a rage she'd never before experienced. She grabbed her chair and hurled it backwards, screaming every obscenity she'd ever heard. Olga reached for her, but she pushed her aside. Sophia sat motionless, staring at Tony as if stunned into absolute silence. Angel screamed at Giovanni in a voice so loud it was raspy with emotion, "I hate you! I hate you!" She called him every horrible name that popped into her mind. "You're not my grandfather!" She spewed. "You're a monster and I hope you die!"

"Angel," Tony yelled and she turned towards him.

"Don't you ever say my name again. Don't ever speak to me. Don't look at me. I despise you," she uttered through gritted teeth and streaming tears. "I'll make sure the Venturini's know you are single-handedly responsible for his death!" For a brief moment she saw fear flash in Tony's eyes because he knew what that meant for him and his family. It meant revenge and certain bloodshed. She was promising to ensure his death and they both knew it.

Olga and Sophia finally managed to drag her, kicking and screaming from the conference room. When the door closed behind them, the men sat in momentary silence.

"She's a feisty one," Chase quipped, trying to lighten the moment.

"Si," Salvatore agreed, nodding his head up and down. "But look at what she is made of, half Maratinzano and half Buscetta."

"A deadly-ass combination," Chase exhaled. "Watch out world."

Tony sunk into his chair with his eyes glazed over.

Once upstairs, Angel, Olga and Sophia collapsed onto Angel's bed. Angel writhed and wailed in mourning and Sophia and Olga held her and wept, exchanging sorrowful moans in Italian.

Hours turned into days and Angel lay in bed, refusing to eat, drink or get up. She stared blankly, through intermittent bouts of sobbing, and stroking the ears of her two cats, Midnight and Mo, who lay on the pillows next to her head. They never left her side, as if they knew her heart was breaking. Olga and Sophia discussed taking her to a hospital but Giovanni wouldn't allow it.

"She must find the strength to live from within herself," he told them. "We will give her more time."

On the third day, Angel got out of bed, feeling dizzy and weak from lack of food and water. She brushed her teeth and drank two full glasses of water, then showered, dressed and began to pack. She had come to a decision; she wasn't going to be forced to live a life of violence. It didn't matter that she was half Giovanni and half Salvatore; she would no longer be a part of all the killing.

Olga tapped on the door with a tray of coffee and cinnamon pancakes. "I made your favorite breakfast," she said. "My famous cinnamon pancakes." Although the pancakes smelled wonderful and it had been days since she'd eaten, an appetite was nonexistent amid the agony of Angel's grief. She opened the door and Olga's face lit with surprise to see her up and dressed. "Merciful Heavens," she gasped. "Aren't you a sight for sore eyes." Olga waddled in, set the tray on the bed and gave Angel a tight squeeze. "I've been so worried about you; I thought I was going to get one of them bleeding ulcers." She shook her head dramatically from side to side. "You know Elsa, down at the hair salon, says people my age don't recover from a bleeding ulcer. She says their stomachs explode like a volcano and then they die."

"You're not going to explode," Angel said. "You don't have to worry about me anymore. I'm leaving."

Olga looked at the two suitcases sitting in the corner and nodded her head up and down. "Okay," she sighed. "I'll go pack."

"Why are you packing?"

"Well, you're not going alone and you're not leaving me here. We're a package deal you and me." Olga winked and squeezed Angel's fingers. "You should know by now that I don't leave my Angel." She scurried to her bedroom to pack. A few minutes later Olga hollered down the hall, "are we going someplace warm or someplace cold? Never mind, I'll pack for both."

Angel was zipping up her last suitcase when there was another knock on her bedroom door. She opened it expecting Olga and slammed it shut again when she saw Tony and her mother.

"Get him out of here!" She screamed.

"Angel," Sophia scolded. "You've got to listen to what he has to say."

"I don't care what he has to say," she seethed. "There is nothing he can say that will make me want him anything but dead."

"I told you this wouldn't work," Tony exhaled.

Sophia leaned in close to Angel's bedroom door. "I need you to trust me. I need you to give Tony a couple of minutes." Sophia leaned her head against the door. "I promise Angel, the next two minutes will change your life."

Angel opened the door a crack. "Fine, two minutes."

Sophia pulled Tony into Angel's bedroom, closed and locked the door. "Wait," she said in a hushed tone, placing her index finger up to her lips to indicate they should be quiet. "Come in here." She opened the door to Angel's bathroom and then closed and locked it behind them. She then turned on the shower and the bathroom fan. "Now we can talk, but we still need to keep our voices down."

"You think we're under surveillance?" Angel squinted at her mother.

"I think the sooner you assume you are always being watched, the safer you will be." Sophia squeezed Angel's hand. "Listen to what he has to tell you."

Angel let go of her mom's hand and crossed her arms, refusing to make eye-contact with Tony.

Sophia stared at both of them and mumbled something in Italian. "You two have to work this out quickly," she said. "I'll wait in your room." Sophia stepped out of the bathroom and sat on the bed with Midnight and Mo. "This is going to take a miracle," she told the cats.

Tony started to speak and without thinking, Angel whirled around and slapped him across the face. She hadn't planned on hitting him. It just happened, an instinctive reaction she couldn't control. Every time he opened his mouth she hit him until he finally grabbed her arms and held her wrists together. Then she kicked him in the shins.

After several kicks, he wrestled her to the floor. "I have a strict policy against hitting a woman, but you're pushing it, Babe."

"Oh, so you can kill innocent people but you can't hit a woman? Nice moral standards you have." She spit right in his face. "I hate you."

"Yeah, I know that." He let her go and wiped his face on the bathroom towel that hung by the shower. Scooting away from her, he leaned his back against the cabinets, bent his knees up and rested his chin on his hands.

Angel leaned against the wall between the shower and the toilet and pulled her knees to her chest. Uncontrollable tears covered her face. "I loved him," she sobbed. "You son of a bitch, I loved him."

Tony nodded his head up and down. "I know." She saw him swallow hard. "I saw it in your eyes a while back. I guess that's why I, uh, wanted to believe so badly that he was a traitor." Tony choked back emotion. "I guess that's why a part of me wanted him dead." Angel started crying harder and buried her face in her hands. "I guess that's why I couldn't kill him."

She wasn't sure she had heard him correctly, but when she looked up and saw his face, she knew. Several tears escaped his manly exterior and Tony didn't try to wipe them away. He closed his eyes momentarily and shook his head side to side. "I couldn't do it, Babe." Angel could barely speak as she scooted toward him and dove into his arms. He grabbed her and stroked her hair, repeating "I couldn't do it," over and over until emotion overtook him and they wept in each other's arms.

Angel slid between his legs, gripping his arms and sobbing against his chest. Tony buried his face in her shoulder and they clung to each other. Angel was overjoyed. Andrew was alive! Tony was not the monster she feared he had become! The black, bottomless pit of despair that had been sucking life from her was gone; instantly replaced by inexpressible joy. She pulled back from their embrace and kissed Tony. She kissed his hands, his cheeks, his forehead, his lips and his neck. They weren't sensual, erotic kisses, but expressions of heartfelt gratitude and tender, genuine love. Angel smiled for the first time in days as she felt life returning to her. "Thank you Tony," she whispered in between kisses. "Thank you."

He brushed the hair from her face and tucked it behind her ear. "Listen, Babe, we're not out of the woods yet. If Giovanni finds out, I'm as good as dead."

Angel swallowed hard. She knew this was true. "He won't find out. We won't let him find out."

Tony was more afraid than Angel had ever seen him. His voice quivered as he quoted Giovanni, "The truth always reveals itself."

She grabbed his face in her palms and looked deeply in his eyes. "Yes, and it has revealed you as the man of character I always knew you were."

"Babe," he started to speak, but his voice faltered so he pulled her in and kissed her.

"We're in this together," she said, taking his hands and interlocking her fingers with his.

He nodded, took a deep breath and Angel watched his softer side become instantaneously replaced by masculine strength. "We need to get to Andrew so he can fill you in on the rest."

"Where is he?"

"He's at Venito Barone's old house. It was the only safe place we could think of."

The Barone property held a lot of meaning for Angel. It was there that Tony had proposed to her and later where he dumped her. It was there that she first discovered Venito was pretending to be her dad's Compare and it was also there that she had found Grayson Galante's body. The mere thought of Venito Barone's house triggered painful memories for her.

"I don't know why I didn't think to look there," she said, more to herself than to him.

"We need to figure out a way to get you there without Giovanni knowing," Tony explained. "I think your mom has some ideas."

Angel watched his lips moving, but she wasn't hearing his words. She was staring at him, letting a barrage of memories saturate her thoughts. How had they gotten here? A couple years ago she was supposed to marry Tony and live happily ever after. How did it all unravel so quickly? There was a time when she loved him more than anything, more than anyone; but now things were different. She gazed at Tony and felt a twinge of guilt for all the hateful things she had said to him, wishing him dead, saying she hated him, and professing her feelings for Andrew; feelings that were evidentially deeper than even she had known.

"Tony, I'm sorry..." she began, but he held his hand up to her mouth to quiet her.

"We're okay, Babe," he gave a half-smile. "Sometimes things between people grow into something else, something better suited for them."

She leaned in and kissed his lips, softly. "I'll always love you."

"And me, you, Babe. Always."

Sophia tapped on the door. "Things have grown quiet in there so either you've killed each other or you've worked it out."

Angel opened the door and hugged her mom. "How did you know the truth?"

Sophia smiled. "I've been in this business a long time. I've seen the cold killers and I've seen the warm family men. I knew the moment I looked at Tony, he was a big 'ol warm Teddy Bear." She looped one arm in Angel's and one arm in Tony's. "Now," she said, "the three of you need to get to the bottom of this and quickly, before your grandfather is any the wiser."

CHAPTER 6

It took some finagling on Sophia and Olga's part, but they managed to convince Giovanni that Angel needed some time away from the Towers to come to terms with what happened. He finally consented to two nights under their close supervision at a local Boutique called the Dana Hotel and Spa, which was located in the heart of downtown, a few blocks up from the Riverwalk.

They arrived at the spa in Angel's Tank, as Giovanni instructed. He had them travel in the Tank because its anti-ballistic features and bullet-proof glass ensured their safety, but Angel knew it was really because he could track her vehicle. Angel was beginning to understand that not only was Giovanni a man of great power, he was also a man who needed to have control over everything and everyone. After her angry outburst in the meeting, she knew he feared she would run away from him; and she felt his reigns tightening around her.

A bellman helped Olga and Sophia out of the Tank and unloaded their luggage, while Angel stepped from the driver's seat. When the parking attendant reached for Angel's keys, he was promptly greeted with a tug at the shoulder by Manuel. Giovanni had sent Milo and Manuel to watch over his women. "I'll handle this vehicle," Manuel said to the attendant, who wisely gave a nod and backed away from the car.

Sophia nodded to the driver. "We'll call you if we intend to leave."

Angel watched as the Tank rolled out of sight and took a deep breath. She didn't like not having a vehicle at her disposal. It made her feel trapped.

"Come along dear," Olga prodded. "We have much to do." They entered the hotel and Olga gasped out loud. "Merciful Heavens, have you ever seen anything like it?" She held her hand to her chest and let her mouth hang open in awe.

The hotel was elaborately decorated with a mixture of wooden and glass walls, gold dim lighting, and dark velvet curtains; a hint of understated elegance. It was simple, serene.

"I'm gonna like it here," Olga said. "I'm gonna like it here a lot."

A tall, slender woman in a black business skirt, nude hose, black shiny pumps and a white blouse approached them. She had perfectly straight, white teeth and a face right out of Vogue magazine. Her hair was dark black, short and stylish; the kind of hairdo you see on other people and think it looks good, but can never see on yourself. "Welcome to the Dana Hotel and Spa. There will be complimentary champagne and strawberries in the Vertigo lounge at five o'clock. You may check in over there," she pointed to a small counter made of marble. "We've designed a spa package specific to each of your needs and will begin your treatments tomorrow morning promptly at eight. Information on each package is located in your suite." She spoke like a European robot. "Enjoy your stay."

"Spa treatments," Olga gleamed. "I say one of us fake suicidal tendencies every couple months so Giovanni has to send us back here for healing." Angel rolled her eyes. "I could get used to this," Olga grinned.

"Let's hurry and check-in, we haven't much time," Sophia whispered and they both followed her to the check in desk.

Once inside the penthouse suite, Olga waddled around like a wide-eyed kid in a candy shop. "Merciful Heavens," she exclaimed. "Come take a gander at this." She yelled down the hall, "I think it's one of them European bidets." The bathroom door closed and a few moments later Sophia and Angel heard Olga whooping and hollering.

"Do you think we should check on her?" Angel giggled.

Sophia dropped her head and laughed. "I don't know how she can hurt herself on a bidet, so let's just give her a moment."

A few minutes later Olga emerged from the bathroom, her face flushed with color. "Merciful Heavens, that's an invasive little gadget. I've only seen them on TV so naturally I had to stick my fanny on it to see what it felt like."

"Naturally," Sophia smiled and Angel laughed out loud.

"You Europeans are all a bit kinky," she shook her finger at Sophia.

"You're just as much Italian as I am," Sophia rebutted.

"Yes, but we didn't have a bidet when I was little and I've lived in the States almost all my life," Olga waddled down the hall. "I can't wait to tell Elsa down at the hair salon."

Angel checked the time on her cell phone and felt her stomach knot. It was almost three o'clock, the designated hour for her to slip out and disappear with Tony. Olga had placed a room service order exactly forty minutes ago and the tray was most assuredly on its way up. When it arrived at their suite, Milo and Manuel would inspect it and Olga and Sophia would provide a distraction so that Angel could sneak out the door. It seemed like a good idea in theory and Angel hoped it would work as well in real life.

Either Angel's expression showed fear or Sophia's motherly instincts detected it, because Sophia sat down on the bed next to Angel and took her hand.

"Not to worry," Sophia said. "Everything will turn out all right in the end."

"It's the in between that scares me," Angel looked at her mom. "I don't know what to do. I feel like people's lives are actually in my hands and if I mess up..."

Sophia cut her off. "People's lives are in God's hands," she said, brushing the hair from Angel's cheek. "You can only do what you believe is right. If you do that, you will come through this."

"I wish I felt stronger," Angel said, taking a deep breath and exhaling slowly.

"You're father said that to me once," Sophia grinned at the memory. "We were sitting on the bed, much like you and I are now, and he was about to announce his peace treaty to the Chicago Bosses."

"He was scared?"

"Petrified," Sophia nodded. "But no one knew it by looking at him." Sophia rose and kissed Angel's forehead. "You have great strength inside you. Trust it." Angel stood and embraced her mom. "Now it is time for you to go. You must return in thirty-six hours whether you've resolved anything or not."

Angel handed Sophia her cell phone. She couldn't take it with her because she assumed she could then be tracked. "You'll reach me through Tony right?"

Sophia nodded. "Now, go say goodbye to Olga before she goes back into the bathroom." Angel grinned. Olga sure loved that bidet.

CHAPTER 7

Sneaking out of the Dana Hotel was the scariest part of the plan thus far, but it went off without a hitch. Room Service arrived and Olga promptly had them wheel the cart into the suite and over by the windows, drawing Milo and Manuel all the way inside. Sophia tipped the room service attendant, and left the door cracked open just enough for Angel to slip out.

As she was sneaking toward the door, Angel heard the sound of a stainless dome being lifted from a plate and Olga gasping, "Merciful heavens, will you look at this!" Manuel moved closer to inspect the tray of food.

"Is there a problem, ma'am?" He asked.

Olga put her hand to her face and fanned herself. "It's just the most beautiful thing I've ever seen." She waddled across the room and tugged Milo's arm to follow her toward the serving tray. "Lookey here, see how they lined the strawberries up to make a little smiley face?" She sighed loudly and gripped her chest. "It's the little things that make life so special." Then she shook her index finger at them and said, "you'd do well to remember that, boys. In fact, follow me and I'll show you one of the simplest pleasures in life."

Angel slipped out the door and down the hallway, as Olga led the men on a trip to the bathroom to see the magical wonders of the bidet. Angel giggled to herself, imagining Milo and Manuel standing there with blank stares and mouths agape.

By the time the men were back at their post in the hallway, Angel was long gone.

The drive to the Barone property was quiet, though Angel's stomach twisted in noisy little knots. She was certain Tony felt as awkward as she did about where they were headed, both physically and metaphorically. After all, confessing her feelings for Andrew changed the whole dynamic of their relationship. *Or did it?* She wondered.

Tony reached over and took her hand in his, giving it a gentle squeeze. "Relax, Babe," he said, shooting her a sideways glance.

She blew her bangs from her face and gave a slight nod. *Easy for him to say,* she thought. *His heart isn't about to beat right out of his chest from nerves.*

Approaching the Barone house was as intimidating as she remembered. A long gravel road wound through a heavy patch of woods and ended in a circular drive in front of the two-story, white stucco home. There were no neighboring homes for miles. A concrete staircase led up to the over-sized front doors, with large wrought iron handles and concrete lion statues on either side. It had the warmth of a fortress.

Inside the front doors was a split-level landing with steps leading upward and downward. The moment she stepped through the front door, flashbacks of the weekend she and Tony had spent there filled her mind. It was right before college graduation. The night he proposed. A wave of emotion swept over her. She stared, almost dazed, allowing her mind to replay bitter sweet memories of her relationship with Tony.

"Babe," Tony blurted, bending down and waving his hand in front of her face. "I've said your name three times."

She shook off her feelings and took a deep breath. "Sorry, I was...I was in another place."

Tony grinned, "That's too bad. I was in the same place but at another time."

Their eyes met and Angel's heart ached. Was she still in love with Tony? Or did she just miss a time when life was easier? She closed her eyes before they could display her confusion.

"I shouldn't have said that," Tony dropped his head. "My bad."

Angel took a deep breath. Part of her wanted to lean against his strong, solid chest and whisper, 'I love you,' knowing there was no truer phrase to describe her heart for him. The other part of her wanted to fall into Andrew's arms. She exhaled and straightened her shoulders. "Where's Andrew?"

They descended the steps, which opened into a large family room. The ceiling was two stories high and the entire back of the house was windows. The floor was plush white carpeting, the kind that feels soft and squishy under your toes and a two-story, stone fireplace was in the far corner, with an enormous stone mantel that must have weighed a ton. Immediately to the right of it was a bar that ran the length of the room. It was topped with smoke colored marble and the mirrored wall behind made the room look even larger. Angel stared for a moment at the half-circle shaped, white suede-silk sofa and remembered lying in Tony's arms. She shook the memory and it shook her heart as she continued to walk to the left of the stairs, where another stairway led down to a wine cellar.

There were thousands of bottles of wine in the cellar. Angel stopped walking and gazed around the room. The shelves were constructed of Prime Mahogany and the floor was ceramic tile in deep brown tones. The room was lit with small track lights in pale yellow. It was extravagant and something one would expect to see in a wine magazine.

"Now that Venito's dead," Angel cleared her throat, "who gets all this wine."

Tony's eyes sparkled and his smile grew from a smirk to an ear-to-ear grin. "We do, Babe."

"I mean, legally, who does it belong to?"

Tony shrugged. "Dunno. Don't care."

Angel ran her finger over the top of the bottles. "So," she bit her lip, "we could drink one and no one would notice?"

"We can drink all of it if you want."

A moment of silence filled the cellar. *What's wrong with you?* Her senses screamed. *One minute you're crying and professing your love for Andrew and now you're feeling desire for Tony?* Angel tried to shake the voice from her head, but it kept talking. *You can't love them both,* the voice ranted and her stomach wrenched with nerves. Her conscience was right; she was taking fickle to a whole new level. The problem was she felt a sudden pressure to have to choose, or maybe a sudden regret for having already chosen. Was she second-guessing her profession of love for Andrew? *Maybe I thought I was in love with him simply because I was overwhelmed with emotion when I thought I had lost him forever?* Her thoughts taunted her and it was clear, after this whole mess got sorted out, that she needed to have her head examined; or better yet, take a long vacation. *A long vacation away from both of them,* she told herself.

"I'll tell you what," Tony interrupted her thoughts. "We'll get everything worked out with Giovanni, Andrew and the Russians and then we'll have a big party and drink all this wine. Deal?"

"Deal."

They maneuvered through the cellar to the edge of one of the shelves. Tony studied the shelves and Angel studied Tony. She was just about to ask what he was doing, when he twisted the seal on one of the wine bottles, lifting it up and to the left. Then he turned the cork like a combination lock, to the left then to the right and back to the left. There was a slight click and a door opened. Angel felt her jaw drop. "Pretty cool, isn't it," Tony grinned and Angel nodded, stepping closer to get a good look at how the mechanism worked.

"It looks exactly like all the other bottles," she uttered in amazement.

"I know." Tony said. "I've been down here many times and it still takes me a minute to figure out which bottle opens it."

They stepped through the doorway and Tony pulled it shut behind them. The hall was dark and Angel opened her eyes wider, straining to see. "Did you lock Andrew up like a prisoner in here?" She asked, only half-teasing.

"Don't give me any ideas," Tony quipped, slipping his hand in hers to lead her through the darkness. "The door opens from the inside, so you can easily get out once you're in here; but you have to know the combination to get in."

They walked down the hall and through another door that opened into a tiny apartment. There was a small kitchenette, with a stove, microwave and refrigerator to the immediate right. A round kitchen table and two chairs sat on a patch of ceramic tile in front of the refrigerator. Along the back wall was a flat screen television and surveillance system monitors, all inset into the wall, surrounded by bookshelves and pieces of decorative art. In front of the shelves sat a brown leather couch, mahogany coffee table and a leather arm chair. In the far left corner was a queen size bed with a chocolate colored comforter and decorative pillows adorned with golden swirls. A mahogany nightstand and lamp were beside the bed and to the immediate left of the doorway was a bathroom and a small closet.

"What's this place used for?" Angel asked.

"Because of Venito's imposter lifestyle, I think he knew one day he'd have to go into hiding so he built a secret little nest for himself," Tony explained.

"He spared no expense," Angel dragged her fingertips across the leather couch.

Tony sat down on the couch and grabbed the remote from the coffee table. "Come sit down, Babe, I'll show you my favorite channel."

Angel sat down and Tony draped his arm around the back of the couch, letting his fingertips rest mere centimeters from her shoulder, sending a flutter of nerves through her. Being with Tony was comfortable and there was something to be said for comfort. Tony clicked the remote and a picture of a crackling fire appeared on the screen. It even made popping noises like a real fire. "This is your favorite channel?" Angel asked.

"It's soothing," Tony said. "Lean back, close your eyes and listen to it." Tony leaned his head against the back of the couch and closed his eyes. Angel stared at him. He cracked one eye open and returned her stare. "You're not doing it," he said. "Lean back," he sat up and grabbed her legs, pulling her down until her head rested comfortably against the back of the couch. "Now close your eyes," he instructed, swiping his hand gently over her eyelids until she closed them. "And listen."

Angel abruptly sat upright. "Where's Andrew?" She stared at Tony, this time with doubt. Surely he hadn't lied about Andrew being alive? Surely he didn't kill him and lure her here in some feeble attempt to force her to forgive him? Angel's breathing quickened and she felt a clammy uneasiness crawl up the back of her neck.

"Trust me, Babe, he'll be here. Now lean back and relax."

Angel flopped back on the couch but she couldn't relax. She was having a wrestling match between logic and emotion; unsure of which would win. Emotion told her Tony was not a liar, nor a cold-blooded killer. Much as he didn't trust Andrew, he wouldn't have killed him. Logic danced around the ring, throwing punches of doubt. Would Tony kill Andrew out of loyalty to Giovanni? Even Andrew himself had once told her that when the Capo Di Tutti Capi makes you an offer, you don't refuse it. Angel opened her eyes, turned her head and silently gazed at Tony, who sat stone still with his eyes closed. *He wouldn't kill Andrew,* she reassured herself, *because it would hurt me and Tony would never hurt me.*

"Close your eyes, Babe," Tony whispered. "He'll be here. I promise."

Angel must have dozed off because the next thing she knew she was startled awake by a creaking sound and footsteps. She jumped to her feet, whirled around and found herself face-to-face with the Shark. She gasped, suddenly aware that Tony was gone and she was alone with this monstrosity of a man. She froze, unable to speak. He didn't speak either, just gave Angel a slight nod and headed for the hallway.

"Wait," she called out. "Where did you come from?" He didn't say anything, just pointed toward an opening in the floor that hadn't been there before. It was a light-weight tile over by the bed that matched the other ceramic tiles, but opened on hinges. She rushed toward the opening and looked down, hoping to see Andrew ascending the ladder; but there was nothing there but an empty corridor.

Angel rushed down the dark hallway after the Shark. "Wait!" She hollered. "Where is Andrew?" He didn't turn around. "Where's Tony?" The Shark opened the cellar door and then slammed it shut. She ran her fingers along the wall, searching for a handle or knob or mechanism to open it from the inside. There was nothing. She turned back down the hall, reaching in the back of her jeans for her gun; but it was gone. She felt her way down the hall and into the apartment; her pulse quickening. When she entered the apartment Angel stopped abruptly, throwing her hands to her mouth in disbelief. There, seated on the couch, was Kristen.

CHAPTER 8

"Angel, how nice to see you again," Kristen hissed with hatred so strong it could be tangibly felt filling the space between them.

Angel's jaw tightened and she narrowed her eyes. "Where's Andrew?"

"He'll be here," she said, flipping her blonde hair over her shoulders and exhaling as if she were bored.

"What are you doing here? What's going on?" Angel inched toward the bed and the opening in the floor. "Did you come here with the Shark? Where's Tony?" She tried to nonchalantly peek into the opening to see if Tony or Andrew were by chance hiding in the tunnel, waiting to make a grand entrance; but no one was there. Her mind whirled with possibilities. Are Tony and Andrew both traitors, working for Denny and now Kristen? She forced the thought away, telling herself it was impossible. Was Tony the real traitor and Andrew found out about it, so Tony killed him and lied to Angel to lure her here? Did Tony somehow set Andrew up so Giovanni would order him killed? Reigning in her imagination, she focused on Kristen and demanded a second time, "what is going on?"

Kristen laughed out loud. "Oh, Angel, Angel, Angel, you're not so quick on the uptake, are you?"

Angel felt a powerful urge to punch Kristen in her perfectly rounded nose. "Where are they?" She yelled, approaching Kristen with her fists clenched. Kristen didn't stand up or move, but raised her eyes and glared up at Angel; who for the first time noticed the restraints around Kristen's ankles.

Her lips curved upward into a smile and she raised her left eyebrow and crossed her arms. "Oh, I see you're not here voluntarily," Angel grinned. "I'm starting to feel better about this whole thing."

"Feel good while you can," Kristen quipped.

"What's that supposed to mean?"

"Don't listen to her," the Shark gruffed from behind, startling Angel. She jumped, flailed her arms and landed atop his foot. He gave a silent wince and lifted her off.

"Sorry," Angel cringed. "I didn't hear you come in."

"That's part of my charm," he uttered, as he lifted Kristen from the couch and flipped her over his shoulder so her torso dangled down his back. "I'll take the trash out," he said and Angel could have sworn she saw the sides of his mouth start to curl into a smile.

Kristen raised her chin and glared at Angel with pure hate in her eyes. "You have no idea what you're up against."

The Shark quickly turned his body, causing Kristen's head to bash into the wall by the door.

"Ow!" She shrieked. "You did that on purpose."

"I don't know what you're talking about," he mumbled, turning quickly the other way and bashing her head against the opposite wall. He looked back at Angel. "I could do this all night."

Angel laughed out loud. It was the first time she had seen a playful and comedic, albeit violent, side of the Shark.

"By the way," the Shark said, "I'm supposed to tell you he wants to see you now, if you're ready."

"Who?" Angel asked. "Andrew?" The Shark disappeared down the hall without answering her questions.

Angel felt breathless with anticipation, darting her eyes back and forth between the hall and the opening in the floor. *Who wants to see me now?* She wondered. *And where will he come from.*

Moments later, her questions were answered. He entered through the hallway and Angel couldn't believe her eyes. She stood face-to-face with the man from the Pub, the one to whom she had served the chilled vodka and the one Andrew had helped sneak out the backdoor. He was dressed all in black, just as she remembered. Dark hair, brown eyes and unshaven olive skin made him attractive in a mysterious sort of way.

"Hello, Michelangela," he spoke English but his Russian accent was thick. "My name is Vadim Scotrovi. You may or may not know who I am."

Anger boiled inside her. "You were at Tetterbaum's. You're working with Andrew. Why?"

Scotrovi reached inside his jacket and retrieved a pack of cigarettes with the name Sobranie across it and a silver lighter. He opened the pack and held it out toward Angel, offering her a cigarette; but she shook him off. She didn't smoke and even if she did, she didn't like the look of his cigarettes. They were solid black with gold filters and she wasn't entirely sure whether he was lighting a cigarette or a skinny cigar.

He inhaled deeply and blinked slowly, as if the nicotine fix healed him. Then he slid the pack back into his jacket and sat down in the leather arm chair. "Please," he motioned Angel toward the couch. "We sit and discuss matters."

"I want to see Andrew," she crossed her arms and remained standing.

"He will be here," Scotrovi uttered while exhaling a ring of smoke above his head.

"I won't discuss anything until I see him." Angel sat down slowly on the arm of the couch and kept her eyes on Scotrovi.

"Very well," he took a drag from his cigarette. "Then we sit in silence and wait."

Questions whirled through her mind. *Why did Tony bring me here and then leave me? Who took my gun and why? Where is Andrew? Why is Kristen here?* She chewed on her left index fingernail and tried to force herself to think calm, rational thoughts instead of fear-driven, emotional ones. It was easier said than done.

"You shouldn't chew on your fingernails, Sweetheart," his voice came from behind her. "It isn't becoming of a lady." Angel leapt to her feet the moment she heard his familiar voice. She spun toward the door and held her breath when she saw him. "Scotrovi, you mind giving us a moment," Andrew asked and Scotrovi gave a nod.

"I will finish my cigarette and return," he said.

Angel's feet felt glued to the floor by the weight of her feelings for Andrew. She couldn't take her eyes off him and she couldn't stop them from filling with tears. When Scotrovi was gone, Andrew walked to her and engulfed her in his arms. He picked her up, carried her to the couch and sat with her on his lap, her arms wrapped around his neck and her legs draped over his. "Sweetheart, everything's okay now," he whispered.

"I thought you were dead," emotion and anger competed for a stronghold and she tightened her lip. "For three days I thought you were dead."

He stroked her hair and kissed atop her head. "I'm sorry. It wouldn't have been safe for me or for Tony if I contacted you."

Angel pulled her head from his shoulder and looked him in the eyes. "When I saw the tape from the pub, I tried to call you and then I drove everywhere looking for you, but I couldn't find you. When I was at the meeting and I saw the look Giovanni gave Tony," her voice cracked, "and I saw Tony nod, I knew you were..." her voice faded. "I knew you were..." she broke into sobs.

"Shhh," he held her close. "It's over. I'm here and I promise I'll never disappear like that. I'll never leave without saying goodbye."

If only that were true, but Mafia life didn't allow for such promises. People often disappeared without saying goodbye. In the time it takes to pull a trigger, people vanished and lives were destroyed. That was Mafia reality. It was a code of ethics where, for the most part, loyalty to the Capo Di Tutti Capi trumped personal morality and Angel wasn't sure if she could stomach it any longer.

"I prayed and prayed for you to be alive," she sniffed.

"Well, it worked. I'm alive," Andrew smiled. "But I like it best when we pray together." He was making reference to their once shared prayer time which led to an evening of passion. It was the only time they had made-love; agreeing afterwards not to let it happen again due to the complicated nature of their current situation. Relationships between two bogata members were difficult enough without the extra challenge of him being a cop and her being head of mafia family. Talk about a conflict of interests.

Angel leaned toward him, wanting to feel his lips on hers, but Andrew lifted her chin and met her gaze. He wiped some straggler tears from her cheeks with his shirt sleeve and sighed. "We have a lot to discuss and we don't have a lot of time."

This was par for the course with Andrew. *Always practical*, she thought, *to a fault.* She sniffed in deeply and exhaled, nodding her head to indicate she had regained composure. *But you didn't tell him that you love him!* Her heart beckoned, but her mind knew it would have to wait. Andrew had moved on to business and there was much business at hand.

Angel wiped her eyes with the back of her hand. "I need to ask you one thing. Why did you risk my life and Chase's at the pub the other night? Why did you allow sixteen innocent people to die?"

Andrew closed his eyes and shook his head, "it wasn't like that, Sweetheart. The plan got messed up."

"The plan? What plan?" Angel stared deeply into his eyes.

"It's too hard to explain," he shook his head. "It wasn't supposed to happen like that."

"Why would you let it happen at all?"

Andrew's jaw tensed. "I didn't. At least, I didn't mean to."

Their conversation was interrupted when Scotrovi, Tony and the Shark returned and sat down; Scotrovi in the arm chair, and the Shark in a kitchen chair he pulled over across from the couch. Tony sat on the far end of the couch so Angel was between him and Andrew. *Talk about sitting in the hot seat.*

"Where's Kristen?" Angel asked.

"Locked up for the night," the Shark uttered in his natural deep voice.

"Kristen isn't a part of this," Andrew explained. "At least not right now." Angel shrugged her shoulders to indicate she was in the dark on how everything fit together, and Andrew gave her knee a small squeeze. "This will all make sense in a little while, Sweetheart," he looked from Angel to Scotrovi. "Why don't you start explaining and the rest of us will jump in."

Scotrovi lit another cigarette and exhaled slowly. "I am a Russian government agent, working for the Sluzhba Vneshney Razvedki or SVR for short. The SVR handles intelligence and espionage activities outside the Russian Federation." He took a deep drag from his cigarette and held the smoke in his lungs for a few seconds, then exhaled it above his head. "The SVR has several objectives. Counter intelligence, border security, surveillance within and abroad and counter-terrorism, the last of which has been my assignment for many years."

"Counter terrorism?" Angel narrowed her brows. "How does any of this tie into terrorism?"

Scotrovi shook his head, "it is a long, how do you say, complicated story."

That must be the universal male species favorite word. Complicated. It's like an easy out to having to explain details or indulge in any form of deep conversation, Angel thought. *It's like they can just say, 'it's complicated' and badah bing, badah boom, end of story.* Angel was naturally sensitive to the use of the word complicated, as just last week both Tony and Andrew used it to describe the nature of their feelings for her.

Scotrovi stood up and began to pace behind the arm chair. "My country has dealt with Rossiyskaya Mafiya for a long time."

Andrew interjected, "that's the term for Russian Mafia."

"Yah," Scotrovi nodded. "What you call Bratva." He continued. "Russian Mafia criminals are in virtually every area of our society. They deal in illegal oil trade, drug trafficking, smuggling of weapons and nuclear material, money laundering; the list is ongoing."

"How does any of this tie into us?" Angel's lack of patience was beginning to show in her face and tone of voice. A part of her wanted to blurt, *all right, get to the point already!* But she restrained.

Scotrovi continued. "After the September 11, 2001 attacks on your country, we began to discover links between Al-Qaeda and certain Russian mafia groups. I was sent in undercover to one of these groups to gain intelligence."

"You've been working undercover as a Russian criminal for ten years?" Angel stared at him.

"Yah," he nodded and blew a smoke ring over his head. "I infiltrated the Vamloskaya Gang, who are vastly known for their weapons trade and drug trafficking; and

I have since become a trusted, high-ranking member."

"This is where the blonde bimbo comes in," Tony interjected, referring to Kristen.

"Actually, it's where her father, Denny, becomes relevant," Andrew corrected.

"Yah," Scotrovi gave a nod. "Sean Denarius Moloney, or Denny as you call him, contacted the Vamloskaya Boss and worked a deal. We provide him with the weapons and Intel he needs to eliminate Giovanni, Salvatore and their families, in exchange for majority mob control over two of your major cities."

"Chicago and New York," Angel said, the pieces now beginning to fit together.

"So Denny, over the course of many years, connected Bratva members here in the States, who had no real sense of organization, with Vamloskaya members there..." Andrew was cut off by Scotrovi.

"...who pride themselves on strict internal discipline, organization and loyalty." He exhaled smoke and leaned back in the arm chair.

"You following all this, Babe," Tony grinned at her. "I know how much you loved poli-sci and foreign affairs in college," he teased.

"Obviously, I should have paid more attention," she rolled her eyes and leaned forward, placing her elbows on her knees and interlocking her fingers. "So, the Russian government or SVR sent you undercover into the Vamloskaya gang, who made a deal with Denny; and then the Vamloskaya Boss sent you here to the States to increase Bratva presence. Is that the gist of it?"

"There is more," Scotrovi said.

Angel stood up and walked behind the couch. "Of course there is, there's always more," she uttered under her breath.

"There was already a Bratva weapons dealer here to be the liaison between Denny and the Vamloskaya," Scotrovi explained.

"Selovich," Andrew interjected.

"When Selovich was killed and his weapons stolen, Vamloskaya took it personally," Scotrovi's eyes narrowed. "He had much money invested."

"This is where the blonde bimbo comes in," Tony snapped his fingers.

"Yah," Scotrovi said. "Kristen informed Vamloskaya of your involvement, of her father's death, and her intent to honor her father's agreement. The Vamloskaya Boss agreed and sent me here to ensure there were no more errors."

Something in Scotrovi's voice made Angel stop pacing and study him. His expression grew more and more intense and his eyes seemed lost somewhere between sadness and fear.

"How are you supposed to ensure there will be no more errors?" Angel asked.

He pulled a photograph from his inside jacket pocket, gazed down at it for a moment and then handed it to Angel. His eyes softened as he spoke. "This is my wife, Alyona, and my little girl, Zhanna. She is five years old."

Angel's heart skipped a beat as she looked down at the picture. "The Vamloskaya Boss took your family?"

His head moved up and down as he lifted another cigarette from the pack. "Yah, he will hold my family until I succeed here and return home."

"And if you don't succeed here and return home?" Angel already knew the answer. They all knew the answer.

"That is not an option for me," Scotrovi uttered.

Angel chewed on her bottom lip. "Have you notified the SVR that your family is in danger?"

"This is where it gets hairy," Andrew said.

"THIS is where it gets hairy?" Angel's eyes widened. "I'd say it's already pretty hairy."

Angel handed the picture back to Scotrovi. "Vamloskaya sent some boys to make sure you were out of the picture," he explained to Angel, taking one last look at the photograph and then returning it to his pocket.

"The two shooters at the pub?" Angel asked.

"Yah. I met with them the day before the attack to solidify our plans. We would first hit the Pub, and then as your family mourned your loss and were weak, we would hit them."

"Sounds like you had it all worked out," Angel fought back angry sarcasm as she thought of the sixteen patrons that left the pub in body bags.

"During our strategic meetings, I discovered Vamloskaya had a mole inside the SVR. I knew then if I reported to the SVR that Vamloskaya had my family and that information fell into the wrong hands..." Scotrovi dropped his head and shook it. They could all see he was fighting back emotion and no one finished his sentence. They all knew what it meant. It meant Scotrovi's wife and daughter were as good as dead; and it didn't need to be said out loud.

Scotrovi grit his teeth. "I will die to protect my family," he uttered in a voice of desperation.

Angel began pacing again and chewing on her fingernail.

"Uh-oh," Andrew said in a loud whisper, obviously trying to lighten the mood. "She's pacing."

"What does that mean?" Scotrovi asked.

"It means she's thinking," Tony quipped. "And it's always scary when she's thinking."

Angel stopped, put her hands on her hips, and gave Tony a sideways smirk. Then she started pacing again. As questions popped into her brain, she blurted them out for one of the men to answer.

"Scotrovi," she said, "if there is a mole in the SVR, isn't your undercover identity in the Vamloskaya gang already compromised?"

"No," he explained. "As part of a small select group of counter-terrorist agents, my identity is sealed. Only the very top ranking officials can access my information."

"How many top ranking officials are there?" Angel questioned.

"Three."

"I want their names," Angel ordered and she saw Scotrovi's eyes widen with surprise.

"That is top-secret, confidential information. I cannot disclose their identities." Scotrovi shook his head, as if offended by the mere request.

Angel leaned down into his face. "I don't have any reason to trust you, so if you want my help in saving your family, you'll give me exactly what I ask for." She stood up and went back to pacing.

"How did you find out there was a mole?" She asked. "Did one of the Vamloskaya boys tell you?"

"No," Scotrovi sighed, "I saw the markings on their guns."

Angel remembered how intrigued Chase was with the guns, stating they were Russian made weapons and there was no way the Bratva in the States could have them. She also heard Salvatore's words ringing in her head. "If we're dealing with the Russian mob backed by the Russian government," he had warned, "it will be a bloody battle."

"Their guns are Russian-made..." Scotrovi began but Angel cut him off.

"PM's, or Pistol Makarovas, I know," she gloated inwardly when the Shark and Scotrovi glanced at her in amazement. It felt good to be in the know. "Are you certain there is no other way the Vamloskaya boys could have gotten mint condition PM's?"

"No, these guns were made specific by the Russian government. There is a tiny mark below the regular emblem, a mark only a high-ranking SVR member would recognize as relevant."

Andrew piped in, "that's why it was important for the Shark to take their guns after he killed the Vamloskaya boys in the pub. If the police got a hold of the guns and were able to trace them back to the Russian government, we'd have problems of National security on our hands."

"Not only that," Scotrovi added, "but if national attention were drawn then the Vamloskaya would know our mission here had been compromised and they would kill my family."

"And there was no way to kill the Vamloskaya boys before they murdered sixteen of my customers?" Angel fought to keep her anger under control.

"First of all, Sweetheart, it was fourteen customers because two of the bodies belonged to the shooters," Andrew noted and Angel glared at him.

Scotrovi spoke poignantly to Angel. "I know you are angry at the injustice. I am sorry for those lives." His eyes softened. "But if I did not go through with the attack as planned, they would have known and my family would be murdered."

Angel bit her bottom lip and mumbled under her breath. "So we sacrificed fourteen innocent people to try and save two."

"Yah," Scotrovi hung his head, slumping back into the chair.

Angel exhaled and shook her head back and forth. It wasn't right. There was nothing right about the injustice of innocent lives being taken. She hated it. It was one thing for the mob to kill each other, but an entirely different matter for bystanders to be gunned down in cold blood. She still couldn't believe it had actually happened, but even more so, she couldn't believe Andrew had gone along with the plan.

"Andrew," she blurted his name with such force they all stared up at her. "You're telling me there was no other way?"

Andrew shook his head. "Once it was set in motion, we didn't have a choice, Sweetheart."

"That's a load of crap!" Angel could feel her temperature rising and her heart beating faster. "You, Andrew, YOU could have come into the pub earlier and have cleared all of the people out." She paced frantically behind the couch. "YOU," she pointed at Andrew, "could have let me in on what was happening so that I could have made sure no one got hurt."

Andrew jumped to his feet. "That wouldn't have worked," his voice elevated.

"Why not?" Angel crossed her arms and stared at him. "It might have worked, but instead you let fourteen people get slaughtered and you risked my life and Chase's too."

Andrew shook his head. "It wasn't supposed to happen that way!" Andrew yelled. "I knew you two would have time to get into hiding safely."

"And if we hadn't?"

"I knew you would." Their eyes locked.

"And...if...we...hadn't?" Angel over-enunciated each word, through clenched teeth.

"There was nothing I could do," Andrew stared at her, his words piercing through her heart in such a way that made her feel suddenly hollow. "Somehow it got all screwed up and there was nothing I could do."

"We don't know who the mole in the SVR is or where he is. He could be watching every move so we had to follow through with the plan," Scotrovi emphatically explained. "The only thing we could do to stop future massacres was to have the Shark kill the shooters so that they would be unable to hunt down and kill your family as well."

Angel couldn't shake the feeling that Andrew wasn't telling her the whole story. She hated that.

Tony jumped up and clapped his hands together one time, undoubtedly trying to break the tension in the room. "I'm starving. Let's take a breather and get some grub." He moved toward the door. "Shark, man, you want to help me in the kitchen upstairs?"

They left while Angel and Andrew were still in a stand-off. Scotrovi rose slowly from the arm chair, put his cigarette out in the ashtray on the coffee table, and walked toward the doorway. "I will see if I can assist them with supper," he said and then paused and drew in a breath. "Michelangela?"

"Yes?" She met Scotrovi's eyes.

"How many people would you have sacrificed to save your father?"

Scotrovi didn't wait for an answer, not that she would have been able to give him one. He abruptly left the room and Angel dropped her chin and closed her eyes. She could still feel Andrew's stare. She walked to the couch, slumped onto it and buried her face in her palms. "I'm so angry I can feel it burning all the way down to my toes."

"You have a high sense of justice, Sweetheart," Andrew said, sitting down atop the coffee table, leaning toward her with his elbows on his knees. "That's a good trait."

It bothered her that Andrew had risked her life, but she knew they couldn't waste time arguing about it. What was done was done. She had to ignore that part for now. *Tony would never have put your life at risk,* her mind taunted. *Never!* Maybe what was so hard was that it all hit too close to home. Seeing Scotrovi's wife and daughter in the picture made Angel remember being the five year old little girl whose daddy never came home. It paralleled her story just enough to make her feel edgy and uncomfortable. What's more, Scotrovi made her face something about herself that she didn't want to admit. Would she have sacrificed fourteen innocent people to save her father? Or her

mother? Or Aunt Olga? The truth was
undeniably yes.

CHAPTER 9

Over the course of the next few hours, they talked while dining on spaghetti with olive oil and fresh basil, warm bread and wine. They huddled around the coffee table and the small kitchen table in the underground apartment.

"Sure would be nice to sit at the large table upstairs," Tony said, shoveling in a bite. "But we have to keep dead-head here out of sight." He pointed to Andrew.

"You can all eat upstairs. I just can't risk sitting in front of a window and having my brains splattered by a sniper," Andrew answered.

"Table talk," Angel moaned.

"Agreed," the Shark gruffed.

"None of us should be seen coming and going from here," Scotrovi added. "We must only use the underground tunnel and do so cautiously."

"Where does that tunnel lead?" Angel asked, holding up her glass for Tony to fill with wine.

"There's a whole network of tunnels beneath the house. It's really pretty cool, Babe. I'll show you later," Tony said and he and Andrew met eyes. Angel noticed their exchange and felt her face flush. It was that all-too-familiar tension rising from within, reminding her that she had feelings for both of them; as if she needed a reminder. What bothered her even more than her fickle heart was the obvious fact that Andrew didn't want Tony to take her through the tunnels. Was it that he didn't want her alone with Tony? Or that he didn't want her seeing something in the tunnels? She flagged it in her mind to revisit later.

"I'm not going into the tunnel without my gun," Angel said, raising an eyebrow at Tony. "Why'd you take it?"

He pulled her 9mm from his waistband and handed it to her, handle first. "I thought it best to give Scotrovi a fighting chance, Babe. I was worried you'd have blown his head off the minute you saw him."

Angel stood up and slid the gun into the waistband of her jeans. "I might have," she admitted.

Scotrovi raised his wine glass in toasting fashion toward Tony. "Thank you."

Throughout the rest of the conversation Angel came to understand what role each person in the room played. She learned that the Shark lied about killing his brother, Gerald, because Gerald agreed to spill the beans on all Denny had planned.

"So if it wasn't Gerald, then whose body was found in the building across from the Towers?" Angel asked.

"One of Denny's men," the Shark answered while chewing a large bite of garlic bread. "Denny sent everyone out in pairs to make sure the job got done."

"Denny was a wise man," Scotrovi added. "All Russian gangs send men out in groups, usually groups of six broken into fragments of two each. Should they meet with resistance, the job will most likely still be accomplished."

Gerald also proved influential in helping the Shark infiltrate Denny's group and was killed when Giovanni's men took down the Iowa compound. The Shark later contacted Andrew and informed him about Kristen's plans to carry out her father's revenge, the treaty with the Russians and the planned meeting with Scotrovi.

Scotrovi added, "I was scheduled to meet with Thomas Boglevich, who was a Vamloskaya member, but your Shark here showed up instead. He brought Andrew in on the situation and here we all are."

"See, Sweetheart," Andrew explained, "because Scotrovi's family is in danger, and until we can find the mole in the SVR, we've got to make the Vamloskaya Boss believe that everything is going as planned."

"Which is why the Shark couldn't get rid of the blonde bimbo," Tony added.

"Yah," Scotrovi leaned back from his empty plate and pulled out his cigarettes. "We need the blonde bimbo, as you call her, to continue her communication with the Vamloskaya so they believe everything is on schedule."

"Speaking of Kristen," Angel raised an eyebrow. "Has anyone fed her?"

The Shark rose from his seat and exhaled loudly, "I will take care of her."

As he walked toward the doorway Tony quipped, "I think someone has a little thing for the blonde bimbo."

Instantly two large hands came from behind and gripped Tony's shoulders. His eyes bulged with surprise. "I wouldn't say that again friend," the Shark snapped.

"Got it." Tony smirked and sunk back into the couch as the Shark released his shoulders. Angel pursed her lips together to stifle a laugh.

After Kristen had been fed and Scotrovi had another cigarette, they were ready to tackle the problem at hand. First, how do they find the mole in the SVR before he or she figures out Scotrovi is an undercover agent? Second, how do they make the Vamloskaya Boss believe the deal with Kristen is being executed without error and with no one dying? Third, how do they ensure the safe return of Scotrovi's family? They needed to develop a plan in the next thirty-six hours, which was when Angel had to sneak back into the Dana Hotel and Spa and return to the Towers with Sophia and Olga.

Angel paced behind the couch. "We need more manpower," she said. "Each of us must have one or two people we trust with our lives." She studied their faces. "I say we bring in those people."

"Babe, if someone leaks that I didn't follow Giovanni's order, I'm dead," Tony said.

"We're both dead," Andrew added.

Scotrovi shook his head. "If we don't find the mole in the SVR, my family is dead; and so am I."

"He's right," Angel crossed her arms and stared at Andrew. "You had no problem taking a chance when it was Chase's life on the line," she said. "Not to mention when my life was on the line."

"You can't argue with that," Tony smirked.

"You're not helping." Andrew glared at him.

"I know," Tony grinned ear to ear.

"I'm going to bring Chase in on what's happening," Angel said matter-of-factly. Her tone clearly implying this decision was not open for discussion. "I believe his weapon contacts, previous knowledge of Selovich and his operation here, and his technological skills will be an asset."

"We might be able to utilize his pilot skills too," the Shark added.

"Now, who do you want to include?" Angel nodded at Tony to speak first.

"I dunno, Babe, I'm a little gun shy after the whole Dane thing. Let me think on it." Tony got up and walked toward the door. "I'll grab another bottle of wine and check in on the bimbo."

Angel had forgotten about Dane. He worked for the Andriachinni family and although he wasn't a Made member yet, Tony trusted him. They all did, up until the point where he tried to kill Tony, Angel and Sophia with a car bomb. Dane met with a sudden death via Andrew's .45 when he drew his gun and pointed it at Andrew in the middle of a meeting.

"I think the only person who would prove beneficial is Sal, my long-term contact in the FBI," Andrew said. "I know I can trust him. Maybe he even has a trusted contact in the SVR to help us find the mole?"

Angel looked to Scotrovi, whose eyes drifted to a far away place. "Anyone you trust to bring in on this?"

"No," his jaw tightened. "I trust no one with the lives of my family."

Tony walked back in, carrying a bottle of Cabernet. "You're trusting us, Ace," he said, removing the cork and giving it a sniff.

"There's got to be someone at SVR you can trust. Someone high up in the organization?" The words were fresh off Angel's lips when Scotrovi jumped to his feet and grasped her by the shoulders.

She gasped, wide-eyed and he yelled, "I trust no one at SVR. No one!"

The moment Scotrovi's hands clutched Angel, Andrew leapt from the couch and Tony cleared the chair and drew his gun in one swift motion.

"Take it easy, Ace," Tony hollered; his aim steady.

"Let go of her and slowly step away," Andrew instructed. Angel and Scotrovi were nose to nose. A trickle of sweat ran down the side of his clenched jaw and his eyes pierced through her with an intensity she couldn't identify. Was it anger? Fear? Hate?

Scotrovi removed his hands and held them, palms up for a moment. "My apologies Michelangela, and to everyone. I fear the stress of the situation and my concern for my family has overcome my senses." He stepped away from Angel and made his way toward the door. "I think I should resign for the evening. Good night." He disappeared down the hall.

"You okay, Babe?" Tony asked, disarming his .45 and slipping it into the back of his jeans.

Angel nodded. "I'm fine. What do you think all that was about?" She raised an eyebrow.

"I think he's stressed out, Sweetheart, just like he said," Andrew shrugged. "Stress can make people do crazy things."

Angel bit her bottom lip. Something didn't feel right. She knew stress all too well. She'd had her share of freak-out moments, but something in Scotrovi's stare revealed more. She couldn't put her finger on it, but she saw something beyond a flash of panic in his eyes.

The Shark stood from his chair, and set his wine glass on the kitchen table. "I'm turning in for the night too," he said, disappearing through the doorway.

"Me too," said Tony, setting the wine bottle on the coffee table. "I'll leave this here for you two." He started to walk toward the door and Angel felt an awkward tug in her heart. Was Tony leaving her here with Andrew, a bottle of wine and one bed? Was he implying that they would sleep together and he was okay with it? *Well, you DID tell him you loved Andrew,* the little voice in her head taunted. *But I told him I loved him too,* she answered back in the quiet of her mind. It was one thing to sleep with Andrew at his house, and that only happened once. It was another thing entirely to be with him under the same roof as Tony.

"Where do I sleep?" Angel blurted out and it stopped Tony in his tracks. Shock shown on his face and his eyes darted from her to Andrew and back to her again. She could tell he was not only taken aback by her question, but pleasantly surprised. "I mean," she cleared her throat, "is there a guest room I can use?"

"Sure thing, Babe," Tony smiled the sort of smile that glows from internal happiness. "Top of the steps, down the hall, last door on the left."

"Thanks," she gave Tony a smile, "for everything."

Tony walked down the hall and Angel turned around to see Andrew, sitting on the couch, leaning back with his arms crossed over his chest. She took a deep breath and closed her eyes, trying to make sense of her own heart. She stood behind him and gently touched his right shoulder. "I guess I'm going to go up to bed now, too," she gave his shoulder a tender squeeze and headed for the doorway.

"You're never gonna trust me again, are you?" His question took her by surprise and she didn't know how to respond. "You don't have to answer, Sweetheart." He stood up and walked toward her, taking one hand in his and looking intently in her eyes. "I can see it."

"You let them into Tetterbaum's," she shook her head, still in disbelief. "You let them attack innocent people." She stared in his eyes. "You let them attack me."

Andrew hung his head. "I know you don't understand, hell, I don't even understand what happened." He shook his head. "You have to believe me when I tell you it wasn't supposed to go down that way."

"I want to believe you. I do, but something doesn't feel right." She slid her hand from his and started toward the hall.

"Angel," he reached for her arm. "Have I lost you?"

How can you lose something you never really had? She didn't say it, but she felt it. "Let's just get through this and then maybe we can sit down and talk."

"Goodnight, Sweetheart," Andrew mouthed quietly but Angel was already gone.

She walked slowly up the hall, her heart tormenting her mind and her thoughts muddling up her heart. She didn't know how they were going to make anything work, but of one thing she was certain. She would not let Scotrovi's family die.

CHAPTER 10

Angel crept up the last flight of steps in the Barone fortress, to where the bedrooms jetted off down the hallway. Tony told her she could sleep in the spare bedroom, down the hall, last door on the left. She opened the door and was startled to see Tony sitting on the bed.

"What are you doing?" Angel asked, aware of the intensity in his face.

"You want the truth, Babe?" Tony's tone indicated agitation.

Angel nodded, closed the door and sat down next to him. "I always want the truth."

"I still don't trust him and it's killing me."

"Who? Andrew? The Shark?"

He pursed his lips together. "There's somethin' not right and I can't put my finger on it." Angel had the same feeling but she didn't want to fuel Tony's doubt by telling him. It was the feeling that there was more to the story than Andrew, Scotrovi or the Shark was telling. "It's probably just me and I'm letting all this crap in my head cloud my judgment."

"What do you think is clouding your judgment?"

"Fear," Tony shook his head.

"Fear?" Angel was surprised, as Tony was one of the most fearless men she knew. "What are you afraid of?"

"Giovanni, for one, and..." Tony stopped mid-sentence and took a deep breath. "I'm afraid of losing you, either to a bullet or to someone like Andrew." He turned to face her, bending one knee up on the bed and taking her hands in his. "You're not mine anymore, Babe, and I guess it's killing me because there was never a time when I stopped wanting you to be mine."

Angel hadn't ever seen his perspective. When Tony left her, she thought it was because he had found someone else or had fallen out of love. It wasn't until she learned about her Mafia roots that she came to understand Tony had left to protect her, to protect her identity.

"See, Babe," he continued, "you got over me, but I never got over you. I've loved you since the day we met and even when I left I didn't stop."

Her mouth went dry and her heart sped up. Who was she kidding? She had never gotten over him. She tried. She grieved the break-up and got angry, fell into Grayson's bed to take her mind off of him, but if she were completely honest with herself, she'd have to admit that she had never completely gotten over Tony. He was her first true love.

Tony stood up and moved toward the door. "Lock this when I leave," he said.

"Tony?" She jumped up and called out his name, not knowing what she was going to

say next. She just didn't want him to leave.
"Can I use your phone to call Chase?"

"No, Babe. It's too risky. I'll contact
him tomorrow for you." Of course, he was
right. They had to assume that Giovanni had
eyes and ears watching all his people and one
stupid move could mean the end of both Tony
and Andrew. Any contact with anyone had to
be carefully thought out.

Tony reached for the doorknob and
Angel reached for him, grabbing the back of
his black t-shirt and tugging. She felt a flush
of nerves as he turned around and looked at
her. "Will you stay with me?"

"Babe..."

She put her fingers to his lips. "I don't
want to be alone." *Is it that you don't want to
be alone or that you want to be with him?* An
internal voice taunted her but Angel shook it
off. "Will you hold me?"

"Only if I get to pick where I put my
hands," Tony teased and Angel playfully
smacked his arm.

They lay down on the bed, Tony on his
back and Angel snuggled into his chest. It felt
good. Comfortable. Safe. He wrapped his
arms around her and held her tightly against
him. "Is this too weird?" She asked.

"Nah," he sighed, "it's just right."

Angel awoke to a gun shot and the
sound of shattering glass. Tony was already
on his feet, .45 in hand and heading for the
bedroom door. She grabbed her 9mm from

the nightstand and followed him. "What's happening?" She whispered.

"Dunno, Babe, but we gotta get to the wine cellar before whoever it is starts searching the rooms."

Angel checked the clip on her gun, shoved it back in and took the safety off. Tony cracked the door slightly; just enough to hear voices moving in their direction, then closed and locked it. He went to the window and looked out. "Change of plans, Babe," he said, pushing the window open quickly and quietly.

"We can't go out this way; it's almost a two story drop." Angel peered down.

"It's less than two-stories because of the way the house sets on the land; and we don't have a choice." Tony shoved his gun into the waistband of his jeans. "Here's what we're going to do. I'll hang out the window and you're going to climb down my body and then drop to the ground."

"What!" Angel could feel her eyes bulging as Tony put one leg out the window. "Tony, I can't. I can't do that. We'll both fall."

He tugged her arm and pulled her closer to the window. "You have to do it. You can do it. Babe, it's either this or a bullet and I think we got a better chance out this window."

Angel peeked out the window and down to the ground. Her stomach went queasy. The good news was that they weren't landing on a patio, pavement or rocks. No one had groomed the property since Venito's death, so the grass had grown quite thick and long, incurring the softest possible landing. The voices grew louder in the hallway and Angel started to panic. "Okay, let's go," she said, shoving her 9mm into the back of her jeans.

Tony climbed out the window, keeping the base of the window in his armpits for a sturdier grip. "Keep your legs together when you land and bend your knees," he instructed. She began to climb out, straddling his head and shoulders until she could get her body turned around piggy-back style.

"Are you okay?" She cringed.

"Yeah, Babe, I actually like it when you wrap your legs around my head."

She could hear the smile in Tony's voice even though she couldn't see his face. *Men!* She slid down his back until her cheek was against the small of his back and her arms were wrapped around his groin area.

"Watch your grip, Babe," he winced and she tried to lower her hands. "That's not a handlebar." Angel would have laughed out loud had their lives not been on the line. She worked her way down his legs and on a mental count of three, dropped into the weeds. She felt the impact of the ground in her knees and hips the most, as she hit and hurled backward into the tall grass. Tony slid down from his armpits to his hands, gripping the base of the window and preparing to jump. Seconds later, he hit the ground, rolling beside her. "We have to head south to the tunnel opening," he panted, pulling out his .45. "We need to move fast and stay low."

Angel nodded, pulled out her 9mm and they took off through the weeds. Seconds later they heard voices behind them. Angel looked over her shoulder and saw two men standing in the window from where they had escaped.

"There, in the grass," one man yelled and pointed, while the other man fired off several shots with a rifle.

Angel instinctively ducked down and Tony grabbed her by her shirt, dragging her forward. "Keep moving," he barked. "Chances are they're not a good shot."

When they reached the tree line, they stopped to rest. Angel looked back at the house. Through the lighted windows, she could see four men, but was unable to make out their faces. They had Kristen, but there was no sign of Andrew, Scotrovi or the Shark.

"Who do you think they are?" Angel asked. "Do you think they're working for Kristen and came to rescue her?"

Tony shook his head. "I think they work for you." She stared wide-eyed at him. "I think Giovanni sent them to retrieve you and kill the rest of us."

"How could he know we were here?"

"I dunno." Tony pulled his phone from his pocket and checked the call log. "You didn't call anyone while I was asleep did you?"

"Of course not." Angel wrinkled her brow.

"C'mon Angel!" Tony spat through gritted teeth. "First you ask to use my phone, and then you want me to hold you so they'll know right where to find me. You played me!"

Angel couldn't believe what Tony was saying. Talk about paranoia. "I would never play you," she glared at him. "I didn't use your stupid phone and I didn't ask you to hold me so someone could find you, you jerk. I asked you to stay with me because I wanted to be close to you." She angrily stood up and started to move through the trees when Tony dove, caught her by the hips and pulled her to the ground.

"What are you doing?" Angel yelled and Tony clasped his hand over her mouth.

"Sshh, someone's here." Angel heard it too. Quiet footsteps. Slow, quiet footsteps. Her heart raced and her breathing quickened. Tony put his lips directly to her ear and whispered. "When I count to three, we get up and separate. You run as fast as you can to the right. I'll go to the left. If you see anyone, shoot 'em." Before she could voice an objection Tony counted down and on three she instinctively jumped up and ran. She dashed through the trees and the darkness, with the cool air, making a whirring sound in her ears and her heart pounding wildly. She ran, not knowing where she was going, but too afraid to stop.

Shots rang out and Angel could hear the popping sounds of bullets hitting trees. Were they shooting at her or Tony? Was Tony shooting at them? She wanted to stop and look but fear kept her moving. Out of the corner of her eye she saw what looked like a large brush pile of broken limbs and overgrown shrubs. She purposefully ran passed it and then circled back and wedged her body as far as she could into the pile. She tried to slow her breathing so she could hear if someone was following her, but she was panting too hard. Her skin was cold but the rest of her felt hot and clammy. She quietly worked her way deeper into the brush pile until she was certain she couldn't be seen from the outside. Then she crouched down, clutched her gun tightly and squinted through the branches. *Where is Tony?* She wondered. *Had Giovanni's men realized I was missing from the hotel?* She pondered, but then dismissed the thought, knowing Sophia would have called Tony's phone at the first inkling of suspicion. *Unless Giovanni had taken her phone away and was keeping her under watchful eyes.* If these were Giovanni's men they wouldn't be chasing Angel, they would be after Tony and Andrew. That is, if Giovanni somehow discovered Tony didn't kill Andrew as ordered; but how could he have known? It just didn't make sense.

The crunching sound of footsteps made Angel's hair stand on end and she hunched down further, curling into a ball. She saw the silhouette of two men pass by, one carrying a rifle and the other a .38. The beep of a cell phone stopped their movement and the one carrying the rifle slung it over his shoulder and pulled a phone from his pocket.

"They said they got him," he said, reading the text. "We can move out."

"What about the girl?" The other man asked.

"Our orders were to get Tony. Besides, they already got the blonde girl."

The man with the .38 chuckled. "Lucky bastard was up here with two ladies all to himself."

"He ain't lucky no more."

"Yeah, but talk about going out with a bang." They chuckled. "Gives getting whacked a whole new meaning." They laughed again. Angel wanted to shoot them both just for their perverted humor, but she refrained.

"Do we get to hit him tonight? If so I think we should do it now and dump the body here."

"This ain't where we dump."

"It's as good a spot as any."

"Don Venturini is very particular about where we make 'em and take 'em. We got places for that and this ain't one of those places. Besides, he told us specifically to bring him in."

Angel silently gasped. *Don Venturini!* That meant Giovanni probably still had no idea that Tony didn't follow through on his orders to kill Andrew, but neither did any of the other families. The information must have hit the street and now Andrew's family had put a hit out on Tony.

"What if we was to, say, accidentally shoot him here?" The man holding the .38 asked.

The one holding the rifle shook his head. "Then Don Venturini might have to, say, accidentally shoot us." They started to walk back toward the direction of the house. "You ain't never gonna be made if you can't follow simple instructions."

"I'll be made. I'll probably be made before you are."

They sounded like two little boys arguing over who could run faster, climb higher or hit a ball the farthest. *Guys never grow up,* Angel thought. *They just compare different stuff as they age; like who has the more expensive car, the cooler gadgets and the bigger penis.* She gave a mental eye roll and sighed. When she was certain the men were gone, she made a dash for the house, sprinting through the trees and the darkness. She knew she had to get to Andrew as fast as possible, before his father officially ordered Tony's death.

CHAPTER 11

Angel climbed through the windows that had been shattered by the Venturini men as they broke into the house. She ran across the room, straight down the stairs to the wine cellar and started beating on the wooden shelves near where Tony had opened the secret door. She didn't know which bottle opened the door or the combination. Her best bet was to bang and yell and hope that Andrew, Scotrovi or the Shark were inside and would hear her.

When Andrew finally opened the door, Angel breezed past him. "We've got trouble," she panted. "Big trouble."

He followed her down the hall. "I know. I caught some of it on the surveillance screens."

Angel stopped dead in her tracks and glared at him. "You saw what happened and you didn't do anything to stop it?"

"Whoa, Sweetheart, what was I supposed to do? Go charging in against four heavily armed men?"

"To save Tony, the one who saved YOUR life? Yes!" Angel threw her hands up in the air.

"Save Tony?" Confusion shown on Andrew's face. "I thought you were talking about Kristen." Andrew went to the surveillance console and pushed some buttons and then grunted. "I don't know how to pull up what's been recorded, or if it was actually recorded; but I saw four armed men come in through the windows here." He pointed at the surveillance screen. "A few seconds later they left with Kristen." Andrew met eyes with Angel. "What happened to Tony?"

Angel filled him in on the details, minus the fact that she and Tony had been snuggling when Venturini's men arrived. There was no sense in going into that right now. "You had to have recognized the four men?" She said. "They are from your own bogata."

Andrew shook his head. "Those guys aren't part of the Venturini's, Sweetheart."

"They have to be. I heard them say Don Venturini sent them to get Tony and he was their next mark." Angel was emphatic in her argument and keenly aware that the time was ticking on Tony's life.

"They aren't Venturinis unless they're brand new recruits, brought on within the last couple days." Andrew's tone was skeptical.

"That must be it," Angel shrugged. "Now you need to call your dad and tell him not to kill Tony."

"That doesn't make sense. Four new recruits aren't going to be sent on a job like this, and especially without the guidance of a trusted member of the family." Andrew stared through her and she could see his brain churning. "Something's off here."

Angel threw her hands up in the air. "Tony needs you now. Right now!" She was panting, partly from emotion and partly because she was still recovering from her sprint through the woods. "Your dad is going to have him killed and you have to stop him."

Andrew's eyebrows rose higher. "Wait a second," he pursed his lips together and then popped them apart. "How did my family know where to find Tony?"

"It doesn't matter," Angel blurted. "Just call your dad and tell him you're alive and not to kill Tony." Her frustration was building. "The solution isn't all that complicated, Andrew. Pick up the phone. Tell Don Venturini you're still alive and stop him from killing the man who spared your life. Nothing else matters."

"It does matter," Andrew shouted. "We need to know who knew of Tony's whereabouts and why they would have leaked that information."

Angel's arms were now flailing in frustration. "It could have been anyone. Maybe word of your demise just now hit the street."

"Sweetheart, you're missing my point." Andrew ran his hand through his hair. "Someone knew Tony was here which means he was probably followed or being tracked; and if that's the case, whoever it is might also know that the rest of us are here. Besides, the four men I saw were not after Tony. It looked like they had come for Kristen."

"What are you saying?" Her stomach flip-flopped like she was on a giant rollercoaster.

"I'm saying a lot of things don't make sense. If the Venturini's came to hit Tony, he'd already be dead and they wouldn't bother taking Kristen." Their eyes met in a steely stare and Angel felt fear growing in her gut. "I think we need to leave," he said, pulling a .38 from the nightstand drawer and stuffing it into his pants. He then took his .45 in one hand and Angel's arm in the other and headed down the hall.

"What about Scotrovi and the Shark?" Angel whispered.

"For all we know they're behind this whole thing." Andrew answered in a tone that told her this idea wasn't new to him.

Angel stayed close behind Andrew as they opened the door to the wine cellar, crept up both flights of stairs and exited through the front doors. Tony's SUV was sitting in the driveway where he had parked it. Andrew stopped at the lion statue to the left of the front door, crouched down and reached his hand behind it.

"What are you doing?" Angel asked, crouching down next to him.

He winced as he tried to bend his wrist under the statue and then up. "I'm trying to get the car key."

"There's a car key in the lion's butt?" She stood up, looking around to see if there was any sign of the Shark or Scotrovi.

"Get back down," Andrew barked and she quickly dropped back into a crouching position. "We don't want to make a sniper's job easy."

Angel gripped her 9mm tighter and could feel her palm getting sweaty from fear.

"Got it," Andrew blurted, pulling out a key. "You drive." He tossed Angel the key as they hurried down the steps and into the car.

"Why am I driving?" She asked as she pulled the gear shift into drive and sped around the circle and down the gravel road.

"Because I'm dead, remember?" Andrew crawled into the back seat and crouched down.

"How did you know where to find the car key?" Angel glanced at him through the rearview mirror.

He was peering out the windows as he spoke, making sure they weren't being followed. "It was Tony's plan. In case we discovered someone couldn't be trusted and we had to escape, we would have a backup key."

"Why the lion's butt?" Angel smirked when she saw Andrew grin and shake his head as if amused.

"Tony said it would be an easy place to remember. He said, 'if we find out someone's an asshole, the key is in the asshole.'"

Angel laughed out loud. "That sounds like him."

An expression of introspective concern replaced his smile. "He's a good man," he said.

Angel could see warmth in Andrew's eyes when he talked about Tony. Whatever had happened between them the day Andrew was supposed to die, it had impacted him; maybe even changed him. She wanted to ask about it, but this wasn't the time. Right now, they had to get to the Venturini's so Andrew could return the favor.

They rode in silence for a few moments and then Andrew instructed her to pull over at a gas station. "I want to call my father and find out if those really were his men."

"We can use On-Star," Angel reached for the button but froze when Andrew yelled.

"Don't touch it!" He dove toward her arm. "Don't touch the call button! We'll show up on GPS and until we know what the hell is going on, we need to stay hidden." Angel stared at him, her mouth half open. She couldn't remember a time when she'd seen Andrew so jumpy. "I didn't mean to scare you, Sweetheart."

Angel pulled behind the station and next to a single pay phone that stood between the car wash and the air pump. She angled the SUV so it would shield Andrew from other cars while he used the phone. As he climbed back into the backseat, Angel could tell by his expression that something was terribly wrong. His brow was narrowed and there wasn't much color left in his face. "What is it?" She asked.

"My father sent two men to find Tony but they never checked back in." Andrew leaned forward, elbows on his knees.

"What does that mean?" She turned and studied his face. "I heard one of the guys say they had him, so where is he?"

Andrew pursed his lips together and inhaled slowly. He didn't answer her question and she knew it was because he didn't have an answer.

"What do we do now?" Angel asked. "I need to get in touch with Olga and my mom so maybe we should drive to the hotel, but then Giovanni will know you're alive but I guess that doesn't matter now because Tony is already missing..." she was thinking out loud and rambling.   Their eyes met and Angel saw fear, though he attempted to conceal it with a slight grin and a wink. "Calm down, Sweetheart. Let's take this step by step." Andrew leaned back against the seat and exhaled. "My father didn't sound right."

"What do you mean?"

"His voice was different somehow. Shaky. Weak." Andrew closed his eyes.

"Maybe finding out that you are alive was emotionally overwhelming for him."

Andrew shook his head. "I thought of that, but it doesn't feel right." He sat up straighter. "I feel like he was trying to tell me something but couldn't say it outright."

"So let's drive to his house and talk to him face-to-face."

Andrew squint his eyes as if he were considering the idea and then shook his head. "We need more information first."

"It's two o'clock in the morning. Where do you want to go to get information?" Angel again felt frustrated, as she shifted into drive and pulled out of the station, heading toward the city.

"How many men did Giovanni send to watch you at the hotel?" Andrew asked.

"Two. Milo and Manuel. They're stationed outside the suite door and they're pretty easy to manipulate."

"Top floor?" Andrew asked.

"Yes," she peered at him through the rearview mirror. "How'd you know?"

"It's safer and harder to escape from the top floor. He locked his princess in a tower." They rode for a moment in silence and then Andrew asked, "Why were you three at a hotel in the first place?"

She could feel his eyes on her and she deliberately avoided eye contact through the rearview mirror. *How do I explain this one?* She wondered. *I can't just blurt out that when I thought he was dead I professed my love for him and then went into a crazy rage.* Her heart sped up and she swallowed hard. *Or can I?*

"Sweetheart?" He leaned forward. "Everything okay?"

Angel cleared her throat. "Yes, sorry. I was zoning."

"It doesn't make the passenger feel secure when the driver openly admits to zoning out," he teased and she gazed up at him in the mirror and smiled.

Angel pulled the car into a Denny's lot and went inside to use the bathroom and payphone. She looked up the number to the

Dana Hotel and Spa and called. Hearing Sophia's voice made Angel relax a little. She explained what had happened and how they needed to keep a low profile. "We need information," she told her mom. "Can you get in touch with Chase?"

"Yes," Sophia replied. "Bring Andrew here. Olga and I will take care of Giovanni's watchdogs. When you get here, call the room using the lobby phone and let it ring one time. Then head up."

"Okay," Angel sighed.

"Be careful," Sophia whispered. "I love you."

"I love you too," Angel said and disconnected the call.

An hour later they knocked on the suite door and Olga motioned them inside. "Merciful Heavens," she said. "The mess you get yourself into, child."

"Nice to see you too," Angel hugged her tight.

"Looks like you raised the dead," she smiled at Andrew. "Good to see you alive."

"Great to be alive," he nodded and gave her a grin.

Angel peered around the suite. "Where's mom?"

"Oh," Olga waddled toward the hall. "She's finishing up in the bathroom."

"How'd you get rid of Giovanni's men?" Andrew asked.

Olga snickered. "We didn't really get rid of them, per se."

Angel's eyes grew wider. "What would you say that you did with them?"

Olga grinned ear-to-ear. "We zapped 'em." She smacked her hands together.

Andrew and Angel exchanged quick glances and then darted their eyes back to Olga. "You did what?" They exclaimed almost in unison.

"We zapped 'em. You know, with one of those little taser thingies. Like that Grayson Galante did to you." She looked at Angel and plunked down on the couch. "I ordered us some room service. It should be here any minute."

"Where are they?" Angel gasped.

"Merciful heavens child, you're not keeping up very well," Olga rolled her eyes. "They're in the bathroom with your mother."

Angel started for the hallway and the bathroom but Andrew held his palm up. "I got this one," he said. "You'd better stay with her in case room service arrives. Keep your gun handy."

Angel sat down next to Olga. "Where'd you get a taser?"

"Off the internet," Olga answered matter-of-factly. "Elsa, down at the hair salon, told me about this woman who was mugged by these hoodlums and the only reason she lived was because she had one of them taser thingies so she zapped 'em and got away." Olga sighed, "I knew right then and there that I had to get me one of them gadgets. Besides," she grinned, "I saw how powerful they worked when Grayson zapped you."

Ugh! Does she have to keep bringing that up? Angel did a mental head slap. *It was not one of my prouder moments.*

Sophia entered the room and Angel jumped to her feet to give her a hug. "Everything okay in the bathroom?" She asked.

Sophia smiled. "Your aunt zapped them pretty good."

Olga grinned, held her hand out and made a zapping noise. "They dropped like a sack of potatoes." Her face beamed with pride. "Been a long time since I dropped anybody," she said. "Reminds me of the good 'ol days when I was young and nimble. Of course, we didn't have Tasers back then, you had to use sheer physical force."

Sophia interjected, "Andrew wants me to contact Chase and ask him to bring some duct tape when he comes."

Sophia stepped into the other room to dial Chase and Angel returned to her seat on the couch next to Olga. "How did you get them into the bathroom?"

"That's where I tasered them."

Angel shook her head and smirked. "You were in the bathroom with both men and you tasered them?"

"Merciful heavens, no," Olga gripped her chest. "Your mother was in the bathroom pretending to stop you from killing yourself."

"What?" Angel's mouth fell open.

Olga patted Angel's knees. "Oh, child, you've been in quite a depression while you've been here."

"I have?" Angel grimaced.

"Yes, you've stayed locked in the bathroom most of the time."

"Good cover," Angel smirked.

"It was my idea. You didn't know that your old aunt was so creative did you?" Olga leaned back and chuckled. "Merciful heavens, you should have seen your mom's eyeballs bug out of her head when she opened the bathroom door and those two big thugs came barreling toward her." Her little rounded cheeks glowed red as she laughed out loud. "See, I ran screaming for help, because you were trying to kill yourself."

"I got that part," Angel said.

"They rushed in and I pointed to the bathroom and cried, 'please, save her, get her out.'"

Angel rolled her eyes. "Oh, brother."

"Mark my words missy, if my performance were on the big screen I'd win an academy award." Olga gloated.

Angel shook her head and exhaled. "Then what happened?"

"They banged on the bathroom door and I zapped 'em from behind," Olga mimicked holding the taser and making a zapping sound again. "They fell against the door and when your mother opened it, they just about landed on top of her." Angel's eyes widened.

Sophia returned to the room after calling Chase. "I had to jump up on top the bidet to keep from getting smashed."

Andrew came sauntering down the hall with a smirk on his face. "Well," he raised his eyebrows, "one of them lost a couple teeth, but other than that I think they're both gonna be okay."

Sophia winced. "It was the big one on the right, wasn't it? He hit the counter on his way down."

"Told ya they fell like a sack of potatoes," Olga quipped.

Room service arrived and so did Chase. After Andrew and Chase duct taped Giovanni's men and dragged them into one of the bedrooms, so the bathroom could once again be used for its normal purpose instead of as a holding cell, they all snacked on chocolate cake and coffee.

"They didn't have any pastry on the menu," Olga complained. "That takes this place down a few notches in my book."

"The cake is perfect," Angel said, "just what we needed."

Olga threw her hands in the air and waddled into the small kitchen to fetch some creamer, mumbling something under her breath about the audacity of any hotel failing to include pastries on the room service menu.

When Chase's computer equipment was set up in the living room area, they all huddled around the screen. "I pulled up any surveillance I could tap into on your father's place," he said to Andrew. "There's not a lot of action and no sign of Tony." Chase played it forward quickly and there were no comings or goings from the front, side or back entrances during the last several hours. "You sure your dad's in there?" He asked.

Andrew nodded. "I just talked to him a little over an hour ago. He said he was home."

"Well, I'm no mob-ass-know-it-all, but something tells me somebody would have gone in or out of the place this evening," Chase said.

"Maybe not if they're mourning your death," Angel said.

"Or plotting to avenge it," Sophia added.

Andrew leaned toward the computer. "Can you pull up surveillance on the house from earlier today?"

"How far back?"

"How far can you go?" Andrew asked.

Chase hit some keys. "About twelve hours without having to hack into an archived security database."

He backed the surveillance feed up twelve hours and they stared at the screen. Nothing happened for a long time. No one came and no one went. Chase sped the feed up to save time. Still nothing.

"Something is wrong," Andrew shook his head. "Even if they're mourning or plotting revenge, men would be coming and going." He walked across the room and ran his hand through his hair. "My dad and brothers might stay inside, but the bogata members would be active."

Olga piped in, "they would at least be coming to pay their respects for his loss."

Sophia nodded in agreement.

They continued watching the feed and were ready to shut it down when a black limousine pulled to the front entrance. The driver stepped out, opened the back, driver-side door and a man in a long black coat and black fedora stepped out. The front door was immediately opened and he disappeared inside.

"Get me a visual of that man's face," Andrew barked and Chase tapped away at the keyboard. He backed up the frame to show the man stepping out of the limo, and then zoomed in on his head. They all instinctively squinted and leaned toward the screen.

"I can't get a clear picture of his face," Chase grunted.

"What about a different camera angle?" Sophia asked. "Can you grab a feed from somewhere else that may show his face?"

Chase sat for a second, his knee bouncing up and down spastically and his brain, undoubtedly contemplating whether or not Sophia's suggestion was doable. His fingers then danced wildly across the keyboard until the picture morphed into one recorded from an angle to the left and backside of the limousine. He zoomed in on the man's face again, this time revealing a clear profile view.

Andrew leaned in close. "That's Vincent Galante."

"He's probably dropping by to pay his respects," Angel said.

Andrew frowned. "I doubt that. There's no love lost between my father and Don Galante."

Chase hit some more keys. "Let's see if we can get a make on the driver."

The angle of the image turned and Chase zoomed in on the driver's face as he opened the back door. Angel gasped. "That's Thomas Boglevich."

Andrew and Angel's eyes locked. They both knew what this meant. The Shark had lied. Again. He had implied that Boglevich was killed when he kidnapped Kristen. Now, Boglevich was clearly alive, Kristen had escaped their holding and the Shark and Scotrovi were MIA.

Angel felt her anger rising.

"I never liked that Galante fellow," Olga scowled. "He's got evil little beady eyes."

Angel paced back and forth across the suite. "Where would they take Tony?" She was addressing everyone in the room, but no one answered. "C'mon let's think about this," she demanded. "Why would they want him and where would they take him?"

Chase grunted, "That's assuming he's not working with them and the whole kidnapping him thing wasn't a fake."

Angel felt the last thread of self-control unravel, and in one fluid motion she pulled the 9mm from the back of her jeans and pushed it against Chase's forehead. "You almost got Andrew killed and now you're trying to convince us that Tony is a traitor. I think YOU'RE the problem." She cocked the gun and Chase threw his hands above his head, outwardly trembling.

She could feel Andrew's stare piercing through her, though she didn't look at him. "What are you doing, Sweetheart?" He asked, using an overly calm, soothing tone.

Olga pushed herself up from the couch, fetched her taser and stood next to Angel, with the taser outstretched. "You want me to zap him? It's cleaner than shooting him."

"Il mio Dio, la famiglia intera è andata matto!" Sophia leaned against the back of the couch and threw her hands up in the air.

"Covenuto," Andrew agreed.

"We are NOT crazy," Olga blurted in their defense. She nudged Angel with her elbow and whispered, "They forget I can understand what they're saying."

Angel lowered her gun. "Maybe we are crazy."

Chase exhaled loudly and slumped his shoulders. "You almost made me pee myself with that crazy ass look on your face."

"Sorry," Angel mumbled. "I'm just sick of not knowing who to trust."

Chase sat up straighter and grinned. "It's okay. It sort of turned me on."

Angel rolled her eyes. *Everything turns you on!*

CHAPTER 12

It was 6:00am and they had been up all night. Olga was in the hotel suite kitchenette, brewing another pot of coffee, complaining that she could only make four cups at a time. Sophia had stretched out on the couch. Andrew and Chase were still huddled around the computer screen and Angel stood in front of the large glass windows, looking out over the city. A few months earlier she would have stood here gazing at the waking city seeing only lights and taxis and regular folks getting ready for another day. Now as she peered out, she saw territories, secret meeting halls, bogata boundaries for body drops and a sea of untrustworthy faces. Now, she saw hidden agendas, weapon and drug deals, revenge and retaliation schemes and she was at the center of it all.

Olga waddled over and stood next to her. "Pretty city ain't she," she said, looping her arm in Angel's and patting the top of her hand. "Your old aunt knows what you're thinking Missy, and you're wrong."

"What am I wrong about?"

"It's not all violent. Not everybody orders their friends dead. Merciful heavens, there are more regular people than the irregular people," Olga sighed. "You're forgetting what it was like before you knew who you were."

"That seems like a lifetime ago."

Olga nodded. "Dios mio, you don't have to tell me." She put her hands on her chubby, round hips. "I've been with you through it all and I'm plum proud of you."

Angel took a deep breath and sighed, feeling the weight of the world pressing down on her. She felt a lot of things, but pride wasn't one of them.

"Your trouble is you don't remember who you were before you found out who you are and you're letting the second one kill off the first." Olga paused and took in a breath. "What I mean is just because your eyes are open now doesn't mean you close off your heart." She gave her a sideways squeeze. "Your grandfather is wise but he makes mistakes. Sometimes he makes terrible mistakes. You came from him but you don't have to be like him." Olga waddled back toward the kitchen, announcing that the coffee was ready.

Angel's heart beat faster, as Olga's rambling filled her with a new sense of revelation. Olga was right. She had been compromising her own beliefs about what is right and what is wrong. She had been allowing Giovanni's experiences to lay a foundation for her future; and it was a foundation upon which she did not intend to build. She hadn't been true to her own heart, and it was time for that to change.

Angel joined Andrew and Chase at the computer. "So, what have we found?"

"The fact that Vincent Galante went to see my father has been bothering me, so I placed another call to my dad," Andrew explained. "Galante came to him with the information of my death..."

Angel cut him off. "How did Galante find out about it?"

"I don't know yet," Andrew shrugged. "My dad's working it and he'll let us know." Andrew exhaled, "anyway, Vincent Galante told my father where Tony was hiding."

"How did he know?"

"Well, you and I didn't tell him, and Tony certainly didn't tell him, so we can only assume that the information came from either the Shark, Kristen or Scotrovi," Andrew answered.

"That would confirm that Galante..."

Chase cut her off, "is definitely working with the Russians."

"We pretty much assumed that was the case the minute we saw Boglevich driving him around," Andrew added.

"I thought all the Bosses hated the Bratva. Why would Galante work with the Russians toward his own demise? " Angel shook her head side-to-side. It didn't make sense.

"He could have cut a deal to secure his own interests," Andrew surmised.

"There's more," Chase said, squirming in his seat and clicking away at the keyboard. "Since your father said the men he sent to retrieve Tony never returned, I hacked into the police database to see if there were any bogata-linked murders within the past twelve hours."

"And?" Andrew asked.

"Two men, with ties to the Venturini Crime Family were found dead last night."

"Dead?" Angel gasped. "Who killed them? They were alive when I left the woods and headed for the house."

"According to the preliminary police report, the bullets came from a semi-automatic Russian made gun. The same guns used at Tetterbaum's," Chase read aloud and Andrew exhaled.

"A PM," Angel said under her breath.

"Damn straight," Chase said. "It's a one-of-kind, sweet-ass gun. I'd love to hold one in my hand just once."

Angel started to pace. "Where were the bodies found?"

"That's the kicker," Chase said, glancing up from the computer. "They were floaters, pulled out of the Chicago River." Andrew stared at Angel, who stopped pacing and narrowed her brows.

"No one dumps in the Chicago River. Every bogata knows bodies are not to be dumped in that River."

Andrew nodded his head up and down. "Every CHICAGO bogata knows."

"It obviously ain't common-ass knowledge among the Russians," Chase quipped.

"What about Tony? Any sign of him?" Angel's eyes widened with anticipation, both hoping for the best and fearing the worst.

"There were no floaters meeting his description, if that's what you mean," Chase said.

Angel paced back and forth, chewing on her index fingernail and forcing her mind to walk step-by-step through the facts. Vincent Galante had sided with the Bratva and was most likely attempting to recruit Venturini and the other Bosses for their cause.

"So what do you want to do now," Chase asked. "You want to send someone to take down Galante?"

Yes! She silently screamed in her mind, but stopped short of verbalizing it. Much as she didn't like Vincent Galante and admittedly wouldn't mourn his loss, she understood that he was a mere pawn in the Russian's game.

"No," she answered Chase. "He won't die for his ignorance, at least not by my hand. Undoubtedly, the Russians will use him to gain advantage and then kill him themselves."

"So we're just going to let him get away with being disloyal?" Chase's fingers had slipped off the keyboard and hung by his sides, and his mouth gaped open in an outward display of disbelief.

"The only thing we know for certain is that he informed Venturini of Andrew's death and told him where to find Tony..."

Chase interrupted; his eyes bulging from his head. "And that he's obviously working with Boglevich."

Angel inhaled and nodded. "Yes, he's working with Boglevich, but we don't know the extent of their agreement, or what information, if any, he has given them."

"Them being the freaky-ass Russians," Chase added.

She looked over at Andrew and rolled her eyes, as if to say 'help,' but all he did was grin.

"Sounds like you're adopting an innocent until proven guilty philosophy, Sweetheart," Andrew said. "I don't think your grandfather's going to like it."

Olga clapped her hands together. "Good for you," she waddled over and squeezed Angel in a sideways hug. "It's about time somebody brought the American Constitution to the Mob."

Chase stared at her. "You're not thinking about keeping Giovanni in the dark on all this, are you?" He fidgeted in his seat. "Because I'm no mob-ass expert, but I'm pretty sure Giovanni hates to be kept in the dark."

Angel held Chase's stare for only a second and then redirected her attention to Andrew. "We need to get Giovanni and probably Salvatore out of the way for a while. How do we do that?"

Chase leapt to his feet. "Are you freaking-ass kidding me? You don't just get the Capo di Tutti Capi and the Head of the Cosa Nostra out of the way."

"Well, it's either that or we let him kill Andrew and Tony," Angel put her hands on her hips.

"You're going to get us all killed!" Chase yelled.

Olga grabbed her taser and held it up. "Either you sit down and shut up, or I make you," she said and Chase sank back down into his chair.

Andrew ran his hand quickly through his dark brown hair and took a deep breath. "First things first, we have twelve more hours until you, Sophia and Olga are due back at the Towers. Let's use this time to gain as much information as possible. We may not need to get rid of Giovanni and Salvatore if we have enough evidence to present to them. Besides, Salvatore and his experience with the Russian mob might come in handy." Andrew was always the voice of reason. Angel was still furious at Giovanni for ordering the hit on Andrew. She wanted to shove a bound and gagged Giovanni in a closet for a couple of days and hope no one would notice; but Andrew was the calm thinker in the group. He was the level head amidst the rampant fear and anger. He was the one she could trust to offer a non-biased approach to any problem.

Sophia slowly shifted into a sitting position on the couch. "I may be able to get Salvatore on board, but no matter what evidence you present to Giovanni, he will still kill Tony for disobedience and Andrew for the appearance of disloyalty. The only person in this room he will not kill is you, Angel."

Olga nodded in agreement and made the sign of the cross over her body. "Giovanni is a stubborn mule of a man. He accepts no apologies and he makes no apologies either. That old coot has probably been dreaming of doing me in for years."

Angel didn't want to admit it, but she knew in her heart they were right. She couldn't risk Giovanni's wrath falling on Andrew and Tony. She needed to come up with a way to protect them.

"Chase, can you hack into the FBI database and run a background check on all the key players?" Andrew asked.

"Easy as pie," he said and started clicking the keyboard.

"I want to know anything on Boglevich, Kristen, the Shark, and Scotrovi. I also want to know of any connection these people have to Vincent Galante," Andrew said. "I'm going to get in touch with Sal at FBI headquarters to get his input on how we handle the Russians."

"Oh, I almost forgot," Chase blurted excitedly. "I ordered new cell phones for us, ones that won't be tracked. They'll be ready for pick up this morning at 9:00am."

"Good thinking," Andrew patted Chase on the back.

"Now," Angel paced, "how do we get rid of Giovanni?"

CHAPTER 13

Their new cell phones were programmed and Chase outfitted them with a tracking frequency blocker, ensuring that no one could lock onto the signal and find them. "I also installed a sweet-ass locator on each unit, allowing us to be able to find each other if needed," Chase explained. "Type in the code STAR 31393 and a GPS grid will display each of our locations."

"Great," Andrew said, punching in the code and checking it out.

Chase handed an extra phone to Angel. "This is Tony's if we ever find him."

"We'll find him," she said, feeling the sting of fear in her heart. *We have to find him.*

Olga waddled down the hall from the back bedroom, carrying two trays of food. "I fed Moe and Curly," she said.

"It's Milo and Manuel," Angel corrected.

"Whatever. They're ungrateful weasels." Olga shook her head in disgust. "I have half a mind to go back in there and zap 'em again."

"No more zapping," Angel sighed.

"One of them has to use the bathroom," she said to Andrew. "I'd be happy to take him if you're too busy," she smiled. "I wouldn't mind seeing if Elsa is right about there being a correlation between a man's height and the length of his ding-dong."

"Olga!" Sophia gasped.

"Well, I can't help being curious," she put her hands on her hips. "It's not like I was gonna touch it or anything."

Sophia mumbled something in Italian and Angel giggled out loud, partly at Olga, but mostly at Andrew's open-mouthed, shocked expression.

"Damn Olga, you're one wild-ass chick," Chase said, high-fiving her as she waddled into the kitchen.

Andrew left to give the Milo and Manuel a potty break while Angel dialed Tony's cell. She listened to his voicemail and the mere sound of his voice brought a lump to her throat. *God, please help us find him and keep him safe, wherever he is,* she silently prayed.

When Andrew returned, Chase announced that he was linked into Sal's FBI database and ready to transmit information. "We're ready to video conference in," Chase told Andrew, who gave a go ahead nod. Chase clicked some keys and Sal appeared on the screen.

"Sal, how are you?" Andrew asked.

"It is good to see your face friend," Sal spoke with an accent Angel couldn't identify and he was older than she had pictured him. He was thin, with protruding cheekbones and hair that looked as if it had once been coal black, but was now mostly gray. Wrinkles around his lips and the rasp in his voice told Angel he was a life-long smoker. His skin was ashen and his light hazel eyes glistened. Even though she'd never met him, her gut told her Sal could be trusted.

"Have you got any information for me?" Andrew said, leaning down near the screen.

"Yes, but I fear it is not what you had hoped for," he shook his head.

"Lay it on us," Chase said.

Sal directed his eyes from Andrew to Chase and back to Andrew. "Friend, are you certain we are in good company?"

Andrew nodded. "This is Chase." He put his hand on Chase's shoulder. "He can be trusted."

"Very well," Sal nodded. "I ran the names you gave me. First, there is no record of a Vadim Scotrovi in the SVR database."

Andrew exhaled and shook his head, "I figured as much."

"But that doesn't mean anything, right?" Angel piped in. "I mean, he told us that his identity was confidential and only the highest ranking officials could access his file."

"Yes, and then he conveniently forgot to give us the names of those three high ranking officials," Andrew noted with sarcasm.

"I am sorry, but there is no one in the system by the name Vadim Scotrovi and without physical data it is impossible for me to trace this man," Sal explained.

Angel narrowed her brows. "What do you mean 'physical data'?"

"Like a fingerprint," Andrew said.

"Or something with DNA, like a big-ass lugie," Chase added.

Angel grimaced at the word lugie. There were few things in life more disgusting than a grown man hocking a big-ass lugie.

"A hair follicle," Sal added.

"Or any other form of bodily secretions," Chase quipped, grinning at Angel as she shivered her shoulders in disgust.

"Let's concentrate on the fingerprint," Andrew scolded and scowled at Chase.

"We have his fingerprints," Angel blurted excitedly and turned toward Andrew. "Remember when he left the room to go to bed? He set his wine glass on the coffee table."

An ah-ha spark lit in Andrew's eyes. "And no one picked it up after him?"

"I don't think so," Angel shrugged. "I left the room and you were the only other person there. Did you touch it?" Andrew shook his head no. "So the glass must still be sitting there…" her voice trailed off as the realization of what that meant rushed over her. *We have to go back.*

"I'll go back and get the glass," Andrew said to Angel. "You stay here."

"No," she shook her head emphatically. "It's safer to go in pairs. I'm going with you."

Andrew assigned Chase and Sal the task of working together to hack into the SVR database and find out if any member of SVR had ties to the Vamloskaya family.

"I fear, friend," Sal sighed, "you will be surprised at the many ties to crime families in the SVR. They have a notorious reputation for corruption."

"So do we," Andrew said, referring to the Chicago police.

Olga's assignment was to keep a watchful eye on Giovanni's men, who were still tied up in the bedroom; and Sophia's task was to contact Andrew's father, Don Venturini, and find out any information she could on Tony's whereabouts.

"What makes you think he will tell me anything," Sophia had asked.

Andrew gave her a wink. "My father has a weakness when it comes to pretty ladies, especially a pretty lady named Sophia."

Sophia's cheeks turned a light rose color and a smile crept across her face. "You Venturini's certainly are charming," she sighed. "Always have been."

Angel looked at Andrew. "There's a story there. I can tell."

Andrew grinned. "Yep, but I've been sworn to secrecy, Sweetheart, so you're gonna have to get the details from your mother."

When they arrived at the Barone property, Andrew instructed Angel to pass the long gravel drive and take a dirt road that wound behind the small lake, the same lake where she had found Grayson Galante's body. She shuddered from the memory.

"We'll enter through the tunnel, just to be safe," Andrew said, as he pulled out his .45 and Angel followed suit, grabbing her 9mm and making sure it was ready.

Angel wondered why Andrew thought the tunnel would be safer, but she didn't bother to ask. After all, he was the cop and knew more about these things. Besides, she was preoccupied with the nagging sensation that they shouldn't be there.

At the mouth of the tunnel, Andrew faced her and motioned with his fingers over his lips for her to keep quiet. She gave a nod of understanding and followed him into the tunnel. It was pitch black; the kind of blackness where you can't see your hand in front of your face; the type of darkness where your eyes dilate, trying to find light, but since there is no light you begin feeling dizzy and disoriented. Angel gripped the back of Andrew's black leather jacket with her left hand and clutched her gun in her right.

They walked for what seemed like forever, though it was really only for about five minutes. Angel wanted to ask how long the tunnel was, but she was afraid to speak since Andrew had told her to remain quiet. A shuffling sound from behind startled her and she tugged on Andrew's jacket.

"Shhhh," Andrew whispered. The shuffling noise came again. "Pick up your feet, don't drag them," he uttered in a hushed tone.

Angel tugged harder on his jacket. "I'm not making that noise," she whispered. No sooner had the words crossed her lips than a hand gripped her left ankle and pulled her to the ground. Angel's nails scraped down the back of Andrew's leather jacket as she lost her grip and fell. Her right hand slammed against the ground, inadvertently firing her gun.

"What the..." Andrew yelled but was interrupted by Angel.

"He's got my leg! Somebody's got my leg!" She frantically kicked and thrashed until she finally broke free. Then scrambling to her feet, Angel took off running in a dead sprint. She was running for her life and the adrenaline rush made her forget that she was blindly running through a pitch black tunnel. The only sound she heard was her own heartbeat and the panting of her own breath. When logic finally conquered the panic, she stopped, placed her back against the left side of the tunnel wall, and squatted down with her gun clutched in front of her. There was no sound. She didn't know how far she had run but the eerie silence was strangely deafening and she felt as if the impenetrable darkness was suffocating her. She fought the urge to panic, but fear manifested itself in clammy skin and trembling fingers. *Where is Andrew?* She wondered. *He couldn't be that much further behind me*; and then a horrible thought hit her. *What if whoever grabbed me now has Andrew?* She had to find out. *I'll walk slowly back the way I came until I find him,* she told herself. *He's probably looking for me and we'll bump right into each other.* The words brought little reassurance because she knew that whoever had grabbed her leg was still somewhere in the tunnel too.

Angel's phone vibrated in her pocket and she pulled it out, giving herself a mental

head slap. *Why didn't I think of this before?*
She could track Andrew with her phone and it
would also provide a light in the darkness.
She quickly slid the unlock icon upward and
saw that a text had come in. It was from
Andrew and it read: Come back. I found
Scotrovi. Angel hurriedly punched the GPS
code into her phone and followed the red dot
back to Andrew. Somehow just seeing the
little red dot on the screen made her feel safe.

They carried Scotrovi back the way
they'd come and out of the tunnel. Angel
winced as the bright morning sky made her
eyes burn. "Your eyes will adjust in a few
seconds," Andrew said.

They leaned Scotrovi against a tree and
Andrew squatted down to get a closer look at
him. He had been shot in the left shoulder
and his left arm, neck and hands were covered
in blood. "He's lost a lot of blood," Andrew
exhaled. "We've got to get him to a doctor
quickly."

Scotrovi's eyes rolled back into his head
and he mumbled in Russian. "Video this with
your phone," Andrew blurted.

"What?"

"Video him with your phone. Quick!"
Andrew barked, while ripping off the bottom of
Scotrovi's shirt and tying it tightly around his
shoulder and under his armpit.

Angel hit the camera and then video
record button on her phone and bent down
toward Scotrovi so that she could record his
mumblings. Angel kept recording while
Andrew slung Scotrovi over his shoulder and

carried him to the Tank. They put the back seats of the Tank down and made Scotrovi as comfortable as possible. Angel crouched next to him, recording every word he uttered.

"How's he doing?" Andrew called from behind the wheel.

"I don't know," Angel shrugged. "He's still talking, but his skin is starting to look gray." Angel stared momentarily. "It sounds like he's praying." She leaned in closer and listened. She couldn't understand anything he said because it was all in Russian, but she caught two words and her heart melted. Alyona and Zhanna. Scotrovi was calling out to his wife and little girl, and Angel choked back the urge to cry. She wondered if her own father had called out her name right before he died. Holding the phone steady with one hand, she reached with the other and intertwined her fingers with his. "Stay with us," she whispered to him. "Fight to live and stay with Alyona and Zhanna." Tears dripped from her eyes as she glanced up at Andrew in the rearview mirror. "Hurry."

CHAPTER 14

It was noon before Andrew and Angel returned to the Dana Hotel. They had managed to get Scotrovi to the hospital and the prognosis for survival was good. He had lost a great deal of blood, but the bullet had made a clean entry and exit. Andrew assigned two cops on the Venturini payroll to guard him. "They're good men," he assured Angel, whose eyes showed concern. "They'll keep him safe."

Upon entering the lobby, the dark haired, robotic-like woman who greeted Angel, Olga and Sophia upon their arrival, made a bee-line for Angel. "I was instructed to give you this the moment you returned." She handed Angel a white envelope.

"Thank you," Angel nodded and the woman paraded gracefully away. Angel opened the envelope to find a note that read: Meet me in the Vertigo Lounge. It was signed Sophia. Angel and Andrew walked down the steps and into the Lounge, immediately spotting Sophia at a corner booth in the back of the room. Three large men dressed in black suits stood in front of the table. Anyone who walked by could tell they were heavily armed as their clothing bulged awkwardly outward in areas where one might hide a weapon.

"Not very discreet, are they?" Andrew shook his head.

"Do you know them?" Angel asked as they approached the table.

"Unfortunately, yes" Andrew sighed.

Don Venturini rose from his seat and greeted Angel with a kiss on each cheek. "Michelangela, it is good to see you," he smiled and Angel was pretty sure this over-the-top gesture of respect was nothing more than an attempt to impress her mother. He then gave Andrew a pat on each cheek and looked at him as only a father, who is relieved and overjoyed to see his son alive, can. "Please, come, sit," he said, motioning Angel into the u-shaped booth. Sophia scooted around closer to Don Venturini and Angel and Andrew slid in on the other side.

A big smile filled Don Venturini's face and Angel noted the family resemblance. "It restores my soul to see you sitting here, son," he said to Andrew.

"I'm glad to hear that, Pop, but I'm afraid the happy reunion will have to wait." Andrew shifted in the booth. "We need some answers and we need them fast."

Don Venturini leaned back in the booth and folded his arms over his chest. "Ahhh," he sighed. "So that is why you sent this beautiful woman to call on me this afternoon."

"No, no," Sophia gently brushed her fingertips across his arm. "Calling you was my idea." He smiled at Sophia and Angel had to stop her jaw from dropping open at the obvious sparks between them.

142

Why hadn't I noticed this before? She wondered and then remembered that the only other time she had seen Sophia and Don Venturini in the same room was when Sophia had found that her husband, Denny, was behind her kidnapping and the attack on the family. She was obviously too shaken up to pay attention to Venturini then, but now it was a different story. Now, there were sparks flying and Angel wondered what had happened between them in the past. She made a mental note to ask Olga about it later. *My mother will hide stuff, but Olga will give me all the juicy details,* she cunningly smirked.

"Let me disclose the occurrences on my end," Don Venturini said, leaning in closer. "Two days ago I received a call from Vincent Galante, informing me that Giovanni had given the order for your hit and Tony Andriachinni did the deed." His eyebrows narrowed and his eyes grew darker. "I was enraged!" He pounded his fist onto the table and Angel jumped. "Galante told me not to seek immediate revenge; that his people were working on it and would help me enact vengeance against Tony and ultimately Giovanni." Venturini stopped talking and directed his eyes toward Angel. "I mean no disrespect."

Angel nodded, "none taken."

Venturini continued. "Yesterday Galante showed up at the house and told me that he had located Tony. He asked that two of my men join four of his to bring Tony back to me." His fists drew up in tight knots of anger. "I trusted him and I sent my men and do you know what happened to them?"

"Yes, Pop, they were dumped in the Chicago River," Andrew said.

"In the River!" Venturini exclaimed, his voice growing louder. He shook his finger at Andrew. "Nobody, and I mean NOBODY in this town dumps bodies in the River!"

"Pop, take it easy," Andrew said, trying to quiet him before he drew unnecessary attention to their table.

Don Venturini leaned back in the booth. "You're right. You're right. I'm sorry, son. I get worked up."

"I know, Pop."

"It's disrespectful to the City, to the people, to our families..." his volume began to rise again but when Sophia gently stroked his arm, his voice tapered off.

"Have you heard from Vincent Galante since?" Andrew asked.

"No, I have not seen him or heard from him since yesterday."

"Do you know anything about Tony's whereabouts?" Angel asked.

"I assumed he was killed with my men, but I have no information to that effect." He looked at Andrew. "Maybe you should have the police scan the River for his body."

Angel fought the lump rising in her throat. Sophia reached over and squeezed Angel's knee under the table.

"For now we're working under the assumption that Tony is alive," Andrew said, giving Angel a nod. "And whoever killed your men have Tony."

"And Vincent Galante is working with them," Angel added with a roll of her eyes. "Big surprise."

Andrew filled his father in on what had transpired since Denny's Iowa encampment had been taken down. Kristen had been found, they had met Scotrovi, Tetterbaum's Pub had been attacked and they appeared to have been betrayed by the Shark.

"Bratva!" Venturini spewed. "I find it hard to believe even a low-down dog like Vincent Galante would link himself to the Bratva. What does he have to gain?"

"Chicago," Angel and Andrew answered in unison.

"The Bratva helps Kristen follow through on her father's revenge by killing Giovanni, Salvatore and Angel. In return she uses her father's resources to help them infiltrate and take Mafia control of the city." Andrew summed it up as if it were quite simple to grasp. "I imagine Vincent Galante was promised a large area of Chicago in exchange for helping the Bratva get rid of the other families."

"That makes sense," Angel's eyes lit with a spark of understanding. "By telling you that Tony had killed Andrew and helping you seek revenge on Tony, he's already succeeded in causing a feud between the Venturinis and the Andriachinis."

"And it's not like it's difficult to cause a war between the bogatas," Sophia added.

"But who is his connection?" Andrew said more to himself than to the rest of them. "Who told Vincent Galante where to find Tony?"

"Non so," Venturini threw up his hands. "He did not speak of his informant and I was too busy mourning your death to worry about how the information was acquired."

Sophia drew closer. "There weren't that many people who knew of Tony's whereabouts so it shouldn't be too difficult to figure out."

"Kristen, Scotrovi, the Shark, Andrew, Tony and Me," Angel counted on her fingers.

"Seems pretty clear who your culprit is," Sophia said. "It's got to be the Shark, working with Kristen."

Angel shook her head. "I know that's the obvious answer, but it doesn't feel right in my gut."

"No one else knew where to find us, Sweetheart. It has to be the Shark." Andrew draped his arm around the back of the booth and a shiver ran up Angel's spine. Only this time, it wasn't a sensual shiver of desire, it was fear. She looked at Andrew and doubt flashed across her mind. *Could Giovanni have been right about Andrew?* She chewed on her bottom lip. *Could Andrew be a traitor after all? Could he have been the one who sold out Tony and even shot Scotrovi?*

"Angel. Hello? Angel?" Sophia waved her hand in front of Angel's face until she was startled back to reality. "Are you alright? I called your name several times."

146

"Yes, sorry, lack of sleep makes me get a little zoned out," she lied. She was really deep in thought about Andrew's actions and possible motives. "I think I'm going to head upstairs and lay down for awhile."

Andrew slid out of the booth and pulled Angel out by her hands. "You want me to walk up with you?"

"No, you should stay here and hash out more details," Angel said, trying to sound nonchalant. "My brain is mush so I won't be much help anyway."

She quickly said her goodbyes and ascended the staircase back to the lobby and toward the elevator, taking it to the penthouse floor. When the elevator opened she stepped out, dropped her cell phone inside a decorative bouquet of flowers that sat on a table outside their hotel room door and made a quick jaunt to the staircase and back down to ground level. If Andrew used the GPS on his phone to track her, and she knew he would; it would appear that she was in the penthouse.

She sneaked across the lobby and slipped through one of the side doors, making a dash down the street toward Northwestern Memorial Hospital. She hoped Scotrovi was conscious because she wanted to talk to him alone. She had a feeling Scotrovi held the answers that could tie this whole thing together.

Angel approached his room and the two cops guarding the door. "Andrew sent me over to check on Scotrovi," she said with forced confidence.

"You armed?" The man to her right asked.

"Are you?" Angel retorted.

"What business you got with this Russian dude anyway?" The man to her left asked, leaning down into her face.

Angel held her stance and raised her chin slightly. "Do you know who I am?"

As soon as the question reached his ears, fear lit his face. "Holy Mary Mother of ..." the man to her left leaned away and stood up straight, his eyes popping from his head. "I didn't recognize you, Ms. Maratinzano. My apologies."

At the mention of her name the man to her right gasped. "You mean she's ..."

"The granddaughter to the Capo di Tutti Capi," the other man interjected. "Yes, she is, so hurry up and open the door, would ya."

The man to her right stared at her as he pushed open the door. "We meant no disrespect."

Angel nodded. "I don't want to be disturbed and I don't want anyone to know I'm here. Capisce?"

"Capisce," they uttered in unison and the door closed behind her.

CHAPTER 15

Scotrovi's chest was bare aside from the bandage covering his left shoulder. He was hooked to a heart monitor and an I.V. and Angel noticed right away that a healthy color had returned to his skin. His eyes were glazed over from the morphine drip and he winced as he tried to sit up when he heard her enter.

"Michelangela," he uttered quietly as she approached the bed. "You saved my life. I am indebted to you."

"Yes," Angel said, pulling a chair next to his bed. "And you can start paying off that debt now, by answering some questions."

"What is it that I may tell you?"

"You said you had no choice but to follow through with the attack on Tetterbaum's the other night. But that doesn't make sense because you could have somehow killed the two Vamloskaya boys before the operation ever took place. Why didn't you?"

"Vamloskaya members are tracked." Angel cocked her head to indicate she didn't understand. "We are tracked by satellite feed so our location is always known."

"How do they track you?"

"With an implanted chip beneath the skin in an area not regularly seen when out in public," he explained. "Every Vamloskaya member has a chip."

Angel's mind drew a list of all unseen areas on the human body and she shuddered to think of which area he meant. "Can it be removed?"

"It is designed to have explosive effects when taken from the body, though I have never witnessed this myself."

"Does this device provide only your location or does it transmit more information?" She studied his face as he spoke.

"Have you ever looked at Google Earth?" He asked and Angel nodded. "The device allows them to track each member's precise location and the satellite allows instant upload of our actions, or lack of action as it may be." He took in a slow breath and exhaled. "There are cameras everywhere and any security or surveillance feed can be used to verify their orders are being followed." Angel dropped her head and sighed. She knew that was true because she'd watched Chase hack into camera feeds throughout the city, searching for any sign of Kristen and the Shark.

"Okay, next question. Did Andrew shoot you?" Angel saw shock in his eyes. She could tell he was not expecting that question.

"No, I did not even see Andrew," Scotrovi answered.

"Did the Shark shoot you?" Angel asked and then watched closely as Scotrovi wrinkled his nose and shook his head slowly.

"No, the Shark did not do this," he exhaled. "The Shark would not shoot me."

"Did you actually see who shot you?"

Scotrovi gave a nod of his head. "Yes. It was your friend, Tony."

This wasn't the answer she expected and although she tried to hide her surprise, she was certain Scotrovi noticed it. "Where did he shoot you?" Scotrovi gave her a cockeyed glance and pointed to his shoulder. "No, I mean where were you standing when he shot you?"

"Near the entrance to the tunnel. I was running from the tunnel and Tony was running toward it. It was dark and we almost collided. I yelled his name and he turned and shot me."

She shook her head and exhaled. This didn't make sense. *Why would Tony shoot Scotrovi?* "Did he accidentally shoot you?"

"I do not believe it was accidental," Scotrovi answered.

Angel stood up and paced back and forth in front of the bed, gnawing on her fingernail.

"Do you always wear holes in your shoes when you think?" Scotrovi asked and Angel grinned.

"Always." She continued to pace back and forth and mull the facts over in her mind. "Did he say anything to you before he shot you?"

Scotrovi scrunched up his face and looked as if he were trying to replay the moment in his mind. "Yes, he said he was sorry."

"Those were his exact words?"

"No, his exact words were, 'I'm sorry man' and then he shot me."

"Did you see where he went after that?" Angel's heart was beating faster. She didn't understand why Tony shot Scotrovi, but that could wait. The exciting news was that this meant Tony was still alive and Venturini's men never found him which was probably why his body wasn't pulled from the River with theirs.

"I didn't see anything after that," Scotrovi uttered. "I may have lost consciousness."

Angel sat back down in the chair next to his bedside. "Can you remember the last place you saw the Shark?"

"It was before the gunmen came. He was coming out of Kristen's room and I passed by him in the hallway. I said goodnight and he said something about making sure the prisoner was locked up tight." Scotrovi gave a one-shouldered shrug. "I did not think anything strange of it."

Angel felt her lips start to curl at the corners. Knowing Tony was alive lifted an enormous weight from her soul. Scotrovi stared at her, as if looking through her. "You are filled with joy, no?" He asked.

Angel grinned. "Relief more than joy," she said.

"Ah, I am relieved too," Scotrovi nodded, "relieved that your friend is a poor shot."

A light came on in Angel's mind and she leapt to her feet. *Tony's not a poor shot! Tony's the best shot! Tony didn't kill Scotrovi because he didn't WANT to kill him.* Angel's mind was racing. "That's it!" She blurted aloud, causing Scotrovi's glassy eyes to widen. She sat back down in the chair and grabbed Scotrovi's hand, squeezing it and shrieking with excitement. "That's it!"

"What is this IT you keep saying?" Genuine confusion covered his face.

She moved closer and spoke quietly. "Tony didn't kill you because he didn't want you dead. He only wanted other people to think you were dead."

Scotrovi lowered his brow and scowled. "Then why shoot me?"

"He shot you cleanly through the shoulder, a place where the bullet could easily enter and exit without too much damage," Angel explained.

"Speak for yourself. I feel damaged," Scotrovi moaned.

"Believe me, if Tony wanted you dead you would be dead. He shot you exactly where he intended."

"How did he know that the bullet would clear?" Scotrovi's skepticism leaked through his tone.

"Because he had just recovered from the same gunshot wound given to him by the Shark."

Scotrovi narrowed his eyes. "The Shark shot Tony through the shoulder?" Angel nodded. "Why? Why would he do this?"

"To save his life," she answered nonchalantly.

"You and your friends have strange customs."

Angel grinned. *You have no idea.*

"So this was some kind of initiation?" Scotrovi asked which made Angel laugh. She could certainly see how it might appear that way.

"It's like this," she explained. "If the Vamloskaya believes you are dead, they will no longer have a reason to hold your family hostage." It was all coming together in her mind. "And if you are dead, then you cannot be detected by Vamloskaya's mole in the SVR."

Understanding lit his face. "Which means Vamloskaya will release my family..."

Angel cut him off mid-sentence. "And then we can concentrate on stopping the Russian uprising without worrying about jeopardizing your family." Angel stood up and looked out the hospital window. "Is there anyone back home who can be trusted to verify the release of your family?"

"There is one man of high power who can find out this information," Scotrovi uttered.

"Who is he?"

"He is high-ranking among Sicilian families and has many informants in place to keep a close watch on the Bratva." Scotrovi drew in a deep breath and winced from discomfort. "He has a deep hatred for the Vamloskaya family in particular and I almost went to him earlier for help in rescuing my family; but I feared that I have been undercover in the Vamloskaya gang for so long that he would not believe me."

"Why does he hate Vamloskaya?"

Scotrovi's eyelids began to close and Angel could tell he was fighting to keep them open. "The Bratva murdered his wife."

"Why?" She sat back in the chair and squeezed Scotrovi's fingers, causing him to open his eyes wider. "Why did they kill his wife?" She repeated.

"It started with a heroin deal between the Sicilians and the Russian Bratva many years ago," Scotrovi slurred. "The Sicilians had made a deal with the Bratva but when the Americans offered more money for the shipment, the Sicilians sold to them instead." Scotrovi's eyes rolled back in his head and Angel squeezed his hand again.

"Then what happened?"

"The Bratva tried to sabotage the shipment, to steal the heroin and pit the Americans against the Sicilians; but the plan backfired." Scotrovi drew in a deep breath. "The Americans and Sicilians killed the men involved and in return the Bratva killed this man's wife."

Angel knew this story all too well. In short, it was the tale of how her grandfather's got them into this mess. Sometime in the late 1960's Salvatore was supposed to sell a large heroin shipment to the Russian Vamloskaya, but when Giovanni offered more money, he sold to him instead. This made the Russians angry so they sent a man named Selovich to intercept the shipment when it arrived in the States. As was a common Mob business practice, two men of neutral orientation were to receive the shipment and verify it was all there before money changed hands. Those men were Moloney and Finnegan. Angel guessed that what happened was Selovich convinced Moloney and Finnegan to steal from the shipment and sell to the Russians themselves; thereby pocketing the money.

"Scotrovi," she squeezed his fingers and his eyes opened wider. She felt guilty for not letting him sleep, but she needed to verify that they were talking about the same people. "Do you know the names of the Sicilians, Russians and Americans involved in this incident?"

"Yah," he nodded, "as do you. The Vamloskaya sent a Russian man named Selovich."

Angel's pulse quickened. "Go on," she said. "Who are the Sicilians and the Americans involved?"

"The shipment was received by Moloney and Finnegan, but they teamed up with Selovich, stealing the heroin and reporting to the Americans that the shipment was short." His eyes closed and his breathing grew deep.

Angel stood and leaned in toward his face. "The Americans you are talking about are the Maratinzano's, right?" His eyes cracked open and he nod his head slightly up and down. "And the Sicilian family are the Buscettas, yes?"

"Yah," he sighed. "When Moloney, Finnegan and Selovich reported to Giovanni that the shipment was short, Giovanni accused Salvatore of trying to, how do you say, rip him off. Salvatore accused Giovanni of trying to steal from him. Giovanni had Moloney and Finnegan killed, while Salvatore had Selovich killed. When the Vamloskaya found out Selovich had been hit, they murdered Salvatore Buscetta's wife in retaliation."

Angel sank back into her chair. *That's why Salvatore was so upset the other night when he learned the Russian's were here.* It all made sense now and it all tied together, except for one thing. "Scotrovi, do you know how Thomas Boglevich ties in?"

"Yah," he blinked slowly, "he is a Russian operative that has gone dark and is suspected of joining forces with Vamloskaya."

"You mean you don't know for sure whose side he is on?"

"No, not for certain," Scotrovi mumbled. "He is on both Vamloskaya payroll and that of the Russian government, but according to my intelligence, he has produced no results for either side."

"So, you don't know if he's good or bad," Angel mumbled more to herself than to him. Angel looked at Scotrovi, whose eyes were closing again. "One more question and then I'll let you sleep. What does the Vamloskaya want?"

"Revenge," he exhaled. "Always they want revenge. You have fueled their anger by killing Selovich's son, stealing their helicopter, and killing Moloney's son, Denarius. They want revenge."

"How do we stop them?"

Scotrovi opened his eyes and drew in a deep breath. He squeezed Angel's hand as if to emphasize his words. "Vamloskaya are ruthless. They will stop at nothing and will murder everyone in their path. They will kill women and children..."

"And innocent people in a restaurant," Angel cut him off.

He closed his eyes slowly and forced them back open. "No one was supposed to die in your restaurant. I do not know what happened." He released her hand. "To the Vamloskaya life is of no value. They will kill everyone to get what they want."

"And aside from revenge, because they've already gotten that, what do they want here in the States?"

"You."

Angel felt her heart momentarily stop, as fear gripped her. "What do they want with me?"

"You represent the betrayal from Salvatore. You represent the murder of Selovich and Denarius. You are their ticket to complete Mafia control over all shipments of drugs, weapons and oil between our continents. If they have you, Giovanni and Salvatore will become powerless. The bounty on your head is worth billions in Bratva longevity." Scotrovi's voice grew weaker. "Their plan is to eliminate every Boss in the States and then use you to eliminate Giovanni and Salvatore, giving them more global power than any other terrorist group." His voice tapered off.

Angel shook him gently. "Scotrovi," she said. "How many Bratva members are here in the States already?" He didn't answer. "How do we stop them?" He was deep in the throes of medicated slumber. Angel stood and gazed at Scotrovi. She couldn't help but feel a certain camaraderie or connection to him. It was probably because he reminded her a little of her father, and being unable to save her own dad, she felt driven to help Scotrovi reunite with his family.

"Rest, friend," she said as she moved toward the door. "I will see you again soon." When Angel opened the door both men stood straighter. She smiled, secretly enjoying the new sense of power she felt. "No one is to be allowed in this room," she said. "Capisce?"

"Yes, ma'am," the man to her left uttered.

Angel walked quickly out of the hospital and then sprinted several blocks back to the Dana Hotel and into the Vertigo Lounge. Andrew looked up, shocked by her arrival, as his cell phone atop the table clearly displayed her location to be upstairs.

"Up to your old tricks of losing your cell phone I see," he sarcastically remarked.

"I'm sorry," she panted, out of breath from running. "I had to speak to him alone and now I need you to call a meeting of the Bosses," she glared at Don Venturini.

"For what purpose should I call a meeting?" The Venturini Boss folded his hands on the table and stared at Angel.

"For the purpose of staying alive." Angel retorted, returning his glare with equal fervor.

"How dare you come in here and threaten me," Don Venturini scathed, while Sophia and Andrew sat quietly with what could only be described as wide-eyed shock.

"This isn't a threat," Angel offered. "If I call the meeting, word will certainly get back to Giovanni. I need YOU to call the meeting as if you and all the Bosses are gathering without me. I will then show up and take over from there."

"What is the purpose of this meeting?" Venturini raised his chin and angled his eyes downward at her.

"I need to know how many of the Bosses have been contacted by the Russians directly or through Vincent Galante, who is presumably working with the Bratva. I need to know how many of our families have been infiltrated."

She looked to Sophia. "Mom, I need you to get in touch with Salvatore and explain to him that we need all the manpower he can give us."

"Honey, his men are in Sicily," Sophia argued.

"I know," Angel nodded. "I need them working against the Vamloskaya overseas. Tie them up. Distract them. Find out how many men they have over here and their course of action."

Andrew rose from the booth and touched Angel's shoulder. "Sweetheart, what is going on? We don't need manpower in Sicily. We have plenty of manpower here to handle any threat."

Angel shook her head. "No, we don't. We have been infiltrated for years. The Bratva is here among us and the hour of their uprising is coming." Angel took a deep breath. "This war started over forty years ago and it's not over."

Andrew grimaced, "it may not be over but we know who the top players are and we have it contained."

Angel shook her head. "No, we don't. The people who we thought were calling the shots are not the top players. They're pawns in a much bigger game," Angel panted.

"I don't know what you're talking about," Andrew scowled.

"I think I do," Sophia said. "The Vamloskaya killed my mother when I was a child. It was over a heroin shipment that Denny's father embezzled. He ended up dead at the hand of Giovanni and Salvatore."

Angel nodded. "It started when Salvatore agreed to sell the shipment to Vamloskaya and then backed out on the deal and sold to Giovanni instead. Vamloskaya sent Selovich to the States to act friendly with Moloney and Finnegan and then sabotage the shipment, which he did by convincing them to embezzle and pit the Maratinzanos against the Buscettas. The plan backfired when Giovanni and Salvatore had Selovich, Moloney and Finnegan killed." Angel spoke faster than she had ever spoken before and at the end of the explanation she drew in a deep breath. "Vamloskaya retaliated by killing Salvatore's wife."

"Why was there no immediate retaliation against Giovanni?"

"Because there was no presence here in the States as of yet. It took time for the children of those men to grow up and plan their revenge," Angel explained.

Andrew mumbled, "You got all this from Scotrovi?" Angel nodded and she could see that Andrew was a little hurt or maybe agitated by the fact that she questioned Scotrovi without him.

"There's more," she sighed, "but its technical stuff and I need you and Chase to work on it."

Angel directed her attention back to the Venturini Boss. "Don Venturini, I know it was my family that caused this conflict, but the Bratva are going to wage war on ALL Italian American bogatas. Their plan is to take out the head of each family." She leaned on the table with flattened palms. "Please, call a meeting with the Bosses and find out how much infiltration has already been done. We need to know who contacted the Galante Boss and convince him that the Bratva makes no deals. They will use him and kill him. The only way we will stop the Russian uprising is if we work together."

Venturini gave a deliberate nod of his head.

Angel started to leave and then quickly turned around. "One more thing," she raised her finger. "Giovanni is not to be in the loop. Capisce?"

"Michelangela, do not kid yourself by thinking that you are capable of holding the Capo di Tutti Capi at bay," Venturini warned.

Angel leaned down into his face, her jaw tense. "Don't underestimate the blood that flows through my veins. What I do is for the protection of your son, Tony, my family and for the protection of all of our families."

"You will not succeed by tying Giovanni's hands," Venturini called after her but Angel was already half way up the steps and heading for the elevator.

It's the only way to protect the people I love.

CHAPTER 16

Angel leaned over Chase's shoulder and starred at the computer screen. "There's got to be a way to deactivate the tracking device Vamloskaya implants inside their members. We need to figure it out before they realize Scotrovi isn't dead."

"Why does it matter if they know he's alive?" Chase asked.

"If they think he's dead, they no longer have a reason to hold his wife and daughter hostage," Angel explained. "If he's alive, his family remains in danger."

"It's almost impossible, when I don't know what type of device their using. It would be a lot easier if I at least had a picture of one," Chase complained.

"Just do your best. Maybe Sal can help." Angel said.

Olga came waddling in from the kitchen, muttering under her breath. "That old coot is a stubborn ass," she spat.

"What's the matter?" Angel asked.

"I tried to get Giovanni to let us stay another night but he is insisting that we return to the Towers immediately."

"What did you tell him?" Andrew asked.

"I told him Angel was still suffering from depression and that she wasn't ready to see his ugly mug yet," she put her hands on her rounded hips. "Humph! You know what he said to me? He said if she could stand to look at my face, then his would be a treat." Olga stomped back into the kitchen. "Old coot."

Angel rolled her eyes and looked at Andrew. "Has Sal called back with any information on Boglevich or the Shark?"

"Not yet but don't worry, he'll come through. He always does." Andrew placed his hands on Angel's shoulders and looked down. "Relax, Sweetheart, if there's any connection Sal will find it." It was obvious that Andrew was trying to reassure her, but it wasn't working because she could see concern on his face.

"We need to find them," Angel gritted and Andrew let his hands slide down her arms, intertwined his fingers with hers and pulled her into the kitchen.

Olga was futzing around in the kitchen, collecting all the sugar and creamer packets she could find. She looked up at Angel and Andrew as they entered. "I'm taking these," she said, with a fist full of packets. "You never know when you'll need travel size packets for something. Or I could give them to Elsa, down at the hair salon. She always has little packets next to the coffee machine."

"You know you can buy those at the store, right?" Angel raised her eyebrows.

"Merciful heavens, what will they come up with next? These are handy little things and just the right portion." Olga waddled out of the kitchen. "I better put these in my suitcase right away so I don't forget."

Andrew chuckled.

"It's not funny," Angel grimaced. "I'm probably going to be just like her at that age."

"I can't wait to see that," Andrew winked and a warm tingly feeling rushed through her. The humor in his tone was quickly replaced by concern as he leaned against the counter and folded his arms over his chest. "What's going on inside that head of yours?" He asked.

"Nothing," she shrugged.

"Something." Andrew shuffled his feet. "And from what I'm seeing behind those eyes, it's something big, Sweetheart; so you want to let me in on it?"

Angel felt her defenses soften just a little as she exhaled and leaned against the counter across from Andrew. "I've been trying to figure out what Tony meant the other night when he said that he didn't trust someone."

"Who did he say he didn't trust?"

"That's just it. He didn't specify who he was talking about. Even when I asked, he sort of evaded the question." Angel bit her lip. "But I think I understand now."

"Go on," Andrew said, never taking his eyes from her.

"See, I think Tony shot Scotrovi because he couldn't trust him to do the right thing, not because he thought he was bad."

"You lost me, Sweetheart," Andrew scratched his head. "Are you saying you think Tony is working with Scotrovi?"

Angel rolled her eyes. "No, I think Tony realized that Scotrovi was only muddling up the bigger picture. I think Tony saw that Scotrovi was too worried about his own family to be able to do what needed to be done overall."

"And what needs to be done overall," Andrew's eyebrows narrowed inward.

"The Vamloskaya has to be stopped and the only way Scotrovi will be able to help take them down is if he isn't concerned about the safety of his wife and daughter."

Andrew raised his eyebrows and licked his lips. "And you think Tony figured all that out and that's why he shot Scotrovi." Angel nodded. "And you don't think that sounds the least bit outlandish?"

Angel shook her head to indicate no. "I know Tony. When he has a hunch, he's almost always dead on." She looked intently at Andrew. "I believe Tony somehow knew that the only way those men found us at Venito Barone's house last night was through the tracking device in Scotrovi. And the reason Tony said he didn't trust him was not because he thought Scotrovi was betraying us, but because he sensed that he was jeopardizing our security."

"How would he have known about the tracking device?"

Angel shrugged. "I don't know, but my gut tells me that somehow he knew."

Andrew nodded. "Okay, for the sake of argument, lets say he did know; why wouldn't he share that information with us?"

"I don't know. Maybe because it was just a hunch?" Angel sighed.

"Where do think Tony is now?" Andrew shuffled his feet.

"I think he's with the Shark and I think they're following whoever took Kristen," she answered matter-of-factly.

"You think Tony is working with the Shark?" Andrew's expression showed obvious doubt. "Tony thinks the Shark is a traitor, remember?"

"I know, it sounds weird, but I think Tony has been onto something the whole time. I think his doubt about the Shark fueled his curiosity and Tony's not one to let curiosity die without finding answers." Angel could see Andrew thought she was way off base.

"Sweetheart, are you forgetting that the Shark lied about killing his brother and then lied again about killing Boglevich?" Andrew shook his head. "Tony was right about the Shark being a traitor."

"No, he wasn't," Angel threw her hands in the air. "The Shark only appears to be a traitor because he's working both sides." Andrew squinted his eyes at her and she gave herself a mental head slap. *How can I make him understand?* Then the idea hit her. *Appeal to his logic and present only factual evidence, not hunches...* Angel took a deep breath. "Besides lying about killing his brother and Boglevich, what crime has the Shark committed against the family?"

Andrew stared at her and Angel watched the wheels turning in his head. "Go on," he said.

"On the flip side, he saved my life several times. He saved your life and Tony's by shooting you both cleanly before Denny's men arrived to kidnap Olga, knowing that his men would have killed you both. He saved our men by taking out Denny's men in the hospital parking lot and in the stairwell." Angel stopped and took a breath.

"Okay, I get it. He's done a lot of good."

"So, why are we labeling him the enemy?" Angel's eyes locked with Andrews. "You, of all people know what it's like to be labeled a traitor."

Andrew dropped his head and nodded. "You're right, Sweetheart."

Angel reached for his fingertips and pulled him closer. "You and Tony just flip-flopped your theories. He thought the Shark was bad, but now believes he's good; and you thought the Shark was good but now think he's bad." She gazed up at him. "We all need to get on the same page if we're going to stop the Vamloskaya."

"For the sake of argument, let's say the Shark is on our side. First, why would he not kill Boglevich and second why would he lie and tell us he did?"

Angel bit her lip. "Because I think the Shark is working undercover with Boglevich." Andrew started to laugh and Angel dropped his hand and backed away. "The Shark couldn't blow either one of their covers and he knew if we thought Boglevich was dead, we wouldn't be looking for him and that would free him up to do his job."

"What's Boglevich's job?" Andrew smirked and raised his hands in the air.

"He's a Russian operative, much like Scotrovi, placed undercover to keep tabs on and if necessary to stop the Vamloskaya."

"Wow." Andrew widened his eyes. "That's amazing."

"I know," Angel said excitedly, "it's all starting to make sense."

"Yeah," Andrew said. "If you live in La La Land." Andrew's lips curled at the corners, like he was fighting the urge to burst into a belly laugh. "You sure do have an active imagination," he teased. Angel didn't like being mocked.

"You can make fun of me all you want," she turned to walk out of the kitchen and Andrew grabbed her wrist.

"I'm sorry, Sweetheart. I just think you're letting your thoughts run away with you."

"Whatever." She twisted her wrist free from his grasp and walked briskly back to the family room.

Sophia entered from the bedroom, carrying her suitcase and Olga's. "We're all packed and ready to go when you are," she said to Angel. "That is, unless Olga wants to use the bidet one last time."

"I heard that," Olga peeked her head around the corner, "and don't mind if I do." She waddled down the hall toward the bathroom. "I'm gonna see if I can have one of these things installed in my bathroom at home," she said, giving a big smile and closing the bathroom door.

"You ladies head back to the Towers," Andrew said. "Chase and I will load up Giovanni's men and go to the Bat Cave until we hear from you." Angel avoided eye contact as she walked by Andrew and picked up her suitcase. "Sweetheart," he touched her arm. "Keep me in the loop on everything."

The only loop you'll get from me is the one I'd like to tie around your neck! She didn't say it, but couldn't stop herself from thinking it. The problem was as much as she loved him, she was still angry because of what he had seemingly allowed to happen at Tetterbaum's. Even though it was for the ultimate protection of Scotrovi's wife and daughter, Angel couldn't help but think there had to have been another way; one that wouldn't have resulted in so many innocent deaths.

"And don't forget to get your cell phone from wherever you stashed it," Andrew said in a scolding tone and Angel rolled her eyes. *Whatever!* She didn't appreciate his condescending tone.

Chase packed up his computer equipment. "I'm still trying to locate Tony through his cell phone," Chase said to Angel. "His phone is old and has slow-ass technology, but hopefully I'll have a lock on him soon."

"Let me know the minute you find him," Angel instructed.

"Will do, Boss lady," Chase quipped.

"Stop calling me that." Angel gritted her teeth and Chase laughed.

"Sure thing, Boss lady," he grinned and she cocked her head and smirked.

"Do I need to point my gun at your head again?"

Chase shivered. "Now you're just trying to be a tease."

CHAPTER 17

Olga, Sophia and Angel stopped in the lobby for a last minute review of the plan before getting into the Tank to head back to the Towers. "Remember we will be under constant surveillance," Sophia warned, "so no conversations about what we're doing."

"Not even in the Tank," Angel added.

"If we absolutely need to discuss something we do it in Angel's bathroom," Sophia said.

"Merciful Heavens!" Olga suddenly gasped. "What are we going to tell Giovanni about Moe and Curly?"

"It's Milo and Manuel and Chase already took care of that," Angel smiled. "He's been corresponding via text from Milo's phone."

"Giovanni will expect them to escort us home," Olga protested.

"Chase handled it." Angel rubbed her hand on Olga's back. "Trust me, Giovanni doesn't know about you Tasering his Moe and Curly."

"Let's keep it that way," Olga said.

As they loaded into the Tank, the conversation became sporadic and rehearsed. "Weren't those spa treatments wonderful," Sophia sighed.

"I've never felt so relaxed," Angel added.

"And that bidet was awe inspiring," Olga blurted and they all laughed out loud. "I can't wait to tell Elsa, down at the hair salon."

Angel felt a twinge of guilt and a ramping up of nerves as she pulled the Tank up to the front of the Towers. Four large, heavily armed men approached and escorted them inside the building and onto the elevator. Angel didn't recognize any of the men and she shot Sophia an uncomfortable glare.

Two of the men unloaded their luggage while the other two boarded the elevator with the ladies. "Four guards?" Angel asked. "Why the ramp-up in security?" There was usually only one, sometimes two men guarding the front entrance. The guards looked at each other but didn't answer.

"Seems to me that's a waste of funds right there," Olga said, elbowing the guard to her right. "How much does the old coot pay you to stand down there at the front doors and do nothing?" The man didn't answer and didn't even acknowledge the fact that she was speaking to him. "See, now he's just being disrespectful," Olga said to Sophia and Angel and then directed her attention back to the man. "I have half a mind to zap you just for being rude."

"No zapping," Angel and Sophia blurted out in unison and the two men looked at each other with obvious confusion. Angel was certain they didn't know whether to laugh or draw their weapons.

When they reached the Penthouse floor they were greeted with two more men, standing guard at the door. "Ms. Maratinzano," the taller man said, dipping his chin in respect and opening the door for her.

"Ladies," the shorter man said, also dipping his chin as a display of respect.

Olga stopped abruptly and turned to the man she had tried to talk to in the elevator. "See," she pointed, "he knows how to treat a lady with respect. You should be taking notes from him." She turned around and waddled through the doorway, stopping to pat the shorter man on the back. "You're a good one," she winked at him. "I can tell."

Giovanni and Salvatore were sitting in the family room when they entered. Sophia gave her father a warm hug. "I trust your vacation was fulfilling to your soul?" Salvatore asked.

"Sì, il padre, era meraviglioso," Sophia kissed him on each cheek.

"And for you Michelangela?" Giovanni rose from the armed chair and faced her. "How was your stay at the spa?"

Angel met his eyes briefly and then looked away. "Eye opening," she answered flatly.

Sophia shot Angel a warning glare. "Don't you want to thank your grandfather for all the wonderful spa treatments and time in such a lovely hotel?"

Angel lowered her chin and cleared her throat. "Yes, I didn't mean to appear ungrateful." Seeing Giovanni was harder than she thought it would be. Looking him in the face after he had ordered Andrew's death was virtually impossible to do without feeling a rush of anger. She swallowed hard. "Thank you for sending us to the hotel. It was truly beautiful."

"Siete benvenuto il mio Angelo," Giovanni grinned, but the intensity behind his eyes stared through her. It felt as if he knew she had left the hotel. *You're just being paranoid!* She told herself. *There's no way he could know.* Her stomach wrenched into nervous knots and her mouth felt dry.

"I'm going to lie down for a while," Angel announced, desperately wanting to escape Giovanni's stare.

"Are you ill?" Salvatore asked.

"I would have thought you would return well rested," Giovanni uttered.

"She hasn't been feeling well," Sophia piped in. "A bit of a stomach virus I think."

"Merciful Heavens, the poor thing had the runs all last night," Olga dramatically jumped on the lying bandwagon and Angel grimaced. "Why, I heard her get up at least four times and you know how draining that much pooping can be." Olga waddled over and took Angel's hand, stroking it gently. "Especially in the middle of the night when you're already so tired and then you get the runs and it burns and..."

"That will do," Giovanni belted and held up his hand, cutting her sentence short.

"Thankfully we had a bidet..." Olga began, but Angel interrupted.

176

"I'm lying down now." She opened her bedroom door and closed it quickly behind her. Her heart raced, as she tried to reassure herself that there was no possible way for Giovanni to know that she had left the Dana Hotel and Spa. Still, the way he looked at her indicated that he knew something. *After all, the truth always reveals itself.* She was beginning to hate that expression. What was once a helpful phrase now felt haunting.

Angel dozed off with Midnight curled up around her head and Mo lying on top of her legs. She awoke to the sound of dishes clanging together, glasses being filled with ice and the smell of warm garlic bread. She sat up and looked at the clock. It was 6:30pm and time to get ready to set their plan in motion. She hopped in the shower, blew her hair dry and threw on a pair of jeans, a black blouse and her black knee-high boots. She wedged her 9mm in the back of her jeans and applied some basic make-up. Lipstick, blush, eyeliner and mascara, adding some silver hoops and a tiny silver cross necklace.

She joined Sophia and Olga in the kitchen where the tension was so thick it could be cut with a knife. They were awkwardly scurrying about in silence. "What's going on?" Angel asked, wherein they both looked up but remained speechless. "What's the problem?"

Sophia grabbed Angel's arm and pulled her near the sink where she was draining noodles. She turned the faucet on full blast and cupped her hands around Angel's left ear, while Olga hummed loudly in the background.

Angel's eyes grew wider as Sophia whispered. "Three of the Bosses have been hit. Not killed. All grazed in non-fatal areas." Angel's pulse quickened. "Everyone except you and Galante." Angel took a deep breath and started to move from Sophia, but her mother pulled her closer. "There's more," she whispered with her lips so close to Angel's ear that she could feel the air leaving her mother's mouth. "Andrew was spotted by one of Galante's men who reported it to Giovanni." Angel's heart raced. *That's impossible. Andrew was heading straight from the hotel to the strip mall, aka bat cave. There's no way he would run into any of Galante's men.* Something felt terribly wrong and one thing was certain, Giovanni's rage would be out of control. "Your grandfather has ordered a hit on Tony, Andrew, the Shark and Boglevich and this time he wants to see the bodies."

Angel's mind spun. She grabbed her mother's head and cupped her hands around her ear. "Where is Giovanni right now?"

Sophia whispered back. "In a private meeting with Vincent Galante, downstairs in the meeting room."

Angel whispered to Sophia, "call Chase and tell him to get over here as fast as he can with as many guns as he has. Tell him to bring the chopper." She then put her mouth next to Olga's ear. "Go get your taser." Olga scurried down the hall to her bedroom.

Angel turned off the sink and grabbed her cell phone, texting Tony on the off-chance that he had his phone and could get her message: "Lay low until you hear from me. Will text when Giovanni is out of the way." She then pulled up the GPS on her phone, punched in the code and located Andrew. He was still in his Bat Cave and Angel breathed a sigh of relief. She text: "Galante's men told Giovanni you're alive. Stay hidden until you hear from me."

She opened the front door and the two guards whirled around with guns drawn. "Ms. Maratinzano," the tall man spoke, "we have been instructed not to let anyone in or out."

"I see," Angel said. "Instructed by whom?"

"The Capo di Tutti Capi."

"Well, we can't go against his orders now can we?" She said with a half-smile. "Since I can't leave, I wonder if you gentlemen might do me a favor and inform my grandfather that supper is ready to be served?"

"Yes, ma'am," the tall man said and nodded for the shorter man to take the elevator and deliver the message.

Angel called after him, "could you also stop at the spare apartment and inform Stefano that he will be dining with us this evening?"

"Yes ma'am," the shorter man nodded and the elevator door closed.

Angel looked at the taller man and gave a smile. "What's your name?"

He cleared his throat, obviously nervous by her presence. "Sean Shepherd, but they call me the Snake on the street."

"Why the Snake? Do you slither around?" Angel moved her neck in a snake-like manner. "Are you sneaky?"

Sean blushed and grinned, displaying a dimple in his left cheek. "Nothing of the sort, ma'am. It came from having two S's for initials."

Angel gave an A-ha nod. "How long have you worked for Giovanni?"

The grin left his face. "Longer than you've known your own identity."

"Touché," Angel smirked. "When did you fly in from New York?"

"Yesterday." He looked down with a sarcastic glare. "Would you like to see my ticket stub or better yet, there might still be a luggage tag on my suitcase?"

Angel stared at him, letting instincts and intuition tell her whether or not he could be trusted. She ran her eyes from his black laced shoes all the way up his six foot, two inch frame to the top of his jet black hair.

"Do you like what you see, ma'am?" He sarcastically asked, letting his ice blue eyes lock onto her stare.

Angel smiled. "I think I do Sean Shepherd." She folded her arms in front of her. "I do have one question though. How long were you in the military?"

Surprise shone in his expression. "Ma'am?"

"Oh, come on, you scream military with the shined shoes laced up so perfect that the end of each shoelace is exactly the same length..."

"Maybe I'm anal about my shoes," he interrupted.

"The way you say the word ma'am..."

"Maybe I grew up in the South?" He interjected.

"You don't have an accent," she rebutted.

"They said you were spunky," he grinned and then nodded his head, "with all due respect I mean."

Angel drew her 9mm and aimed it at Sean's head. "You know I could kill you right here, right now and no one would question my decision."

Sean's eyes widened and he slowly raised both hands above his head. "I meant no disrespect Ms. Maratinzano."

"Army?" Angel blurted.

"Air force ma'am."

"Why were you discharged?"

"I was wounded during a classified mission."

"Why did you start working for my grandfather?"

"He offered me a job as a bodyguard at a time when I needed money."

Angel lowered her gun. "Can you fly a chopper?"

"In my sleep, ma'am."

Angel tucked her gun away and outstretched her right hand. "You can call me

181

Angel instead of Ms. Maratinzano or ma'am."
They shook hands. "I'll check out your story
and if I find that you can't be trusted, I will
kill you."

"Sounds fair enough, ma'am." He
returned to a staunch attention stance and
Angel walked back into the penthouse and
closed the door.

CHAPTER 18

They sat around the dining room table in eerie, thick silence. The clanking and clinking of forks on glass plates was the only consistent sound. Giovanni sat at the head of the table, facing the large windows. Angel sat to his right and Olga to his left. Sophia was next to Angel and Salvatore at the other end opposite Giovanni. Chase, who landed the helicopter on the roof moments before supper was served, sat next to Olga; and Stefano had been un-invited to dinner by Giovanni.

"We do not allow possible enemies to sit at our supper table," Giovanni said of Stefano. "My men will take food down to him."

"We let YOU sit at the table," Olga quipped and snorted a small laugh. Giovanni was not amused.

"Stefano is not an enemy, grandfather," Angel uttered quietly.

Giovanni waved off her words with a scowl. Though he didn't speak, his rage over the perceived betrayal by Andrew, Tony, the Shark and Boglevich was evident.

"You need to calm down," Olga told him, "you're going to give yourself one of them bleeding ulcers or worse yet, a heart attack."

"Bah," Giovanni grunted. "I am healthy as a horse."

"And stubborn as an ass," Olga blurted and Angel bit her lip to keep from laughing out loud.

"I would not speak that way if I were you, Lucia," Giovanni gritted, locking his jaw.

Olga shook her head, "Merciful Heavens, you're a crabby old coot. What makes you so crabby? Are you constipated?" Olga shoveled in a bite of manicotti while the rest of the table sat motionless, eyebrows raised and mouths agape. "You should try using one of them bidets; it might help your constipation problem."

Giovanni pounded his fist on the table so hard that wine splashed out of several glasses. He snapped his fingers and Sean Shepherd and the shorter man, who were standing guard in the foyer, moved quickly toward the table. "Escort Lucia to her room and make sure she stays..." Giovanni stopped mid-sentence, and his head dropped face first into his plate of pasta.

Sean Shepherd and the shorter man drew their guns and took aim at Olga who sat calmly with her fork in one hand and her taser in the other. Everyone stared in wide-eyed shock, except for Angel. She set her napkin beside her plate and rose. "Gentlemen, put away your guns."

The shorter man started to stutter an objection but Sean Shepherd elbowed him and they disarmed their weapons and stared at Angel. She could tell they were certainly curious about what she would say next; though Sean didn't appear overly surprised.

"A doctor will be arriving any moment. You will carry Giovanni to his private apartment downstairs and wait for the doctor. Capisce?"

"Capisce," they mumbled in unison, lifting Giovanni from his chair and moving him toward the door.

"Oh, and clean the pasta from his face before the doctor arrives. No one needs to see him like that," Angel called after them.

"Yes ma'am," Sean Shepherd said and closed the door.

Angel smiled at Olga. "Nicely done."

"That felt even better than I thought it would," Olga giggled. "Almost therapeutic."

Chase's mouth was still half-open. "Damn Olga, you're in some big-ass trouble now."

"I hope I am not next on your list," Salvatore uttered.

"Everyone, please listen," Angel began. "We don't have a lot of time and there is a lot to do." Chase had a sheepish look on his face and raised his hand like a kid in school who needs to use the bathroom. Angel looked at him, "what?"

"Why did we just taser the Capo di Tutti Capi? I'm no mob-ass genius but I think that warrants the death penalty doesn't it?"

Angel took a deep breath. Chase was right. Under normal circumstances it would result in death; however, these weren't normal circumstances. "Giovanni's rage will inhibit us from locating and stopping the Vamloskaya. His attention is on killing

Andrew, Boglevich and the Shark because he thinks they are all traitors, and he ordered Tony killed for disobeying the order to kill Andrew." Angel threw up her hands. "His focus is on killing the only people who are helping us. We won't win unless we work together and Giovanni doesn't know how to do that." They all gave a nod of understanding.

"Do we know what the Vamloskaya want?" Chase asked. "I mean, I know they want total-ass control and power and money, but do we know how they plan to gain that control?"

"Yes," Angel began and was interrupted by a knock on the door. It was Sean Shepherd announcing that the doctor had arrived and was being held in the Lobby. Angel instructed Sean to go retrieve the doctor personally and take him to Giovanni's apartment. "I will meet you there in a few moments." She closed the door and turned to Chase. "Do you have a lock on Tony's phone yet?"

"Yep, we've been tracking him. I text you a while ago."

"Contact Andrew and Tony, the Shark and Boglevich and arrange to pick them up and bring them here via chopper. I want them here as soon as possible," Angel said, checking the clip in her gun and shoving it in place. "I'm going to meet with the doctor."

"How do I know how to find Boglevich?"

"The Shark will know." Angel said.

She turned to leave when Chase asked, "How did the doctor get here so fast?" Angel

186

didn't answer his question but felt her grin grow bigger. Chase stared her down and as revelation dawned on him, he slapped his hands together and leapt into the air. "Holy cow!" He hollered. "You planned on Tasering him the whole time didn't you?" Angel's grin filled her face. "You called the doctor ahead of time," Chase pointed at her with his mouth wide open. "Oh, man, you're as crazy-ass as Olga." Angel winked at him and closed the door.

She met Sean Shepherd and Dr. Harold Rainer in the hallway by Giovanni's apartment, which was one floor below the Penthouse. "You must be Dr. Rainer," Angel said, stretching her hand to greet him with a firm shake. "I'm Michelangela. Thank you for coming on such short notice. Do you have the sedative I asked you to bring?"

"Yes, in my bag."

She led him into the apartment and back to Giovanni's bedroom. Dr. Rainer gasped when he saw Giovanni lying on the bed. His eyes were wide with what Angel could only describe as shock and utter terror as he whirled around and faced her. "Do...do... do you have any idea who that is?" He stuttered.

"Yes," Angel nodded. "He is the Capo di Tutti Capi and he's also my grandfather, which is why I need you to take very good care of him."

"I...I... don't think I'm qualified to handle this patient," he sputtered. "What happened to him anyway?"

"He passed out during supper," Angel lied.

Dr. Rainer felt Giovanni's wrist for a pulse, then lifted each eyelid and looked into his eyes. "He should be taken to a hospital where we can run an EKG and make sure he hasn't had a stroke or heart attack..."

Angel cut him off. "It's not any of those things," she blurted.

"We can't be certain what it is unless we get him to a hospital," the doctor pressed.

"He had a disagreement with his sister at dinner and she tasered him." Angel exhaled and Dr. Rainer raised his eyebrows in surprise.

"I see," he said.

"I'm sure you understand the need to keep this sort of thing quiet. We can't have the Capo di Tutti Capi publically humiliated."

"Yes, I understand," Dr. Rainer spoke hesitantly, taking out his stethoscope and listening to Giovanni's heart.

"One more thing," Angel held up her finger. "I need you to keep him sedated for a while."

"Sedated?" The doctor narrowed his eyes and studied her face. "Why do you need him sedated?"

Angel bit her lip. "It's a long story and if I told you I'd have to kill you, so let's just keep this simple." She walked to the other side of the bed, sat down next to Giovanni and took his hand in hers. "Here's what I want you to do. Sedate him now and when he wakes up tell him he suffered a mild stroke during supper, but he will be fine as long as he rests. Then sedate him again."

"You want me to lie to the Capo di Tutti Capi?" The doctor shifted on his heels. "Do you know what happens to people who lie to your grandfather?"

"Yes," Angel said pointedly. "The same thing that happens to people who have seen too much and refuse a job offer."

"I see," Dr. Rainer's shoulders drooped.

Angel rose from the bed. "You'll be compensated. Five thousand dollars in small non-sequential bills. That's tax free, doctor."

"I'll need some supplies," his voice quivered.

"Sean will see to it that you have everything you need," Angel explained and Sean Shepherd gave a nod.

Angel started for the door and turned back. "I will send supper down for you, as well as breakfast in the morning."

"Breakfast?" Dr. Rainer's voice elevated slightly.

"I will need you to stay at his side night and day. That won't be a problem, will it?"

"No, Ms. Maratinzano, no problem."

Angel felt a tug of compassion. There was a downside to having the power to terrorize people into doing what you wanted. It was called guilt. Dr. Rainer was obviously afraid, terrified even and she knew all too well what that felt like. It didn't feel good. She walked toward the doctor and looped her arm in his. "Dr. Rainer," she sighed, "I understand you're in a difficult position and that you probably feel some trepidation." She turned and gazed at the fear in his face. "Don't be afraid. Do what I ask you to do, which is to take good care of my grandfather, and I promise you will walk out of here unharmed."

"Hey Snake," she called out as she left the apartment. "Assign someone to guard this door and make sure our good doctor doesn't slither away."

"Yes ma'am."

As soon as Chase landed with Andrew, Tony, the Shark and Boglevich, Angel dashed onto the patio and threw her arms around Tony. "Did you miss me, Babe?" He grinned. She pulled back from the hug and punched him half-playfully and half-seriously in the arm. "Ow," he gasped. "What the hell was that for?"

"For leaving me in the woods," she frowned. "And for making me worry you were dead."

Tony rubbed his arm. "I came back and looked for you but you were already gone. I was afraid they had taken you, so I followed them on foot around the house, and that's when I figured out what was going on."

"What do you mean?" They walked inside and into the kitchen.

"I followed the Venturini men until they met up with the four Russians and Kristen on the right side of the lake, just beyond the tunnel entrance. They killed Venturini's men and threw them into a black unmarked van."

Tony stopped talking and gave Olga a hug as she waddled into the kitchen.

"You're on Giovanni's hit list," Olga blurted.

Tony shot Angel a glance. "He knows I didn't kill Andrew?"

"Yep, Galante told him," Angel nodded.

"I never liked that Galante and his beady eyes," Olga scowled. "Are you hungry?" She asked Tony.

"Starving," he said and Olga's face lit up. One of her greatest pleasures was feeding the hungry.

"Merciful Heavens we can't have that," Olga shrieked. "Come sit down and I'll bring you some homemade manicotti, warm garlic bread and some wine."

"The Shark and Boglevich will need supper too," Tony told her.

"Three plates coming right up," Olga moved gleefully about the kitchen. "Out of my way, you two, I have meals to make."

Tony and Angel stepped onto the patio and Tony continued. "I listened for a while but most of what they said was in Russian. What I did manage to get from their conversation was that they were able to find us by way of a GPS device placed in all Vamloskaya members. That's when I started thinking, they hadn't come for Kristen, and they wanted Scotrovi."

"That's when you got the idea to shoot Scotrovi so they would think he was dead?"

"Yeah, I ran back toward the tunnel and hit Scotrovi. I felt bad, Babe, but I shot him anyway, because I thought it would save him and his family in the long run."

"It will."

Tony shook his head. "No, it won't."

"If they think he's dead, his family is safe and so is he," Angel argued.

"I thought that too, but then I remembered that Kristen wasn't a hostage. She willingly got into the van with them. She wasn't restrained or forced. She was one of them."

A sinking sensation filled Angel's gut. "Right then I knew Scotrovi's cover was blown..."

Angel interrupted him, "because she'll tell them he's an undercover SVR agent."

"Bingo, Babe," Tony said. "So I shot the poor bastard for nothing."

Angel's heart sank. She thought all they needed to do was to make the Vamloskaya believe Scotrovi was dead and disarm his tracking device, to ensure the safety of his wife and daughter. Now, his identity was compromised and she didn't want to think about what that meant for his family. Angel walked inside and leaned over Chase's shoulder, looking down at his computer. "You can stop trying to figure out how to disarm the Vamloskaya tracking device," she sighed. "We're too late."

Chase turned around. "Why are we too late?" Angel repeated what Tony had told her. "That's some bad ass news right there."

Andrew draped his arm around Angel's shoulder. "I have two men removing Scotrovi from the hospital and transporting him here."

"Good," Angel said. "Thank you."

"I've been told there is a doctor in the building?" Andrew smirked.

Chase whirled around in his chair and faced Andrew. "Man, you should have seen it. Olga zapped Giovanni and his head fell right into his manicotti. Splat." Chase bounced up and down excitedly. "That was the most wild-ass thing I've ever seen."

Andrew grinned at Angel. "I suppose you had no idea she was going to taser him?"

Chase laughed out loud. "Oh, she knew, man. She totally knew. She called the doctor ahead of time."

"So it was a pre-meditated Tasering?" Andrew raised his eyebrows.

"I'm afraid this is all hearsay, Officer Venturini, and you have no proof," Angel smirked and walked across the room to speak with Salvatore.

At Angel's request the Snake retrieved Stefano and they joined the others in the family room. Boglevich and the Shark unloaded weapons from the chopper, while Chase connected Sal via video conferencing. Salvatore took a seat in the armed chair, usually filled with Giovanni's presence, Sophia and Olga sat on the couch with Stefano and the rest of the men stood around the room.

Angel took a deep breath. "We're in a mess and there's only one way out. We have to stop the Vamloskaya from gaining control of the city. When Scotrovi arrives he will be able to explain their plan in more detail, but until then we need to make sure we're all on the same page." Angel paced around the room. "First, I will be heading up this operation and Giovanni is not to be disturbed. That message must be conveyed to all your men. Capisce?" There was a general grumbling of agreement. "Salvatore, have you heard from your men back home? Is there any word on Scotrovi's family?"

"Not as of yet, but we are still assembling our men to engage the Bratva," he explained. "There is a substantial time difference." Angel nodded. She'd forgotten about the seven hour time difference. It was the middle of the night in Italy, which meant that they probably wouldn't have any answers until tomorrow.

"Until we hear about Scotrovi's family, I want the fact that his identity has been compromised to remain secret." Angel made eye contact with every person in the room. "Scotrovi cannot know his family is in greater danger now than before."

"Why not?" Stefano called out. "Won't he be more motivated to help them if he knows they're in danger?"

Andrew piped in. "Most of the time people acting out of desperation wind up getting themselves and others killed. For now, it's better if he doesn't know that his family is still in harms way."

"Angel," Chase interjected, "I've got Sal on."

Chase held up his laptop so Sal could see around the room and everyone could see him. "This is one of our FBI contacts, Sal. I've asked him to give you a brief overview of what we're dealing with and who our top players are."

Angel stepped to the back corner behind the big armed chair where Salvatore sat and listened as Sal began.

"At Michelangela's request, I have looked into the background of several persons in the room and your tie to the Vamloskaya. I will start with Abrams Finnegan, known to most of you as the Shark." The Shark held up his hand in acknowledgement. "He comes to us by way of the CIA, working with a special counter-terrorism unit. Intel acquired through the 2004 Intelligence Reform & Prevention of Terrorism Act, indicated that there were well-known terrorist groups with ties to some Italian American mob families."

"What kind of ties?" Sophia asked.

"The exchange of vital information and weapons trade were the two more relevant," the Shark explained.

Sal continued. "The Shark was placed undercover and within a year, he became a Made member of the Maratinzanos, working directly with the Capo di Tutti Capi."

The Shark cleared his throat. "Now you know why some of my choices seemed erratic at times," he said in his usual low tone. "My job was to maintain my cover and gain as much information as possible."

"Moving on to Thomas Boglevich," Sal said and Thomas gave a nod of his large, square shaped head. "Thomas comes to us by way of the Bundesnachrichtendienst, or BND for short. It is the Federal Intelligence Agency for Germany."

"Germany?" Salvatore blurted. "I thought his native land was Russia."

Sal spoke up, "Actually, Thomas is Russian born but studied in Germany where he became a specialist in the areas of wiretapping and electronic surveillance of international communities. After a money laundering scandal resulting in the trial of a Russian mafia boss in Germany, the BND began to look deeper into the dealings between the German mob and the Russian mafia. What they discovered was the usual mob laundry list, but with the added goodies of heavy military weaponry most commonly used by terrorist organizations. BND sent Boglevich to the Russian Vamloskaya gang as an undercover counter-terrorist agent."

Thomas nodded his head. "My job was to report any connection between the Vamloskaya and terrorist organizations."

"So, how did you end up in the States, working for Giovanni?" Angel asked.

"When Denarius Moloney contacted the Vamloskaya Boss, I was sent to the United States to meet with Moloney and become the middleman, what you might call a supplier. Denarius, or Denny as he was known to some of you, then placed me undercover in Giovanni's operation with one purpose; to watch over his daughter Kristen and help her escape when the time came."

Chase bugged his eyes out and shook his head spastically. "So, you are like triple undercover. You're like German BND becomes Russian Vamloskaya becomes Italian-American Maratinzano. That's deep-ass multi-cultural undercover right there."

Andrew piped in, addressing the Shark, "How did you know not to kill Boglevich when you went to kidnap Kristen that morning?"

"We exchanged some words and it became clear that we were not enemies," the Shark answered, "just playing in different positions on the same team."

"Why didn't you take Boglevich with you to the initial meeting with Scotrovi?" Andrew asked.

"Because we didn't know yet that Scotrovi was an undercover SVR agent. Had he been a true Vamloskaya member, Boglevich's cover would have been blown," the Shark explained.

"And it was more prudent for me to contact Vincent Galante, a Vamloskaya friendly, and pursue that angle while the Shark, here, handled Kristen," Boglevich added.

"We saw you on surveillance, taking Galante to my father's house. What was the purpose of that visit?" Andrew questioned.

"From the Intel I received, Galante's assignment was to wage war between the bogatas here so by the time Vamloskaya had everyone in place, there would be so much in-fighting, control would be easily acquired. Tony being ordered to kill Andrew was the perfect opportunity for Galante to pit one Boss against another," Boglevich detailed. "And to fuel a hatred for Giovanni."

"How did Galante know where to find Tony?" Angel asked.

"He didn't," Boglevich answered flat. "His job was to make the Venturini Boss think he knew so he would send men to retrieve Tony. Those men were to be murdered and dumped in a forbidden location."

"Like the Chicago River," Andrew added.

"A gesture of disrespect," Boglevich noted. "It is a common practice of the Vamloskaya to intentionally disrespect the customs of other groups."

"They sound like a bunch of pricks," Olga mumbled. "We ought to zap 'em all."

Angel moved from behind the armed chair to the center of the room. "I look around this room and I see invaluable resources. We have CIA training," she pointed at the Shark. "We have FBI training," she pointed at Sal's face on the computer screen. "We have Russian intelligence through Scotrovi and German intelligence through Boglevich. United States Army training with Chase, Air Force training with the Snake, and Chicago Police Training with Andrew. We have resources in the Cosa Nostra," she pointed at Salvatore. "And the representation of three of the top five Mafia families in the States." She took a deep breath and exhaled slowly. "Together we are powerful, so how do we stop Vamloskaya?"

The front door opened and Scotrovi entered in a wheelchair, escorted by the two cops Andrew had assigned to guard his room at the hospital, and one of Giovanni's guards. Andrew moved to talk with them while Tony wheeled Scotrovi over in front of the windows where he could see the computer and the faces of everyone in the room. Angel gave Scotrovi a quick summary of what they'd learned while Olga and Sophia served hot coffee and Cannoli.

"My question before you arrived was how do we stop Vamloskaya?" Angel said.

Scotrovi pulled his cigarette case from his jacket pocket with his good arm, but struggled to open it one handed. "Michelangela," he uttered, "I am in great need of nicotine. I could not smoke in the hospital. May I please indulge here?" Angel nodded while Stefano helped Scotrovi take out a cigarette and light it and Tony opened the patio door so the smoke wouldn't hang thick in the room. Stefano lit it for him and Scotrovi inhaled deeply, holding the smoke in his lungs and closing his eyes. He exhaled slowly. "Aah," he sighed. "Thank you friend."

"Merciful Heavens, he makes that look so good, it makes me want to smoke," Olga said. Scotrovi extended the cigarette case, offering Olga a smoke, but she declined.

Scotrovi leaned back in his wheelchair. "You cannot stop the Vamloskaya by attacking it at the bottom. You must behead it." His words took her back to the night of the attack on Tetterbaum's, when Giovanni likened the Russians to a serpent and said that it must be beheaded. She wished Giovanni could be a part of this now, but she couldn't trust him to reign in his rage. She hoped one day she could explain why she had to take such drastic measures and that he would forgive her; but forgiveness and Giovanni never fit in the same room.

"Vamloskaya's plan of attack here is to cause in-fighting among your families," Scotrovi inhaled and blew a ring of smoke above his head.

"Except the Galante family," Boglevich added.

"Yah, that is correct," Scotrovi agreed. "Then, while there is bickering they will take out the Bosses one-by-one, placing blame on another family, undoubtedly causing a war between bogatas." Scotrovi took another drag from his cigarette. "There is chaos in war and while you are fighting at the front door they will sneak in the back and take control."

"That's exactly why we hit the Bosses earlier this evening," Tony said.

"You what?" Sal exclaimed.

"Hot damn!" Chase blurted. "I did not see that coming."

"We hit all the Bosses except for Galante," Tony answered, "and obviously except Angel."

"You killed the Bosses?" Sal's voice was shaky with shocked disbelief.

The Shark gruffed out a deep laugh. "No, we shot at them."

"More like barely grazed them in non-vital areas," Tony added. "My guess is no one even needed medical attention."

Sal's eyes were wide and looked bloodshot. "Why...why would you do that?"

"Good question," Chase said, "why the hell would you do that?"

"Two reasons," Tony answered. "First, when there's an attack on a Boss the family goes into full-on, protective lock down mode. Those Bosses won't be seen anywhere in public for weeks. So, we just minimized the Vamloskaya's chances of killing them. Second, we didn't go after Galante which will cause the other families to wonder why, and begin to question if Vincent Galante is somehow involved in all of this."

"Won't the other families wonder why there wasn't an attempt on Angel's life?" Chase asked.

"Not after what happened at Tetterbaum's," Tony shot Andrew a quick glance and returned his eyes to Chase. "I'm pretty sure everyone knows her life was on the line."

"I hate that beady-eyed Galante," Olga huffed. "It'd really feel good to zap him."

"You have strange customs of shooting one other," Scotrovi said with his brow scrunched and a scowl on his face.

Tony tapped his shoulder. "Yeah, sorry about the arm, man. I thought it would help."

"I know, friend," Scotrovi said, "but Kristen has surely told them my true identity and Vamloskaya will make my family pay the penalty for my disloyalty." His shoulders drooped with what Angel could only describe as the weight of hopeless despair.

"Now that your cover is blown, can anyone in SVR rescue your family?" Andrew questioned.

"Yah. I have been in contact with them this afternoon and they are trying, but my hopes are not high," Scotrovi hung his head.

"We will get your wife and daughter back," Angel gritted her teeth, anger boiling in her belly. "Salvatore," Angel locked eyes with her grandfather. "Tell your men that Scotrovi's family is their top priority."

"Si, Michelangela," Salvatore gave a nod. "It shall be done."

Angel paced back and forth, intermittently chewing on her fingernail. "So, who is the head of this Vamloskaya serpent and how do we cut off the head?"

Salvatore's eyes grew dark and his boney fingers clenched into tight fists. "My men will destroy Vamloskaya. You have my word."

Boglevich shook his head. "With all due respect Sir, your men are a continent away. The Vamloskaya are already here to take control."

"How do we find them?" Angel asked.

"You don't," Scotrovi exhaled a ring of smoke above his head. "They find you."

"Fine," said Andrew, "then we lure them here, to the Towers, where we will have the upper hand."

Scotrovi chuckled. "There is no upper hand, friend. You are fighting monsters. They have no value for human life and no moral capacity. When they cannot reach you, they will reach the ones you care most about." Scotrovi's hand shook as he raised his cigarette to his lips. "They will kill everything you love and you will be powerless to stop it."

An eerie silence fell upon the room and Scotrovi's words hung thick in the air. Angel couldn't help but feel compassion for him, and the agony he must be going through knowing that the Vamloskaya now know he is SVR and still have his wife and daughter. Angel choked back the urge to allow tears.

"How many Vamloskaya men are here among us?" Angel asked.

Scotrovi shrugged his shoulders, "a couple dozen and the rest are probably in route. The ones that are here have been here a substantial time and are integrated into your organizations. They are your trusted friends, at least in your mind. Vamloskaya have the mindset of terrorists." Scotrovi's eyes narrowed. "They have great weapons, enormous resources and they come to destroy."

Chills darted up Angel's back. "Will the Vamloskaya Boss, himself, come here?" Angel directed her question to Scotrovi but Boglevich answered.

"Not unless the area is completely secure and they have already won the battle."

"No way we're letting that happen," said Chase.

Salvatore rose from the armed chair. "Vamloskaya is lead by a man named Vladimir. He is a ruthless killer and a coward. He never shows his face in public because his enemies are great."

"Is there any way to bargain with them? To give them something they want that might at least buy us some time?" Angel's question brought blank stares from across the room and then Scotrovi spoke.

"Vamloskaya make no bargains and they do not negotiate," Salvatore grit his teeth.

Scotrovi squint his eyes as he exhaled a long column of smoke into the air above his head. "The only thing they consider of value is you," he said to Angel.

It was late when the conversation came to an end. There wasn't an iron clad plan on the table, but there were pieces of a developing plan coming together. Angel instructed Andrew, Tony, Chase, the Shark, Boglevich and the Snake to gather what they needed from their homes or hotel rooms and move immediately into the Towers. "I will provide apartments on the two floors directly below the Penthouse," Angel told them. "You may bring any trusted men, but I want Sal and Chase running background checks on anyone brought into this building."

She paced around the room, assigning tasks. "Chase, I want you to set up all your equipment in the secret meeting room. That's where we will convene from this point forward. Snake, I want you to choose two men and send them for a supply of food for everyone." He nodded. "Get a list from Olga and make it enough to last."

The men began to clear the room and Angel stepped out onto the patio to clear her mind and organize her thoughts. She leaned on the concrete barrier that encompassed the rooftop and stared up at the moon and the stars. *Help us save Scotrovi's family,* she prayed in the quiet of her mind and exhaled, trying to force some of the tension from her body.

"That was a mighty big sigh, Sweetheart," Andrew said from behind her.

She whirled around, startled. "What?"

"I said that was a mighty big sigh," he repeated. "When you sigh that loudly it's because you have deep thoughts dancing around in your head. You want to let me in on the dance?"

Angel shook her head. "I just can't stop thinking about Scotrovi's wife and daughter."

Andrew took her hand and walked her to the farthest edge of the rooftop. "Look out there at the city," he said. "People out there are gonna die tonight. Some from heart attacks, some from car accidents, some will lose their battle with cancer, some will fall asleep and never wake up and some will die in a gang fight."

She scrunched up her face. "Is that supposed to make me feel better, because I think it might be the worst pep talk in the history of pep talks."

Andrew grinned and tucked a piece of her hair behind her ear. "You haven't let me finish, Sweetheart. The point is people die when it's their time and neither you nor I can do anything to save them."

Angel leaned against the wall and put her chin on her hands. "But I feel like I can save Alonya and Zhanna."

Andrew stepped closer to her and wrapped his arms around her waist, leaning her back against his chest. "Things have been rough between us."

"I know," she sighed.

"We're gonna work it out, Sweetheart," he rested his chin on the top of her head. Angel hoped he was right. She wanted to work it out, but she felt like she needed to understand what happened at Tetterbaum's if she were ever to trust Andrew again.

"Have you ever felt like there was something you needed to do, even if it didn't make a lot of sense? Even if you knew that everyone would tell you not to do it?" He turned her around to face him and she could tell he was studying her eyes.

"What are you talking about?"

She lowered her head. "I don't know. I just feel like I can save them."

"That's what I love about you," he said, pulling her in close and stroking her hair. "You want to change the world."

"Not the whole world, just the Mafia world."

Andrew chuckled, "it's nice to know you don't set your sights too low."

She turned around and leaned her head against his chest. "If one person shows mercy to another, then that person will be more inclined to show mercy to someone else and before long people won't be killed for simple mistakes, but given second chances and forgiveness."

"It certainly sounds good on paper, but the Mob doesn't work that way," Andrew exhaled.

"I just keep thinking that the right thing to do isn't always the smart thing. Sometimes it's the dangerous thing, like when Tony disobeyed Giovanni's order to kill you."

Angel cocked her head sideways and looked up at Andrew, seeing his expression soften and fill with a sense of warmth. "I wish I could see the world through your eyes, Sweetheart." He turned her toward him and kissed her forehead, letting his lips linger for a moment. "Maybe I've grown jaded and given up on changing the world."

She slipped her hand in his and intertwined their fingers. "Sometimes your logic and realism pisses me off, but I admire how you balance it all; the whole Mafia and Cop thing." She looked down and shuffled her feet. "I can't even balance my own thoughts, much less my heart..."

He interrupted her sentence with a tender kiss on her lips. "I know," he whispered, and kissed her lips again.

"What do you know?" She whispered back, arching her neck slightly upward and leaning into his kiss.

"I know you're confused," he kissed her again, this time letting his lips linger on hers. "I know I've let you down," his lips enclosed on hers with more determination and his hands slid around her hips and pulled her closer. "I know sometimes you want to escape," his lips brushed against hers, taunting her with temptation and desire. "I know you feel trapped and you want to do what's right for everyone," he kissed her three times, first to the right, then to the left and back to the right; letting his lips brush lightly against hers. Pangs of desire pulsated through her as she leaned forward, running her hands up his chest and pulling him closer. His lips covered hers in a deep, passionate explosion of longing, and his hands moved quickly up her back, pulling her in and holding her firmly against him. For a moment the whole world stood still and Angel lost herself in his kiss. She didn't want the feeling to end. She didn't want to open her eyes and face reality. She wanted to stay in the safety of his arms and lose herself in the magic of his touch; but awareness of their boundaries crept up from the depths of her soul and she forced herself from his kiss.

She turned from him and apologized. "I shouldn't have let that happen." After all, they had agreed that their lives were too complicated to have a relationship right now. *Too complicated. Humph! As if NOT acting on desire makes it any less complicated.*

"It was my fault," he said. "It's hard to fight sometimes." Angel licked her lips and nodded. She knew that feeling all too well. The problem was that most of the time she didn't want to fight it. Sure, her heart was still compromised by her feelings for both Andrew and Tony; but she was certain that she wouldn't mind if Andrew walked in every day and kissed her like this.

"I better get back to work," he turned to leave, but Angel caught his hand in motion.

Her heart was beating hard in her chest as she looked in his eyes and fought the desire to rush back into his arms. "What did you tell Tony that made him not kill you?"

Surprise shone on Andrew's face. He was obviously not expecting her to blurt out this question. She wasn't really expecting to ask it right then, it just sort of jumped out of her mouth. He took a step closer. "Didn't he tell you what I said?"

"No."

Andrew's eyes sparkled as he raised Angel's hand to his lips and kissed it. "I'll tell you after we beat the Vamloskaya."

"Tell me now," she protested, but he walked away, looking back only once to give her wink and a grin.

CHAPTER 19

Angel tossed and turned in bed, unable to stop thinking about Scotrovi's family and the terrible things that could be happening to them. Her heart ached for that little girl and for the fear her mother must be feeling. She was probably longing for her husband and afraid she wouldn't be able to protect her daughter. Little Zhanna was probably praying, like Angel used to do as a child, asking God to send her daddy back home. Angel kicked the covers off and sat up. She couldn't stop the agonizing thoughts from pounding in her head. She got up, threw on a pair of blue jeans and her old, faded Mizzou Tigers sweatshirt from college. She crept quietly to the kitchen, made two cups of hot tea, and then opened the front door.

"Ms. Maratinzano," the man guarding the Penthouse exclaimed, "where are you going at this hour?"

"I need to speak with Stefano," she said. "Escort me downstairs." After three knocks on the door, Stefano groggily answered, with both fear and surprise showing on his face. "I need to talk with you," Angel said. "Now." She instructed the guard to wait outside.

Angel sat at the glass top kitchen table and handed Stefano one of the cups of tea.

"Thank you," he said, taking the tea and keeping his eyes on Angel.

"I'm sorry to wake you, but I need to ask you a question," she began, biting her bottom lip and running her finger around the top of her cup. "When you helped my mother escape, how did you know it was the right thing to do?"

Stefano exhaled what Angel thought to be a sigh of relief. He leaned back in his chair and rubbed his hand along the bottom of his chin. "Oh, geesh! You scared the crap out of me," he sighed. "I thought you were coming here to kill me or have my legs broken."

Angel grimaced. She hated that her presence alone made him think about death or bodily injury. She understood it was par for the course in the mob world, but she didn't like it. "Is there a reason I should have your legs broken?" She asked.

"No!" Stefano gasped. "Definitely no."

Angel stood up, pulled the 9mm from the back of her jeans and laid it on the table. "There, I'll prove to you I come in peace."

Stefano's face softened and Angel could actually see the fear fade from his eyes. "Do you always sleep with a gun?" He joked.

"Just lately," she grinned. "Now, back to my question. How did you know helping Sophia escape was the right thing to do? I mean, it wasn't the smart thing to do because it was dangerous. So how did you know it was right?"

"I didn't know," he said. "I was scared shitless, that's for sure." He rocked the chair back on two legs. "I guess I just couldn't stand the thought of watching Frank hurt this woman who didn't deserve it."

"Were you afraid Frank would kill you?"

"Yeah, but I was afraid of that anyway. I guess something inside just told me that it was what I was supposed to do." Stefano shrugged and took a drink of tea. "This might sound stupid but I have always believed we are put in situations for a reason, and I think my reason for being there was to help your mom; even if it got me dead."

Angel slipped her gun back in her jeans and walked toward the door.

"I wasn't very helpful was I?" Stefano asked.

"Actually, you were," Angel smiled. "Good night."

As she opened the door to leave, Stefano asked, "how long do I have to stay here?"

Angel turned to meet his eyes. "I am sorry Giovanni has made you feel like a prisoner." She shook her head. "You are free to leave anytime you want, but please understand you cannot return to your family without putting them in jeopardy. At least not until we figure out the extent of your uncle's relationship to the Vamloskaya." Angel reached out and touched Stefano's hand. "I will not force you to stay, but I'm asking you to remain until we are certain that it is safe for you to go."

Angel left Stefano and knocked on Giovanni's apartment. Two guards escorted her inside and awakened Dr. Rainer.

"Is there a problem, Ms. Maratinzano," Dr. Rainer asked with a shaky voice and trembling hands as he slid his glasses onto his nose.

"I am sorry to have awakened you, but I need a moment with my grandfather," she said.

"As you requested, he is sedated and will not be able to have a conversation," the doctor explained.

"I understand," she said, walking into Giovanni's bedroom and sitting on the bed next to him. She looked at the IV running into his right arm and the heart monitor as it blinked steadily. "Is he doing okay?" Angel asked the doctor.

"Yes. His vital signs are strong, but Ms. Maratinzano it is against my better judgment to keep him sedated very much longer."

"I know," she whispered. "It won't be much longer."

At her request, Dr. Rainer left the room and Angel slid her hand beneath Giovanni's. She gazed at him, feeling that ever so present twinge of guilt for having done this to him. *It was the only way,* she told herself, but even that justification didn't eliminate the guilt. "Grandfather," she whispered, "I know you can't speak but I'm hoping you can hear me, even if it's somewhere deep in the corners of your mind." She took a breath. "I want you to know I'm sorry for doing this but I saw no other way to protect you and those around you from your rage." She stroked his hand. "I love you so much, but sometimes you make me want to hate you." A tear ran down her cheek and dripped onto her robe. "I've written you a letter and will have Dr. Rainer give it to you when you finally awaken. It explains everything." She stood and kissed him on the forehead. "Ti amo nonno."

Before opening the door to leave Angel slid an envelope from her pocket and handed it to Dr. Rainer. The envelope was marked with Giovanni's name. "You may allow him to awaken tomorrow." The doctor nodded. "Remember my instructions. You are to tell him that he suffered a mild stroke but will be fine with rest. Then give him this letter." Angel opened the door, changed her mind and closed it again. "If you do exactly as I've instructed you, your money will arrive tomorrow evening and you are free to go. If you tell him that he was tasered you will not receive a penny and will be detained."

Dr. Rainer's eyes widened. "I understand."

Angel left Giovanni's apartment and returned to her bedroom in the Penthouse. She punched some keys on her laptop and called up Sal using Skype.

"Michelangela, it is very late," Sal uttered.

"My apologies," she said, "but I need to know where we stand on Scotrovi's family."

"Sadly, I have heard nothing from my contacts in the SVR. They have not been able to confirm even a location of his wife and daughter, much less whether they are still alive."

Angel deflated. "Thanks Sal," she forced a smile. "Keep me posted."

The screen went blank.

Angel paced around her room for the next hour, then showered and dressed. She put on a black skirt that flared just above the knee, a white collared blouse, black jacket and knee-high black boots. She put on silver hoop earrings and let her hair fall long and straight over her shoulders.

It was nearly 4:00am when Angel pulled the Tank into the vacant lot and stepped outside. She had managed to leave the Towers unnoticed because she ordered the security guards to be moved from the lobby to Giovanni's floor. Boglevich approached her with a wire and a vest. "Michelangela, are you certain you want to go through with this?" He asked.

She nodded. "I have to."

She felt him study her face while she thread the wire beneath her blouse and hooked it onto her bra. "Such great courage in one so young," he said.

"Some might call it stupidity," Angel joked and Boglevich grinned.

"I call it bravery." He helped her into the Kevlar vest and closed her jacket around it. "They will search you and remove all of this, but the information we acquire before it is removed could be invaluable."

"Okay," she nodded.

He stared deeply into her eyes. "Remember, to them I am Vamloskaya. I will not be able to communicate with you or help you in any way. I cannot compromise my cover. Do you understand this?" Angel nodded. "It means even though I am there, you are alone in this mission."

"I understand," Angel said, trying to hide the quiver in her voice.

"As you asked, I have arranged a meeting with Vincent Galante. He has been informed of your terms. Once your people receive confirmation that Scotrovi's family has been released into safety, he will escort you to meet with the Vamloskaya here in the city." Boglevich stared at her with an expression of warning. "Vamloskaya are brutal and ruthless. You must understand they will use you to lure Giovanni and Salvatore to them and then kill all of you."

Angel nodded, her mouth going dry and a lump of fear forming in her throat. "I will make them kill me before they can use me to get to my grandfathers."

Boglevich placed both hands atop her shoulders. "Allow me to inform Andrew of the action you are taking so that we have a fighting chance to get you back."

Tears began to fill Angel's eyes but she forced them back and swallowed hard. "No, not until Alonya and Zhanna are safe, and not unless you can guarantee his safety and the safety of anyone he brings with him."

"I cannot." Boglevich dropped his arms and shook his head. "A fight against Vamloskaya is sure to result in many deaths."

"Then we can't fight," Angel said. "Tell them to make the trade."

Angel sat in the Tank while Boglevich made a phone call to inform Galante that they were ready to meet as soon as Scotrovi's wife and daughter were released. She pulled her cell phone from her jacket pocket and punched in Tony's number, then typed a message: "Remember when we were in college and I said that I never felt like I belonged anywhere? Well today I know exactly where I belong. I will always love you, Tony. Always."

She punched in Andrew's number and sat for a moment, staring at the empty text box. *How do you show your heart in one small box,* she wondered, and then began punching the keys. "Sometimes the right thing isn't the smart thing. Sometimes the heart knows better than the mind. Our lives may be complicated but in my heart it is simple. I love you."

Her last text was sent to Chase. She typed: "You're the best bodyguard I ever had. Tell Salvatore, my mother and Aunt Olga I have left them letters on my bed and I love them."

Boglevich tapped on her window and Angel opened the door. "Confirmation on the release of Scotrovi's family is being transmitted now." He handed her a piece of paper with a web address. "You will be able to see live images here." Angel punched the address into her phone and waited for the webpage to appear. She watched as a woman and little girl were escorted from a black limousine and taken into custody by what appeared to be local law enforcement or maybe even SVR operatives. The woman held the child close and cried out with Russian utterances, what Angel could only imagine were tears of relief and joy. Angel saved the website video link and emailed it to Chase with a message. "Please confirm the authenticity of this video."

"You are ready to go through with this?" Boglevich asked and Angel nodded. "I must go now, but I will return with Galante to pick you up."

Angel sat in the Tank and closed her eyes. Part of her wanted to drive away right now, to head back to the Towers where she would be safe; but she knew that would result in more death. Handing herself over was the only way to protect all the people she loved. She began to recite the Lord's Prayer. "Our Father, who art in Heaven, hallowed be Thy name. Thy kingdom come. Thy will be done on earth as it is in Heaven. Give us this day our daily bread and forgive us our debts as we forgive our debtors. Lead us not into temptation but deliver us from evil." Her voice caught on the last phrase and she repeated it. "Deliver us from evil."

"Trasportili dalla malvagità," his voice came from the back of the Tank and Angel jumped and shrieked. "Ssshh," he said. "It's just me." Stefano crawled from the very back into the back seat. "Trasportili dalla malvagità means deliver us from evil. I remember it from when I was a little boy and my grandmother used to pray aloud in Italian."

"What are you doing here?" Angel's heart was racing. "You have to get out of here."

Stefano shook his head. "No way I'm letting you go through with this. This is a crazy plan and you're only going to get yourself killed."

Angel glared at him, her jaw tensing. "This is the only way I can stop all the killing."

Stefano crossed his arms. "How do you know that once the Vamloskaya have you that the fighting will stop? If they kill you, Giovanni and Salvatore are going to go after them and the war continues."

Angel's hands were beginning to tremble. "I don't know. I just want to save that little girl and her mother from being tortured and..." Angel's voice caught in her throat. "I remember being that five year old little girl whose daddy never came home. I remember hearing my mother cry herself to sleep at night, and calling out his name in her sleep. I can't stand the thought of that little girl living without her father or of Scotrovi living without Alyona and Zhanna." She took a deep breath. "I was powerless to save my own father, but I'm not powerless anymore. I can save them."

"What about your mother and Olga and all the people who love you?" Stefano reached forward and touched her arm. "What about them? You're forcing them to make a sacrifice they have no say in."

"Stop it!" Angel yelled at him. "You're trying to talk me out of something I know I need to do."

"No, Angel," Stefano hollered back. "You're trying to convince yourself to do something that you don't want to do; and you're trying to justify it as a sacrifice to save everyone around you, but the truth is the only way you can save them is by staying alive." Angel gripped the steering wheel and fought back tears. "Who's to say Scotrovi's family is even really safe? Are you going to trust a video link on the internet that could easily be fabricated?" Stefano shook his head. "Look at the source. These aren't honest people you're dealing with here."

Angel felt like she was starting to hyperventilate and she leaned her head against the back of the seat. "I don't know how to stop the killing. I can't control the rage in Giovanni and I feel that same rage in my own veins. I can't stop it and I don't want to be this person," she broke into sobs, her hands trembling uncontrollably as she held them to her face.

Stefano leaned forward. "The same blood may be in your veins but the same rage isn't. You protected me. You protected Andrew and Tony. You gave me a second chance, now give yourself one."

Angel sobbed as if her soul were being emptied. "I don't want to be a killer. I don't want to watch the people I love die or wake up every day with the fear that I'm going to lose someone to a bullet. I'd rather die saving someone than sit back and watch the people I love suffer."

Stefano wedged himself between the front seats so he could look in Angel's eyes. "Then be like your father and pave a road of peace, but do it with your life and not by your death." Their eyes were locked together and Angel panted with emotion. "These people don't make deals. They'll kill you and then they'll kill Scotrovi's family anyway."

Angel put her hand up to the keys and turned on the ignition. Thoughts were racing through her mind as she looked at Stefano. "If I drive away they will come after us."

"They were already coming after us right?"

Angel threw the Tank in drive and Stefano into the back seat as she sped out of the vacant lot and toward the Towers. She glanced out the side mirrors and rearview mirror, expecting to be followed but didn't see anyone. By the time they pulled onto the side street adjacent to the Towers, Angel was breathing easier, but then two black vans pulled on either side of her.

"Please tell me these vans are people that work for you," Stefano uttered.

"I wish I could," Angel said and floored the gas. The vans matched her speed. She slammed on the brakes, with the thought to do a quick spin and head the opposite direction, but the vans stayed with her.

Further up the street two more vans appeared, one in front and the other behind; completely boxing her in. Panic rose inside her and she flipped her phone to Stefano. Call Andrew and Chase and Tony right now and tell them what's happening. The minute Stefano held the phone to his ear a barrage of gunfire hit the Tank. Stefano yelled and Angel instinctively closed her eyes for a brief second before remembering that the Tank was outfitted with bullet-proof glass and multi-layered nylon armor.

"Don't worry," she said to Stefano, "they can't shoot through this car."

Stefano got a hold of Chase, who gathered Tony, Andrew, Salvatore, the Shark and the Snake. Stefano put the call on speaker and they had to yell over the gun fire.

"What direction are you headed?" Andrew yelled.

"South," Angel answered.

"I'm locking in on the tracking device in your phone," Chase said. "Give me a second. Okay, we got you."

"We're sandwiched between four black vans," Stefano yelled, "and they're firing on us."

Angel could hear Tony on his phone in the background, calling up manpower from each of the families, with the obvious exception of the Galante family.

"What the hell are you doing out there and why is Stefano with you?" Andrew yelled.

Angel and Stefano stared at each other. She didn't know how to answer that question and she guessed Stefano didn't either because he sat there speechless. "It's complicated," Angel finally hollered.

"I can't wait to hear this one," Andrew quipped.

"They're turning," Chase belted out. "Heading west now." The black vans kept her boxed in, but the shooting had stopped. Either the Vamloskaya realized it was impossible to penetrate the Tank, or the shots were a mere warning for what would happen if Angel didn't cooperate.

"What do you see around you? Vacant buildings? Open fields?" Andrew asked.

Stefano pointed ahead. "There's an airstrip!"

Andrew must have grabbed the phone and held it directly to his lips because all of a sudden his voice was the only one they could hear. "Listen to me carefully; do NOT get on any aircraft. Do you hear me? Take off running away from the aircraft and make them shoot you; but DO NOT let them put you on a plane. Do you understand?"

Stefano and Angel locked eyes. Angel was certain Stefano was filled with as much panic as she was, if not more.

"Do you understand?" Andrew demanded.

"Yes, we understand," Angel answered.

"We're on our way, Sweetheart." The phone went quiet and Stefano grabbed it to see if there was still a signal.

The vans slowed to a stop as they waited for a security guard to open a gate and allow them to pass. They drove slowly down a paved road toward a small airstrip with a hanger that looked big enough to house two, maybe three private planes. The hanger was painted brown and one of the giant sliding doors was open. Stefano looked at Angel through the rearview mirror. "What do we do when they want us to get out of the car? Do we just sit here and let them shoot at us?"

"I don't know," she uttered. "You stay back there and get down. The back windows are tinted so they might not even know you're in the car." Stefano hunched lower in the back seat.

All four vans pulled within fifty feet of the hanger door and stopped, forcing Angel to apply the brake. When the van doors opened and men began to step out, Angel hit the gas with such force it threw Stefano back in his seat. She rammed the van in front of her, threw the Tank in reverse, rammed the one behind her and did it again and again; but she was unable to clear a path to break free. The smell of burning rubber filled the air and Angel beat her palms on the steering wheel. Her car phone rang and Angel pushed the answer button. Chase's voice filled the car. "We have a chopper on the way. You've got to stay put and hold them off as long as you can."

"How long?" Stefano yelled, pulling a .38 from under his shirt.

"The chopper should be there in under five minutes, dude, just sit tight."

Angel looked at Stefano. "I'm sorry I got you into this."

"I got myself into it," he said. "You just got me in deeper."

"You're a good guy," Angel smiled, "and I owe you one."

"Let's just concentrate on living through this and then you can worry about paying me back," Stefano stared out the window. When two men approached the car, Angel grabbed her 9mm. "What are they doing?" Stefano asked.

Angel watched intently. They were carrying large bricks, cinder block bricks and placing them in front of her tires. "They're making sure we don't go anywhere," she said and then Stefano let Chase know what was happening.

"More cars are coming," Stefano pointed.

"Chase, we've got two cars pulling up to my left. It looks like they could be limousines." Angel's view was impaired by the four vans on each side.

"I see 'em. I'm tracking your ass on GPS so I can pretty much see everything you see," Chase explained.

All of a sudden the van in front of them pulled away. "Angel, um, Angel..." Stefano's voice tapered off and his eyes grew wide with terror.

"Oh no," Angel gasped. "They're aiming this thing at us."

"What kind of thing?"

"It looks like a grenade launcher," Stefano said.

"How close are they?" Chase yelled.

"They're right in front of the hanger, so, I don't know, maybe fifty feet away?" Angel's voice shook.

Amid all the noise, they could hear Chase's fingers jumping across a keyboard. "Don't panic," Chase said, "I'm pulling up the schematic of the Tank right now. Hold on. Hold tight. Here we go. Holy shit!" Chase gasped, "Now I know why you call your car the Tank. That is one sweet-ass vehicle."

"Chase!" Angel yelled. "Will it take the impact of a grenade?"

"Without a doubt. No worries. It's got layers of nylon armor and it looks like even a polycarbonate layer between the glass sections. Oh yeah, you're sitting in a freaky-ass ballistic defense machine." Chase's voice was elevated with excitement.

"Are you sure?" Stefano hollered.

"It's gonna jolt the hell out of you so buckle up and enjoy the sweet-ass ride."

Angel and Stefano watched wide-eyed as the man with the grenade launcher took aim. Angel crawled in the back seat with Stefano, both of them strapping on their seat belts. She reached over and grabbed Stefano's hand. Her palms grew sweaty and her heart raced. It was a terrible feeling to be staring down a grenade launcher, awaiting its detonation. Angel made the sign of the cross over her body and began to pray. "Our

Father, who art in Heaven," she looked to Stefano who crossed his body and chimed in.

"Hallowed be Thy name."

"Thy kingdom come, Thy will be done on earth as it is in Heaven," they prayed in unison. "Give us this day our…" The men fired the grenade and the explosion was louder than Angel anticipated. She and Stefano instinctively released their hands and grabbed their ears. Angel squeezed her eyes shut and felt the Tank lift off the ground and slam back down. It jolted them so hard Angel's seatbelt locked around her. When she opened her eyes, she was amazed to see that none of the glass had shattered and there were no holes in the exterior frame.

"Unbelievable," Stefano gasped.

"Everybody okay in there?" Chase yelled through the phone. "That was a loud-ass explosion."

They looked at each other. Her ears rang with a numbing sensation and she opened her mouth to try to pop them. "We're fine for now, but I don't know how many more blasts we can take," Angel hollered.

"Where's that helicopter you were promising?" Stefano yelled.

"They're a few minutes out. Hang tight." They could hear Chase's fingers clicking away on the keyboard.

The van to the left pulled away and Angel's heart skipped a beat. There, a mere forty feet away, on the airstrip was a solid white, private jet and in front of the jet was a man down on his knees, execution style. His hands were tied behind his back and a gun pressed tightly to his head. Angel gasped. "It's Scotrovi. They have Scotrovi."

"What?" Chase blurted. "How did they get him?"

"I don't know," Angel sighed, "but they're going to kill him."

"Something's not right," Chase grunted. "Something's wild-ass wrong about this. How the hell did they get him? He was with us at the Towers."

Angel gripped her 9mm. "They're gonna kill him." She reached her hand for the door handle and Stefano grabbed her.

"Don't go out there! They'll just kill you too," he pleaded.

"Hold your position, Angel," Chase hollered. "Give me two seconds to verify something."

"Scotrovi might not have two seconds!" Angel wailed.

"Hold your position!" Chase yelled.

Angel stuffed her gun into the waistband of her skirt and twisted the door handle. "No!" Stefano screamed and grabbed her wrist.

"I'm sorry," Angel said, twisting her arm free, "but I can't let him die."

She opened the door and slammed it quickly shut behind her. Lifting both hands above her head, she walked slowly toward Scotrovi and the man holding him at gunpoint. Her knees wobbled with every step and she felt a lightheaded sensation from the rapid shortness of her breath. When she reached the airstrip, she was greeted by two men carrying Uzi pistols. They stopped her a mere ten feet from Scotrovi, one reaching behind and removing her 9mm and the other taking steady aim.

"She's clear," he spoke with a thick Russian accent into a headpiece. Whoever was giving instructions must have told the men to stand guard, because they took a flank position, facing her on both sides. Angel's stomach felt hollow as she studied their weapons. There was no way she could take off running and hope they were poor shots. Even if they were poor shots, she knew few targets were missed by an Uzi.

She yelled to Scotrovi, "Are you okay?" He didn't respond to her. Angel yelled to the man holding the gun to Scotrovi's head. "You have me, now let him go. That was the deal. Let him go safely back to his family." The man didn't respond nor acknowledge she had spoken. She turned to the guard to her right, the one wearing the headpiece. "I know you can speak," she taunted, "or are you so weak that you have to obtain permission first." The men didn't move. They stood straight and tall, as if they were at military attention. "You know what we call men who can't think for themselves, who can't speak on their own, but blindly follow someone else's agenda even to the death? We call them cowards." Angel bent over and spit on the boots of the guard to her right.

"Holy shit!" Stefano hollered, "She spit on him!"

"Come again," Chase blurted. "Did you say she spit on him?"

"She just spit on this big Russian dude's shoes!" Stefano exclaimed. "It's like she's trying to piss them off!"

"That is some wild-ass chick," Chase chuckled.

"It's not funny," Stefano yelled. "They're gonna kill her."

"Calm down, the chopper is in range. Stay calm, man. You gotta be my eyes on the ground."

"Just tell them to hurry," Stefano moaned. "I got a real bad feeling."

Angel heard the whirring of helicopter blades approaching and felt a twinge of hope. "Do you hear that?" She taunted the men guarding her. "That's the sound of your defeat. That's the sound of pissed off Italian Americans who have the freedom to think for themselves and to act on their own and do you know what each of them wants to do to you?" She forced a loud laugh. "They want to drop you and they don't have to wait for someone's permission to do it." She saw the man to her right shift his weight and narrow his eyes. "What's the matter?" She spewed sarcastically. "Are you scared? Why don't you use your little headpiece there to ask permission to run away and hide?" The man's jaw tightened. "I see I'm getting to you," Angel hollered. "Too bad you can't use that big gun to shoot me. Too bad you have to wait for permission."

The man to her right turned and grabbed Angel around the throat, squeezing her esophagus so tightly that her eyes bulged. The man holding the gun to Scotrovi's head raised his weapon and shot the guard two times, once through his neck and another into his chest. He fell backward, dragging Angel down on top of him and releasing her throat. Angel pushed off his body and onto her knees, coughing and sucking in air. She reached out for his gun, but the other guard kicked her, picked up the Uzi and slung it over his shoulder.

"Nice try," he uttered with a thick accent.

She moved her eyes to Scotrovi, who remained on his knees with his head down. She was laying only a foot from him and she stretched her arm out to touch his hand, but she couldn't reach him. "We're not alone," she panted. "They're here and everything's gonna be okay," she hollered over the whirring sound of the helicopter. "You're going to be reunited with your family." A single tear ran down his face and dropped to the pavement.

CHAPTER 20

Stefano stared out the window and yelled so that Chase could hear him through the car phone, "he just tried to strangle her!"

"Son of a ..." Chase's voice was interrupted by the ringing of Angel's cell.

Stefano grabbed it and Andrew's voice came through. "What the hell is she doing?" Andrew hollered above the whirring of the helicopter.

"She's trying to save Scotrovi," Stefano yelled, "but I got a really bad feeling about this."

"You and me both," Andrew yelled.

"Put Andrew on speaker," Chase said. "Andrew, we got bad news..."

"Yeah, I'm looking at it," Andrew quipped.

"No man, like worse than that, like really bad-ass news."

"What?"

"I just got confirmation on the video uplink, the one showing Scotrovi's family being set free," Chase paused while he clicked on the keyboard. "The video's fake. It's a cheap-ass fake."

Andrew spewed obscenities as he repeated the information to the Snake, the Shark and Tony who were all in the helicopter.

"What does that mean?" Stefano asked.

"I'm confirming with Sal now, hang on."

"There's a man moving toward her," Stefano blurted. "He's moving toward her. What do I do?" The panic in his voice grew stronger. "What the hell do I do?"

"Hold your position," Andrew yelled. "We've already got two people down there we have to shoot around, we don't need to make it three."

The guard that stood to Angel's left, pulled her to a standing position, away from Scotrovi.

"Someone's getting out of one of the limos," Stefano yelled. "He's walking toward Angel." Two black, stretch limousines were parked between the hanger and the jet.

"I'm zooming in with live feed now," Chase responded.

"We've got visual," Andrew yelled.

"It's that Vincent Galante guy that Olga hates and that Boglevich guy is walking to his right," Stefano said. "I can see them plain as day."

"Andrew, tell the Snake to lift the chopper," Chase warned, "you're low enough to take ground fire, especially when we already know they have a mean-ass grenade launcher."

Andrew relayed the message and the Snake pulled her up. "How many men are on the ground?" Andrew asked.

Tony, who was looking through a sniper rifle, hollered, "I count eighteen, give or take a few. There could also be some on the plane and I don't know how many inside the hanger."

The helicopter circled overhead as Galante and Boglevich neared Angel's location. Galante stopped in front of her. *Olga is right,* she thought to herself, *he does have evil little beady eyes.*

"Michelangela, I knew you would come," Galante said, a grin spreading across his face. "You are so easy to play," he laughed. "It's almost no fun when you play right into our hands like this." He laughed harder. "There was hardly a challenge in luring you here. Too bad you're not more like your grandfather and less like your father." He circled around her. "You might have lived longer." He made a disappointed clicking sound with his tongue. "Such a shame."

"You're a fool, Vincent," Angel spat. "Did you really think the Bratva would give you control over any portion of the city? They're terrorists. They use people like you and then kill them."

"The only one dying today, my little Mafia princess, is you." Galante snapped his fingers and Boglevich drew his weapon and took aim at Angel's head. "Do you see any guns aimed at me?"

Angel looked up at the helicopter and then lowered her eyes back to Galante. "Actually, I'd say there are several guns aimed at you right now." She raised her left eyebrow just slightly and smiled. "Whether I die or not, I can guarantee YOU will be the first one they gun down."

"You are nothing," he seethed at her, "utterly meaningless."

Angel forced a laugh. "Really?" She folded her arms. "If I am nothing then why did you go through all this trouble to get me here?"

Galante stormed passed her. "Keep your gun to her head," he ordered Boglevich, who moved in closer and took aim. "If she moves, kill her."

Stefano yelled into the phone, "Boglevich has a gun to her head!"

"What the hell is going on?" Andrew blurted. "Chase, is Boglevich clean?"

"According to Sal..." Chase began and Andrew cut him off.

"Did you run a check on him?"

"No, Sal did," Chase answered. "No one told me to double-check Sal's work. I mean, I'm not a mob-ass mind reader, man; if you want something you gotta frickin' ask me for it."

"Get Sal on the line," Andrew blurted.

"Right on," said Chase.

Stefano intently watched every move the men made around Angel. "We're running out of time, guys," Stefano exhaled. "They're gonna kill Scotrovi and then they're gonna kill Angel."

"We're not gonna let that happen, Ace," came the voice of Tony through the line. "We'll start picking off men shortly and that'll cause a diversion; take the attention off Angel and Scotrovi."

"That's a big ass negative on that idea," Chase quipped. "You start firing and they're gonna throw her ass on that jet and take off."

"Then what's our move?" Stefano grunted. "I have a gun."

Galante climbed the jet steps and disappeared inside. Angel bounced her knee up and down and made sure not to make eye contact with Boglevich. She lowered her chin and stared at the ground, glancing every so often at Scotrovi, who remained on his knees with the barrel of a gun pressed into the back of his head. She tried not to look at the body lying to her right, or at the blood that pooled around him. The man to her left stood staunch and Boglevich held his aim. Angel wondered if now would be a good time to make a break for it. She could take off in a dead sprint toward Scotrovi, possibly knocking over the man holding the gun to Scotrovi's head. *Maybe Boglevich could shoot the man with the Uzi before he fired off a round?* Angel exhaled and wiggled her fingers nervously. The problem was she couldn't trust Boglevich to take that shot because he had said that he would not jeopardize his cover; and if he didn't take the shot, she would be gunned down by the guard with the Uzi.

When Galante finally stepped off the jet, he carried a black briefcase and a set of handcuffs. He tossed the cuffs to Boglevich. "Cuff her," he said. Boglevich hooked the cuffs around Angel's wrists without making eye contact. He loosely fastened the cuffs to her wrists, placing her hands in front of her body, which Angel took as silent confirmation that he would help her if there was any way possible. Panic began to take hold. *It'll be harder to take off running or defend myself in cuffs,* her mind pointed out the obvious. *But no matter what I have to do, I won't let them put me on that plane.*

"Talk to me, Chase," Andrew blurted. "Is Boglevich clean or not?"

Chase's fingers flew over the keyboard. "He's clean man. Squeaky-ass clean. Everything checks out."

"Guys," Stefano stuttered, "do you see that?"

"I'm showing movement near the hanger, but what do you see?" Chase asked.

"It's a tank," Stefano yelled. "It's a military tank!"

"Leave it to the freaky-ass Russians to bring a tank to a gun fight," Chase quipped. "Andrew, that tank has the power to drop you right out of the sky. If you're gonna make a move you better make it now."

"Roger that," Tony yelled into the phone.

Galante placed the black briefcase in his limousine, then walked to the other limo and opened the back door. He reached his arm in and helped Kristen step from the car.

Angel's eyes widened as Galante escorted Kristen toward her. She flipped her blonde hair over her shoulder and smiled. "I told you to smile while you could," she sneered. "Next time maybe you'll listen to me. Oh, wait; there won't be a next time because you'll be dead." Galante laughed out loud and Kristen snickered. "But don't be sad Angel; before you die there are more surprises for you."

Anger boiled within her and Angel's fingers clenched into fists. She wanted to leap on top Kristen and pound her face into the ground. "Good," Angel blurted. "Because I've got a surprise for you too." She was bluffing. She had no surprise. She was probably going to wind up dead. Her mind raced, trying to come up with a plan to save Scotrovi and herself without blowing Boglevich's cover. *If I only had that Uzi,* she thought; not that she'd ever fired one. She had no idea how to handle a gun that powerful, but she was willing to take aim at Kristen and give it her best shot.

The tank moved closer. "Whatever you're gonna do you better start doing it," Chase hollered through the phone.

The Snake lowered the chopper into a swooping pattern and Tony, using a sniper rifle, hit the man standing to Angel's left. The bullet soared directly through the side of his head and he dropped in a heap, blood splattering all over Angel. She instinctively dove for his gun; but his body landed on it and, with her hands cuffed, she couldn't get enough leverage to pull it out. Boglevich fired at the chopper, but missed. Angel was certain his miss was intentional. Men appeared from everywhere, firing at the chopper. The shots were loud and Angel instinctively rolled into a ball as bullets soared around her. She tried to keep her focus on getting the Uzi, but her fingers were trembling from fear and the rush of adrenaline.

The man who had been pointing the gun at Scotrovi's head turned his attention to the helicopter and fired several shots, leaving Scotrovi unattended. Angel left the gun and crawled toward him. She managed to get to her knees and tried to pull Scotrovi to his feet. The chopper swooped again and this time Tony and Andrew took out the guard who had been holding the gun to Scotrovi's head and another one that was approaching Angel. The helicopter swooped behind the limousines and the Shark leapt to the ground, taking cover behind the limousines, while Tony and Andrew took out several more guards.

Angel tugged at Scotrovi, but he didn't budge. It was as if he was frozen with fear. She screamed his name, but he didn't move. Kristen ran for the chopper and Angel dove for her legs but Galante kicked Angel's arms away, knocking her backwards. Angel scrambled to her knees in time to see Scotrovi rise to his feet and run toward the jet stairway. Angel hollered after him, and then realized what was happening. He wasn't being coerced or forced. He was voluntarily getting on the plane. Everything seemed to be moving in slow motion. Angel saw Kristen turn her head to the left and blow a kiss. Was she trying to kiss Scotrovi? She heard the whirring of the helicopter and more rapid fire of machine guns. Men poured from the hanger only to be gunned down by Tony and Andrew from the chopper. Bodies dropped around Angel and blood splattered across the pavement.

Galante moved quickly toward the plane and Angel dove for one of the guns on the ground. Raising herself up on wobbly knees, she took aim at Vincent Galante. She pulled the trigger and shrieked as the Uzi fired several rounds, knocking Angel backwards and onto the ground. Her ribs throbbed and her head ached from slamming against the runway, but worst of all, she saw she had missed Galante and hit the plane. She wasn't used to the power of the gun.

Angel scurried to her knees and lifted the Uzi again, this time she mentally braced herself for the backlash. Galante whirled around and screamed to Boglevich, "Kill her!"

Before he could even pretend to take aim, Angel fired again and hit Galante. He flew backwards with blood spurting from his neck.

The tank fired at the chopper and the Snake maneuvered it evasively, swooping and turning. With the sound of the blast, Angel instinctively hit the ground and covered her head. Boglevich ran toward the hanger and the tank, taking out every man in his path. His cover was blown. Angel couldn't see where the Shark was, as she clutched the Uzi and dashed toward Scotrovi and Kristen, who were half way up the jet stairway that was beginning to lift as the plane moved forward. Anger consumed her at the thought of Scotrovi being one of them. She screamed with rage, pulling the trigger and swinging the gun with all her might. She hit Scotrovi in the back of the leg and he went down, pulling Kristen to her knees. Kristen jumped up, lifted her gun and fired three shots into Angel's chest.

Angel flew backwards, the impact of the bullets stinging into her skin. She tried to inhale but she couldn't catch her breath and it felt like a weight was pushing her into the pavement. She gasped for air, staring wildly into the sky when everything went black.

Stefano screamed from the car, "She's hit! Angel's hit! She's down!" He grabbed his gun, leapt from the car and ran toward the jet.

Scotrovi managed to gimp his way up the jet stairway with Kristen dragging him. Stefano stopped running and stared at her, the woman he had once loved, the one he had wanted to marry so badly that he went to work for his Uncle Vince so he could make enough money to buy her a ring. None of that mattered now. Stefano took aim and pulled the trigger, then pulled it again and again; sending three bullets into Kristen's chest, just as the plane turned and sped toward the runway. Two men appeared in the jet doorway, kicked Kristen's body off the top of the stairs and pulled Scotrovi into the plane.

The stairway closed and the jet sped down the runway and lifted into the air.

Stefano hit the ground with the sound of the tank blast and the exploding jet. His ears were ringing loudly and a numbing sensation filled his head, as he tried to scramble to his feet and make his way toward Angel. The jet disintegrated into a million tiny burning pieces and so did anyone aboard. Stefano looked over just in time to see Boglevich climb from inside the tank and run toward him.

"She was hit," Stefano yelled and then dropped to his knees next to Angel.

Boglevich felt for her pulse and nodded to Stefano. "She's alive."

As soon as the Snake set the chopper down, Stefano and Boglevich loaded Angel in. "Drive her car back to the Towers," Tony yelled to Stefano. "Bring the Shark and Boglevich with you."

Tony stared down at Angel and quickly turned his head away. She was covered in blood. It was splattered all over her face and her arms, caked down the side of her neck and covering her legs and boots. He swallowed hard.

"You okay, Ace?" Andrew asked when he saw the color drain from Tony's face. Tony nodded. Andrew ripped open Angel's black jacket and saw the Kevlar vest. "Good girl," he uttered, lifting the vest away from her skin.

"I thought you said she didn't tell you about her plan to give herself up to save Scotrovi's family?" Tony said.

"She didn't," Andrew answered.

"Then where'd she get the bullet proof vest?"

Andrew shrugged. "No idea, but whoever gave it to her saved her life."

Tony and Andrew maneuvered the vest off Angel's body and carefully opened her blouse. They both winced at the deep bruises and burn marks. The bullets didn't penetrate the skin, but they had enough force to do some painful damage. "Yikes," Tony grimaced.

"Yeah, she's gonna be sore for a while," Andrew pulled out his cell phone. "I'm gonna call Chase and let him know we're on our way in and to have the doctor ready."

Andrew moved to the front of the chopper next to the Snake while Tony brushed Angel's hair back from her forehead and held her hand. When her eyelids began to flutter slightly, he leaned down and spoke into her ear. "You're okay, Babe, I've got you and we're going home."

She tried to speak but the throbbing in her head and the intense pain in her chest stifled her ability to form words. Her eyes rolled back into her head and the whirring sound of the helicopter carried her back into unconsciousness.

CHAPTER 21

When the chopper landed, Andrew and Tony carried Angel into the Penthouse and placed her on top the dining room table. Sophia gasped and put her hand to her mouth, her eyes instantly watering with concern.

Olga stopped dead in her tracks. "Merciful heavens," she blurted, "is she alive?"

"She took three high-powered shots to the chest, but she was wearing a vest so there was no actual penetration," Andrew explained quickly, making a beeline toward Chase, who was hunched over his computer in the family room.

"Giovanni's awake," Chase said. "Angel left him a letter and according to the doc, he's reading it now."

Andrew sighed. "I hope to hell it asks him not to kill me and Tony."

Olga overheard their conversation. "Don't you worry about that old goat," she sputtered, "I'll zap him again if he comes near you."

Salvatore piped in. "We will all vouch for you. We have seen your loyalty in action."

"Grazie," Andrew nodded.

"Father," Sophia looked to Salvatore, "will you summon the doctor?"

"Si," Salvatore made his way toward the front door.

Sophia squeezed Angel's hand. "It hurts my heart to see her like this," she sniffed.

"I know what you mean," Tony uttered quietly.

Olga left the room and returned moments later with dishtowels and a bucket of warm, soapy water. "We gotta clean her up," she said matter-of-factly, dipping the dishtowel in the water and rubbing it gently against Angel's skin.

"Is this all her blood?" Sophia winced.

"No," Tony answered, "thankfully most of it isn't hers."

"Boy, when you guys have a shoot out, you really have a shoot out," Olga quipped, ringing the blood out of the dishtowel.

Andrew stepped on the patio to take a phone call. They couldn't hear what he was saying but it was obvious his voice was raised. When he stormed back inside, it was with a mixture of anger and frustration on his face.

"What's up, Ace?" Tony asked.

Andrew grunted and rubbed his hand quickly through his hair. "The Captain frowns on mob shoot outs, especially those involving Russians." Andrew rolled his eyes. "Looks bad for the Mayor."

Tony laughed. "It's all politics."

"I bet the Mayor's got his panties in a real tight wad over this," Chase chuckled.

"Yeah, well, I gotta get to the station or I may not have a job," Andrew grimaced.

"How do they even know what went down?" Tony asked.

"Media choppers, man," Chase said, "there were two of 'em approaching as you guys were pulling out. Didn't you see them?"

Andrew and Tony exchanged glances. "This isn't good," Andrew exhaled.

"There's gonna be a shit storm," Chase said. "A real-live ass shit storm."

Dr. Rainer entered the Penthouse, followed by Salvatore and then Giovanni.

"Faccia una pausa il portello," Giovanni uttered to his men, who moved quickly in front of the door, blocking it. He glanced around the room. "No one leaves," he said in a tone that would tolerate no argument.

"Guess the Mayor's gonna have to wait," Tony whispered to Andrew.

"Yeah," mouthed Chase, "we got our own shit storm going on right here."

Andrew and Tony stared wide-eyed at Giovanni, but his eyes passed over them and landed on Angel, still bloody and sprawled across the table. "Michelangela," he mumbled, making the sign of the cross over his body. "My Michelangela."

Sophia and Olga moved to the side to make way for Giovanni, who took Angel's fingertips and pressed his lips against them. He turned toward Andrew, Tony and Chase and seethed, "Chi ha fatto questo a lei!" He demanded.

Chase's eyes bulged and he elbowed Tony. "What did he say?"

Giovanni's jowls tightened and his brows grew narrow. "I asked who has done this to her!" He yelled.

"Vamloskaya, sir," Tony uttered.

Giovanni's face turned a deeper shade of red and he clenched his hands into fists. "Bratva!"

Dr. Rainer used his stethoscope to listen to Angel's heart and lungs, and then checked the wounds on her chest. "Can someone take these cuffs off her?" The doctor asked. "I'd like to make sure there's nothing broken."

Andrew pulled a ring of keys from his pocket and went to work on the cuffs. A few moments later, her wrists were free and Dr. Rainer had completed his exam. He waved smelling salts beneath her nose and Angel's eyes opened.

"Scotrovi," she blurted. "Kristen," her words slurred. "My head..." her voice tapered off and Angel slipped back into unconsciousness.

"Why won't she stay coherent?" Giovanni barked and the doctor jumped, startled by the sheer volume of his voice.

"She has obviously undergone tremendous trauma," Dr. Rainer answered. "Did she hit her head?" He looked to Andrew, Tony and Chase.

"She hit everything," Chase blurted.

"She took a pretty hard backlash when she fired the Uzi," Tony said and stunned silence filled the room.

"Hot diggity dog! How do you like that?" Olga slapped her hands together with glee. "Our Angel fired an Uzi!" Olga was beaming with pride. "Let that be a lesson to any man who thinks a woman can't handle herself. Humph."

"She more than handled herself," Chase added, "she took out Vincent Galante, and shot Scotrovi..." Chase shut up when he saw Giovanni's eyes bulging from his head.

"She took out Galante?" He repeated.

"Yes, sir," Andrew finally spoke. "Were it not for Angel, Vamloskaya would have proven a fatal threat to all of our families."

"I see," Giovanni uttered, walking across the room and settling into his arm chair.

Dr. Rainer put his supplies back in his bag and cleared his throat. "I don't believe she has any fractures, though I would recommend an x-ray of her skull and rib cage. These appear to be the areas that endured the most impact. She probably has a concussion so I'd like someone to wake her every hour for the next couple of days. If you feel you can't handle this I can admit her to the hospital."

"We can handle it," Sophia said, obviously not wanting to let Angel out of her sight again.

"Very well," Dr. Rainer nodded. "I'll leave you a prescription for a pain killer. She'll be achy and sore for several days, but there is no permanent damage." He scribbled down the script and handed it to Sophia.

"Dr. Rainer?" Giovanni's voice came from the arm chair. "My note here says that I owe you some money." He held up the letter Angel had left for him.

"Yes, sir. Your granddaughter promised me payment upon the completion of the job."

"Is your job complete?" Giovanni asked.

"I believe I have done all that I have been asked, sir," the doctor answered.

"Si," Giovanni nodded. "I believe you have." Giovanni snapped his fingers and spoke to one of his men in Italian. The man left, returning moments later with a large manila envelope, filled with five thousand dollars in small, non-sequential bills. "Show the doctor to his vehicle and make sure he is returned safely to his family."

"Thank you, sir," Dr. Rainer said, dipping his head in respect.

Giovanni stared down at the letter and then looked up at Andrew and Tony. "We have much to discuss," he said. "Where is the rest of your team?"

"Stefano is bringing Boglevich and the Shark back with him in Angel's car," Andrew answered.

"When they arrive, we will convene in the meeting hall downstairs." Giovanni rose from the chair. "I want all of you present." He walked back to where Angel lay and kissed the top of her head. "Take good care of her," he said to Olga and Sophia. Then he placed his hand on Salvatore's shoulder. "Walk with me to my apartment," he said and they left.

Angel snapped awake as Olga placed the smelling salts beneath her nose again. "Olga," Sophia scolded, "the doctor said to wake her every hour. It hasn't even been fifteen minutes."

"I just wanted to see how they work. Powerful little suckers aren't they," she grinned and took a sniff, then let out a yelp and plugged her nose.

"You're quite a case," Sophia laughed.

Angel's eyes stayed open and she was finally able to focus on faces and speak in complete sentences; although she didn't have the energy to say much. When she felt strong enough to stand, Sophia escorted her to her bedroom and helped her shower and dress in clean clothing. Just getting all the blood off made her feel a lot better. She moved slowly because every inch of her body ached. Her ears rang and her head throbbed, but she was alive and so was everyone she loved and that was all that really mattered.

Stefano and Boglevich returned without the Shark.

"Where's the Shark?" Andrew asked.

"We couldn't find him," Stefano said.

"We looked everywhere," Boglevich added, "but there were police coming so we couldn't stay any longer and risk being seen."

"Was he hit?" Tony asked.

"He wasn't among the bodies we saw," Andrew answered. "And we saw a lot of bodies."

"How many bodies?" Olga blurted from the dining room, where she was busy cleaning the table.

Stefano shuttered. "A lot."

Tony shook his head at Andrew, "you lost the Shark again, Ace," he teased.

"WE lost him this time," Andrew rebutted.

"Hey, I don't know about you, but I was too busy shooting bad guys to see where he went," Tony smirked.

"Oh," Andrew scoffed, "like I wasn't up there shooting bad guys right next to you?"

"I think I took out more than you," Tony grinned.

"Keep the dream alive," Andrew quipped.

"The Shark's a big boy, he knows where to come," Olga interjected. "Now come sit and I'll get you all something to eat." She fed them sandwiches, salad and minestrone soup. When Angel was feeling a little better, she crept to the kitchen and peeked around the wall into the dining room.   Andrew sat at the end of the table, facing the windows and Tony sat on the opposite end, facing the front door. On one side sat Chase and Stefano and on the other side were Boglevich and the Snake.

Olga waddled over and wrapped her arm gently around Angel's waist. "Why don't you go in and talk to them?" She prodded.

"I'm not ready."

"Angel May," Olga put her hands on her rounded hips, "don't you know by now that you are ready for whatever life throws at you.

Merciful Heavens child, you were born ready."
She gave Angel's arm a squeeze. "You're the
only one who doesn't know it."

Angel peeked around and stared at the
six men eating at her table. "I'll talk to them
in a while." She carried a cup of coffee back
to her bedroom, set it on the night stand, and
curled up in her bed; Midnight and Mo
snuggling in close and purring loudly. She
knew there would be questions and so many
things to explain but right now just the
thought of the conversation felt overwhelming.
Her body begged for sleep and she didn't have
the energy to fight it.

CHAPTER 22

Everyone gathered in the downstairs meeting hall around one of the long, rectangular mahogany tables. Giovanni sat at one end and Salvatore at the other. Down one side sat Chase, Stefano, Tony, Andrew and an empty chair. Down the other side sat Sophia, Olga, Angel, Boglevich and Sean Shepherd, aka, the Snake. Giovanni cleared his throat. "We have much business to discuss before the big meeting this evening. Has anyone heard from the Shark?"

No one spoke.

"Very well," said Giovanni. "Chase, we will begin with your video surveillance."

While Chase made his way to where his computer was set up, Angel asked, "what big meeting?"

"We will meet with the Bosses this evening. There are many concerns following the death of Don Galante and we need to address them," Giovanni explained. "First, I want to see what occurred this morning."

With the punch of a few short keystrokes, a video transmitted from Chase's computer to the projector screen on the far wall. "During the incident, I was able to track Angel's location and zoom in using a GPS satellite link. I tracked her phone first, then by the GPS in her car, but once I had her location at the air-strip I was able to pull up live video feed.   It's crazy-ass new technology," Chase excitedly explained. "Sort of like Google Earth on steroids."

"Remain on task," Giovanni prompted.

"Right on," Chase said. "Anyway, what I forgot was that there were also cameras on the chopper. Remember, Andrew had ten tiny surveillance cameras installed around the chopper before I flew the Shark to Denny's Iowa compound?"

There was a general utterance of remembrance around the table.

"I pulled the feed from each of those cameras and talk about a wild-ass ride!" Chase fidgeted in his chair, tapping at the keyboard and glancing up intermittently to make sure everyone was following. "I've taken footage I thought was relevant from the GPS link and the chopper cameras and sort of put them into one presentation." The video appeared on the projector screen and Chase warned, "This is not for the faint of heart, if the blood alone doesn't make you wanna hurl, the 3D flying effects from the chopper cameras will."

Chase sporadically froze the screen so that he or one of the others could point something out or explain what was taking place at that very moment. Angel closed her eyes through most of it. She had no desire to relive the gore.

When the presentation ended, Giovanni leaned on his elbows and folded his hands in front of his face. "It must not become common knowledge that Michelangela was the one who killed Vincent Galante," He said. "Capisce?"

Angel wrinkled her brow. "Why?" She shrugged her shoulders. "Why does it matter who killed him?"

"There will certainly be retaliation from the Galante bogata and I do not want you at the center of it," Giovanni answered in an authoritative tone that let everyone know the matter was not up for debate.

"Agreed," Andrew said. "The official police report and media release will state that he was gunned down by the Russian Bratva."

"Perfetto," Salvatore nodded, kissed his fingertips and threw the kiss into the air. Salvatore would agree to anything that would make the Russians look worse or suffer more.

"I noticed that Michelangela is standing alone for a long period of time, speaking to the Vamloskaya." Giovanni tightened his lip. "Why was she unaccompanied?"

The room grew quiet. Giovanni's angry tone undoubtedly made everyone fearful to speak. Angel licked her lips. "I thought they were going to kill Scotrovi so I got out of the car and approached them."

"What did you say to these men?" Giovanni asked.

"I don't remember." She honestly didn't. Maybe it was due to some type of traumatic stress syndrome, commonly suffered by soldiers after war; or the result of slamming her head on the pavement.

Whatever the cause, she didn't remember what she had said to the Vamloskaya men.

Chase punched around at the keyboard. "You're in luck," he said. "Boglevich put a wire under her vest so I've got a recording of everything she said. Chase backed the video up and enhanced audio. It'll take me a second to eliminate the background noise out." His fingers moved wildly across the keys. "Not sure if I can perfectly line up the video with the audio since they're two separate feeds, but I'll get it close."

They all turned their attention toward the screen. The audio faded in and out in areas and was drowned out by the helicopter sound.

"She's clear," the Russian man said.

Angel yelled to Scotrovi, "Are you okay?"

She yelled to the man holding a gun to Scotrovi's head "You have me, now let him go. That was the deal. Let him go safely back to his family."

Giovanni held up his hand and gestured for Chase to pause the video. He turned his attention to Angel. "You made a deal with these men to trade your life for Scotrovi's freedom?" Angel wasn't sure whether it was anger or shock in Giovanni's eyes. "Why would you do such a thing?"

Angel folded her hands on the table. "I thought he had a wife and a five year old little girl. I thought if I could somehow save them..." her voice tapered off and she shook her head. "I don't know how to explain it."

"Because there is no good explanation," Giovanni huffed and then motioned for Chase to resume the video. Chase hit play and they all looked toward the screen.

"I know you can speak," Angel addressed the guard to her right, "or are you so weak you have to obtain permission first. You know what we call men who can't think for themselves, who can't speak on their own, but blindly follow someone else's agenda even to the death? We call them cowards." Angel bent over and spit on his boots...

Chase paused the video feed. "That right there is priceless," he blurted.

Salvatore's lips curled at the corners into a grin of disbelief. "Did you spit on his boots?"

Angel rolled her eyes. "Evidentially."

Chase hit play and they watched and listened.

"Do you hear that? That's the sound of your defeat. That's the sound of pissed off Italian Americans who have the freedom to think for themselves and to act on their own and do you know what each of them wants to do to you? They want to drop you and they don't have to wait for someone's permission to do it. What's the matter? Are you scared? Why don't you use your little headpiece there to ask permission to run away and hide? I see I'm getting to you. Too bad you can't use that big gun to shoot me. Too bad you have to wait for permission."

Chase paused the video as the man reached to grab Angel by her throat. Angel swallowed and looked down at the table. She felt flushed and awkwardly embarrassed and she didn't want to make eye contact with anyone.

After a moment of stone silence, Tony scooted his chair out from the table, stood up and applauded. Angel met his eyes and he smiled at her from ear-to-ear. "That was awesome, Babe."

Chase jumped in with applause. "It was like wild-ass Rambo kind of awesome!"

Andrew's voice rose above their applause. "It was unnecessarily dangerous."

Angel glared at Andrew. "No, letting killers into a bar where innocent people are dining is unnecessarily dangerous," she uttered through a tensed jaw.

"I told you, no one was supposed to get hurt!" Andrew's voice rose.

Tony sat down. "Well aren't you Mr. Buzz-kill," he said to Andrew.

"I thought it was totally hot," Chase quipped, sitting back down and bouncing his knees up and down like a spastic Chihuahua.

Giovanni's eyes grew dark.

"That is what we refer to as verbal combat," Boglevich added. "It's a form of psychological warfare. There are grown men with years of training who freeze up in similar situations, but she came by it naturally. What she has shown here is great strength of will."

"Whether she was good at it or not, it was a dangerous decision and the wrong one to make," Andrew argued.

The Snake tentatively stood up and cleared his throat. "I have flown a lot of missions and I've seen more than a handful of trained men who could not have engaged the enemy the way she did." He nodded to Angel and sat back down.

"You got big 'ol kahunas," Chase grinned, leaning back in his chair and twirling a pen between his fingers.

Giovanni pound his fists against the table. "Michelangela risked her life because of an error in judgment, not because of strength of will or tactical skill." He exhaled loudly. "Andrew is right, it was unnecessarily dangerous."

Angel stared at Giovanni and a rush of emotion filled her. Had it not been for the pain in her chest and the throbbing of her head, she might have leapt from her seat and threw a chair at him. Instead, she raised her eyebrows and met his eyes in a glare of disbelief and disdain. She wanted to be respectful of his position and authority, but every time he opened his mouth it became more difficult to respect him. "Andrew is right?" She mumbled with enough sarcasm that Chase's eyes bugged out of his head. "Did you just say Andrew is right?" She pushed her chair away from the table and rose slowly. "You mean the same Andrew you tried to have murdered because you thought he was a traitor?" She flattened her palms on the table and leaned down. "And why did you think he was a traitor? Oh, I remember," she blurted, her voice rising slightly. "It was because he believed Scotrovi. In fact, he believed Scotrovi's story enough that he allowed fourteen innocent people to be gunned down in my restaurant." Andrew tightened his jaw, dropped his head and stared downward, while she moved away from the table and pointed her finger at Giovanni. "You were wrong to order Andrew's death and you're wrong to agree with him now, because he's wrong," she pointed at Andrew. "He is wrong again."

"Sit down," Giovanni ordered but Angel didn't budge from her stance. She wasn't backing down no matter the consequence. Giovanni slowly rose from his chair. "Sit down," he gritted but she didn't move.

"I will not sit," she said and you could hear a pin drop in the room as their eyes locked in a deadly stare.

"Your disobedience is noted," Giovanni seethed.

"And so is your rage," Angel rebutted.

"You are just like your father," he mumbled and dropped back into his chair.

"That is the highest compliment I can be paid," Angel blurted. "My father wanted peace and in that quest we are alike. But as a friend told me this morning," she met eyes with Stefano and her face softened, "it makes more sense to pave a road of peace with my life than with my death."

Stefano grinned back at her and it was the first time she could ever remember seeing him smile.

Her voice softened. "I am guilty of being deceived by Scotrovi. I admit it. He played on my emotions and I fell for it." She circled around the table. "I fell for it, as did Andrew and the Shark and Boglevich and Tony and many, many others." She walked toward Giovanni. "And maybe my choices were dangerous, but they were made out of a longing to save lives and to hold families together."

"Compassion clouds judgment and THAT is when good men die," Giovanni muttered.

Angel stopped moving toward him and stared at him. This time it wasn't anger that filled her, but a mixture of disbelief and disappointment. He hadn't heard a word she said. It was as if he was incapable of understanding her heart. "You're wrong," she said softly. "My compassion only caused the bad people to die today, but your rage almost killed several good ones."

No one spoke as Angel moved toward the door. Sophia scooted her chair out and followed Angel.

"This meeting is not adjourned," Giovanni's shoulders moved up and down as he panted.

"Look at you, you old goat," Olga said while pushing herself to a standing position. "You look like the big bad wolf all huffing and puffing like that. Humph!" She followed Sophia and Angel toward the door.

Salvatore spoke to Giovanni, "if you lose control of your people you have nothing."

Angel turned and faced him, "that's not the way the world works, at least not anymore. If you have to control your people then what you have is forced, fearful obedience, not loyalty."

"Bah," Salvatore waved his hand and spoke something in Italian that caused Giovanni to give an arrogant chuckle and Sophia and Olga to gasp. Angel looked to Andrew and Tony, but neither volunteered to translate.

Salvatore and Giovanni's arrogance sickened her and it took all of her energy to hold her anger back. It was hardening like a pit in her stomach, burning her esophagus with acid as it tried to climb upward and spew hatefulness across the room. She counted to ten, telling herself to remain composed. Angel took several steps toward the table and addressed Giovanni.

"After you ordered Andrew's death I made a decision. I was leaving. I was leaving you." She inched her way closer. "I was leaving the power-hungry arrogance that fuels your rage and the title of authority that makes you think it's acceptable to kill people." She never took her eyes from Giovanni and spoke as if no one else was in the room. "The only reason I stayed was because I found out Andrew was alive and I went to meet him."

"As I suspected, you did not stay at the Hotel and Spa," Giovanni gritted his teeth.

"No, I didn't; and in case you were wondering, you didn't suffer a mild stroke either." He looked up and met her eyes.

"What?" Giovanni's face turned red.

"Sul mio Dio!" Salvatore burst.

"I tasered you and then paid the doctor to keep you sedated." His mouth fell open.

"Actually, she didn't taser you, I did," Olga interjected. "And it felt really good." Olga shook her fist at him. "If I'd have had a taser years ago, I'd have done it then." Olga made a zapping motion with her hand and a buzzing sound with her lips.

Giovanni lowered his eyes and Angel didn't know whether he was hurt or enraged. "It was the only way to stop you from killing good men, MY men." Angel walked closer and narrowed her eyes. "You cast judgment on me for believing Scotrovi's lies when you, yourself, sat in a meeting with Vincent Galante, the greatest traitor of them all, and believed his story." Angel's pulse quickened and she sucked in a deep breath. "You judge and judge and judge but who judges you?"

All eyes were on her, most of them wide-eyed with fear and all of them shocked. Angel glanced around the table, her heart pounding in her chest. "Grandfather, you are my family, but so are these men," she rattled off their names like a school roll call. "Chase, Stefano, Andrew, Tony, Boglevich, the Snake." She took a deep breath. "These men are mine, not because I control them but because I trust them." She began to circle around the table. "I have known some longer than others but each of these men has protected me, defended me and saved my life." Emotion welled up within but she stifled it, knowing that if there was any way to reach Giovanni, it had to be through proven strength and not womanly emotion. "Not one of them would have sent me out there this morning. They would all agree with you that my actions this morning were dangerous, which is why I told no one that I was going. But all of them rushed to my aid and support once I was there. All of them backed me up."

She neared Salvatore and leaned down closer to him. "We WON today." She resumed walking around the table. "We took the Vamloskaya down today. We should be gathered here celebrating but instead you want to point fingers and judge the men who have served you well." She shook her head. "If you want to find fault, then you and Salvatore should go stand in front of a mirror, because in case you've forgotten, ALL of what happened began with the two of you."

She saw Salvatore and Giovanni exchange glances.

"When will you two see that unjustly judging people doesn't make you powerful?"

"We do not unjustly pass judgment," Salvatore barked.

Sophia crossed her arms and glared at Salvatore. "Siete un bugiardo, il padre. Un Bugiardo!" She yelled.

Olga waddled toward Giovanni, shaking her fist. "Siete un più grande bugiardo che lui," she hollered.

Chase leaned over to Tony and whispered, "What are they saying?"

Tony whispered back, "Sophia called her father a liar and Olga said Giovanni was an even bigger liar."

Chase's eyes were as wide open as his mouth. "Damn, these Maratinzano women are some wild-ass chicks," he grinned.

Tony rolled his eyes. "You have no idea, Ace."

Angel looked from Sophia to Olga and back to Giovanni. "I don't know what they just said, but I'm sure it was the truth." She walked closer to Giovanni. "You always say, 'the truth will reveal itself' and you're right; it does and it has." She walked behind Tony and placed her hand on his shoulder. "It's revealed Tony as a man of character who, despite an order from the Capo di Tutti Capi, did what was right by letting Andrew live." Tony gave her fingers a tender squeeze.

Angel moved toward Stefano. "It revealed Stefano as someone who despite being scared to death, risked his life to save my mother; and risked it again today to rescue me." She smiled at Stefano. "Thank you." She walked toward Boglevich. "It revealed Boglevich, though seemingly guilty, as a good man working undercover to find and stop any link to terrorism within our bogatas." She circled around the table. "It revealed Chase as someone who was smarter than we all thought..."

"Hey!" Chase blurted, making Angel smile.

"... with skills and commitment essential to overtaking our enemies," she continued and Chase grinned. "And it revealed Sean Shepherd, the Snake, as a damn good pilot who was willing to jump in on a rescue mission to save a woman he barely knows." She took a deep breath and exhaled slowly, making her way toward Andrew. "Most of all, it revealed Andrew as a man who desires peace as much as I do, who walks a fine and very complicated line between familial obligation and career aspiration. It revealed a man whose logic often gets in the way and who has a hard time understanding that the right thing to do is not always the smart thing." Andrew turned to meet her eyes with a spark of affection.

She circled back toward her seat. "It revealed good men who made terrible decisions," she darted her eyes between Salvatore and Giovanni, "decisions that have come back to bite us in the ass today." Angel exhaled and bit her bottom lip. "When does it stop? When will we realize that every act of violence results in another act of violence and it just keeps going and going?"

She turned her attention to Giovanni, walking closer to him and kneeling down at his side. "It revealed a grandfather who holds great power and bears the burden of responsibility that comes with it." Giovanni turned his chair slightly and looked down at Angel. "And it reveals a granddaughter who loves her grandfather but fears the death toll of his rage."

Sophia and Olga stood by the door, clutching each other as Giovanni took his hand and patted the side of Angel's cheek. Salvatore rose from the end of the table. "Parla la verità," he said.

"Si," Giovanni gave a nod and translated, "she speaks truth indeed."

He leaned down and kissed each of Angel's cheek. "La verità la ha rivelatore è pronta," he said.

Chase hit Tony's arm. "What'd he say?"

Before Tony could answer, Giovanni gave an over-exaggerated eye roll and exhaled loudly. "I said the truth has revealed that she is ready."

"Right on! I love this family," Chase quipped and slowly leaned his head toward Tony. "Ready for what?" He whispered.

CHAPTER 23

Angel stood in front of the full-length mirror in her bedroom, staring blankly at her reflection. A clump of nerves had burrowed into the center of her belly, an all too familiar uneasiness that came before any meeting with the Bosses. The fact that Giovanni and Salvatore said she was ready did little to boost her confidence; especially when she didn't understand what they thought she was ready for. Mo rubbed up against her leg, shedding his calico hair on her black pants. She bent down and scratched behind his ears until he purred like a motor boat; then she picked him up and set him on the bed next to Midnight. Returning to her reflection, Angel sighed. Her black pants were pressed and creased to perfection. Her white blouse and black jacket fit perfectly and her black heels glistened almost as much as her silver hoop earrings. All she needed was a black fedora and a machine gun and she'd look like a gangster right out of the 1920's.

Olga tapped on her door and waddled in. "Merciful Heavens, don't you look hot," she said, making Angel laugh out loud. It felt oddly uncomfortable to have Olga call her hot. Sophia slid in the door and closed it behind her. "I have something for you," she said, and then stopped abruptly when she saw Angel.

She put her hand to her chest and tilted her head. "You look bello," she said. "Così bello."

"Is bello a good thing?" Angel asked.

Olga plunked down on the bed and shook her head. "We've got to get you Italian lessons."

"It means beautiful," Sophia smiled and tucked a piece of Angel's hair behind her ear. "Here," she handed her a black velvet box. "These belonged to your father." Angel opened the box and saw two silver cufflinks, each of the letter M. Inlayed in the center tip of the M was a tiny diamond. "He would have wanted you to have them." With a needle and some black thread, Sophia quickly attached the cufflinks to Angel's black suit jacket and looked at them glisten in the mirror.

"They're beautiful. Thank you." Angel hugged Sophia and Olga stood up and nuzzled her way in until they had a three way embrace.

"I wish we could be in there and hear your speech," Sophia said.

"Merciful Heavens, if it's anything like the one from this morning you'll have them eating out of your hand in no time flat," Olga added.

"That's right," Sophia squeezed Angel's fingers. "You just speak from the heart like you did earlier and you'll be great."

Angel exhaled. "I hope so."

"Go out there and nail 'em," Olga said, giving her a wink and making a punching motion with her arm. "Oh, that reminds me, do you want to borrow my taser in case any of them get mouthy?"

"No," Angel and Sophia blurted in unison.

"I'm just saying, it feels really good to taser someone that's pissing you off," Olga waddled toward the door. "I have a right mind to go zap your grandfather again, just for fun." Olga made a buzzing noise as she waddled out.

"What are we gonna do with her?" Angel sighed.

"I don't know," Sophia shrugged. "She certainly is a live wire."

After Sophia left, Angel sat on her bed and breathed slowly, trying to release the tension she felt. She'd met with the Bosses before, but this time it was different. This time she would be leading the meeting, laying out instructions for the replacement of the Galante Boss and ordering a bogata house cleaning that would result in many deaths. She didn't like the killing, but realized that allowing the disloyal to live jeopardized the lives of the loyal members. Like it or not, it was the reality of the Mafia world and Angel was smart enough to understand the need for such protection.

A quiet tapping at her door drew her from her thoughts. She opened it and met eyes with Andrew. He was dressed in a black suit, light gray shirt and black tie. He smelled of musk scented aftershave and Angel's stomach quivered nervously when she saw him. "Can I come in?" He asked.

270

She closed the door behind him and then sat down on the bed. "Do you want to sit down?" She gestured for him to sit next to her.

"I would, but I see your demon cats are standing guard," he smirked. Andrew had a love hate relationship with Angel's cats. Actually, it was just a plain hate relationship. Midnight hissed and moaned every time Andrew came near and Mo, who was usually the snuggly one, ran and hid whenever he heard the sound of Andrew's voice.

"I promise not to let them get you," Angel grinned and Andrew hesitantly sat down on the furthest corner from the cats.

"I wanted to talk to you before the meeting because, well, I'm not sure if I'll have a chance afterwards." He took a deep breath and exhaled, then ran his hand through his hair and stood up. "I owe you an apology," he blurted with an awkwardness Angel had never seen in him. "I underestimated you and I way over-estimated myself." He shook his head. "I let you down. I let me down and I almost got you killed; and for that I can't forgive myself." His voice cracked with emotion and Angel stood up. She reached for his hands but he moved away. "I didn't come in here for your sympathy. I just wanted to tell you that I'm sorry and that I fully acknowledge my responsibility regarding the innocent lives that were lost at Tetterbaum's and in..." Andrew stopped talking and clenched his fists.

"And in what?" Angel prodded.

"And in losing your trust," he said in a tone that dripped with regret.

Angel lowered herself back on the bed and stared at the floor. Had he lost her trust? Could she rely on his judgment again? Those were questions she couldn't answer, at least not right now. They'd have to be left to the unraveling of time. She didn't know what their relationship held for the future, but of one thing she was certain. She wanted him in her life. A momentary silence fell between them and Angel was torn between desire and fear, logic and emotion, her heart and her head. She wanted to kiss him, to feel his arms around her, to have his hands caress her and melt all the bad stuff away; at the same time, she wanted to understand what happened that night at the pub and how so many innocent lives were lost.

"Can I ask you something?" She said, standing back up and looking him in the eye.

He nodded.

"What made you trust Scotrovi?" She could tell by his surprised expression that he wasn't expecting this question.

"He answered all of my questions with precision and ease. He was detailed and every detail lined up. He never faltered, never paused, and never changed his story." Andrew shook his head and Angel could see his jaw tighten. "That and the fact that Sal checked him out and couldn't find any reason to throw up a red flag." He exhaled and closed his eyes for a moment. "I've been a cop for a long time and I'm good at it. I'm really good at it. I can read people. I can sense when they're lying or hiding something; at least I thought I could." His shoulders slumped. "I'm sorry, Sweetheart. I blew it and I'm so sorry."

"What do you mean Sal didn't find any reason to throw up a red flag? I thought he couldn't find any information on Scotrovi at all without fingerprints or some sort of DNA sample?"

"I gave him a blood sample after we found Scotrovi shot, and Scotrovi's story checked out. He had the highest security clearance in the SVR and his identity was sealed." Andrew shrugged. "Sal confirmed the name of his wife and daughter, everything."

Angel had a flashback of Scotrovi on his knees in front of the jet. She remembered seeing a tear drip from his face to the pavement. Her stomach suddenly felt hollow and she stared at Andrew. "Oh no," she said almost inaudibly.

"What?"

Angel cupped her hands around her mouth. "Oh no," she uttered breathlessly.

"What?" Andrew grabbed her shoulders.

"I've had this horrible feeling all along that Scotrovi was telling the truth."

Andrew shook his head. "No, he wasn't, Sweetheart. Believe me; I've played this over and over in my mind. I don't know how he did it, but he deceived all of us."

Angel pursed her lips together. "I don't think he was the one playing us. That person is still here." Angel's mind was a whirlwind of flashbacks and tiny red flags she either hadn't noticed at the time or had flat out disregarded as irrelevant. Now, it was starting to come together. "We flip flopped the motive. We thought he was good, going undercover as bad only to help good prevail in the end." She paced back and forth. "But that was backwards. He was first bad, went undercover as someone who was good so that we would send him back to pose as someone who was bad."

"You're losing me, Sweetheart," Andrew watched intently.

Chase knocked on the door. "Giovanni says it's time to head downstairs," he hollered and Angel pulled open the door with such force it startled Chase. "Whoa, hello," he jumped.

"Is your equipment still set up in the meeting room? She asked.

"Yeah, why?"

"Go get it and bring it up here. I need you to set the video from this morning to the place where the Shark jumps out of the helicopter. Then get Sal on video conferencing. And tell Tony to come up here." Chase nodded and hurried off.

Angel stuck her head outside her bedroom door and hollered to Olga and Sophia. "I need to stall the meeting. Can you serve everyone something to eat?"

"How long do we gotta stall," Olga questioned, "long enough for a snack or a full meal?"

"Just some hors d'oeuvres should do it. Just keep them preoccupied for a few minutes."

Angel was panting now as the adrenaline surged through her. "You want to calm down for a minute and tell me what's going on in that head of yours?" Andrew asked.

"It's the Shark," she exhaled. "The Shark is the traitor."

"Sweetheart, we've been down this path and it doesn't check out."

"I know it. I can feel it and better than that, I can prove it."

"How?" Andrew's eyes lit with interest.

"When Sal looked up information about the Shark he made the comment that the records were sealed by the highest authority. We all breezed over it, assuming that just because his name appeared in the CIA database was enough to prove he was good." Angel stared at Andrew. "It bugged me, so I contacted Sal and asked him if it was normal for the CIA to seal records. He said it was, but usually only when the operative was going undercover in other parts of the world; and he added that the name of the officer who sealed the files was almost always listed."

"Except in this case, right?"

"Right," Angel sighed. "Whoever sealed the Shark's identity sealed their own too."

"That's still speculation," Andrew said.

"Hear me out." She took a deep breath. "The Shark didn't kill any of the bad guys. Not his brother Gerald. Not Kristen. Not even anyone in Denny's compound.   And I didn't see him shoot anyone this morning, did you?"

Andrew had a distant look in his eye like he was struggling to remember. "Now that you mention it, I don't recall him firing on anyone, but I wasn't paying attention to what he was doing. My focus was," he paused, "elsewhere."

Angel knew what elsewhere meant. It meant his eyes were on her and ordinarily that would have given her tiny chills of longing affection, but there wasn't time for that now.

"The other night at the Barone house when Scotrovi jumped up and grabbed me by the shoulders, you and Tony stood up to confront him, but the Shark sat there holding his wine glass." Angel narrowed her eyes. "And Scotrovi said that right before the Russians attacked the Barone place, he saw the Shark coming out of Kristen's room."

"I hear what you're saying, Sweetheart, but none of this is concrete evidence."

"As soon as Chase sets up his computer, I'll show you concrete evidence." Angel shook her head and cursed out loud. "Why didn't I see it?"

Chase poked his head in, "we're up in the family room."

Angel and Andrew joined Tony and Chase at the computer. "What are we looking for, Boss?" Chase asked, with his fingers perched and ready to pound the keys.

"I want to see the surveillance video from this morning when the Shark gets out of the helicopter."

Chase pressed some keys and they all watched. The chopper swooped low and held position just long enough for the Shark to jump out behind the limousines and run toward the hanger.

"What was he doing in the hanger?" Tony asked.

"I don't know," Andrew answered.

"You're missing the important part," Angel said. "Look, he passes several Vamloskaya men and he doesn't shoot at them."

"And they're not shooting at him either," Chase uttered with a shocked tone.

"I can't believe we missed that," Andrew shook his head.

"We were a little preoccupied at the time," Tony quipped. "I don't know about you but I was focused on shooting the bad guys."

"Now, can you go to the part where Kristen and Scotrovi are on the jet stairs?" Angel asked and Chase moved the video forward. "There, pause it there," Angel pointed. "Can you zoom in on Kristen?"

"It would help to know what we're looking for." Chase quipped.

"When Kristen pulls Scotrovi up, she leans in like she's going to kiss him, or at least that's what I thought she was doing at the time; but I was wrong." Angel pointed to the screen. "Look at her eyes and the direction she's looking. She's blowing a kiss to the Shark."

"Holy freaking shit!" Chase blurted, zooming the screen in closer and closer.

"She's right, man. Kristen's definitely looking to the left and it's at the Shark."

"Zoom in on the Shark and see if his eyes are on her," Andrew said and Chase did.

"Sure as shit!" Chase blurted.

"Now, pull up the feed from the night of the attack on Tetterbaum's," Angel said, "only this time, can you pull surveillance from the cameras in the front of the building?"

"It'll take me a few minutes, but I can do it," he said.

Andrew narrowed his eyebrows. "What are you doing?"

"You kept saying something went wrong that night and it wasn't supposed to happen like that," Angel began and Andrew cut her off.

"It wasn't," he interjected. "We had a plan and no one except the two shooters was supposed to die."

"I believe you," Angel said, "and I think the video surveillance from the front of the building is going to prove what really happened."

Olga and Sophia left to carry hors d'oeuvres and drinks to the meeting room. "We're running out of time," Tony warned. "People downstairs are gonna get suspicious and wonder what's going on; and trust me, Babe, you do not want a room full of armed mobsters getting anxious."

"I'm going as fast as I can," Chase belted. "You think you can do it quicker?"

"Nope, you're lookin' good Ace," Tony patted Chase on the back.

The video popped on the screen and Chase forwarded until they could see the two shooters enter Tetterbaum's. A few minutes later Scotrovi entered. Chase fast forwarded and Angel narrated. "During this time I'm serving Scotrovi a chilled vodka with no ice and Valerie is serving the two shooters a beer." Chase continued to fast forward. "I've now noticed that something is strange about these men and walked back to the kitchen to get Chase and my gun."

"I'm not tracking with you," Andrew said and Angel held up her finger to say just a minute.

"There," she pointed to the screen and they all watched as the Shark entered through the front door carrying an Uzi pistol."

"I'll be a son of a..."Chase blurted. "I can't believe we didn't catch this before."

"We didn't catch it because we only watched the surveillance video from the back door," Angel explained.

"I'm lost, Babe," Tony said, squinting at the screen.

"Before Chase and I went into hiding, we heard a couple single gunshots. Then, all of a sudden we heard a barrage of gunfire, like the kind that would come from an Uzi pistol."

"Man, I feel like a dumb-ass idiot," Chase hit the top of the table with his palm. "No way two guys killed fourteen people with just pistols. Soon as they shot one person the other thirteen would be running for the door." He shook his head. "Un-freaking-believable!"

The light of recognition went on in Andrew's eyes. "I can't believe I didn't pick up on this." Andrew ran his hand around his chin. "I was so shocked that people died and then so worried that you were among the dead that I never stopped to analyze the scene." He slowly walked to the other side of the room. "The plan all along was that Scotrovi would get a drink at the bar and then excuse himself from the bar, walk to the backdoor where I would let him out and let the Shark in. The Vamloskaya boys were told Scotrovi was going to go back to the kitchen and kill Angel and the staff. Their instructions were to wait exactly three minutes from the time Scotrovi got up from his seat at the bar before they started shooting. That would give the Shark plenty of time to kill the two shooters before they ever even drew their weapons." Andrew shook his head. "No one else was supposed to die."

"One of the Vamloskaya men kept looking at his watch, which made me nervous," Angel recalled.

"So, when Scotrovi left the bar, the Vamloskaya didn't wait the full three minutes," Chase said. "Either something spooked them into shooting sooner, or they had different instructions because Angel and I heard single gunshots before the Uzi was fired."

"Maybe someone else in the bar fired at the Vamloskaya shooters first?" Angel posed. "Anyway, it doesn't matter. What matters is that the Shark killed everyone in the restaurant, then went back outside, ditched the Uzi, walked around to the back waited for Andrew to open the door and free Scotrovi; then went inside and killed the shooters using a different gun."

"Not just a different gun, a sweet-ass PM," Chase quipped.

Andrew looked like the weight of the world was pressing on his shoulders. "No one was supposed to be killed except the two shooters, that way it would appear that Scotrovi went through with the mission as planned but got ambushed and barely escaped with his life."

"I hate to throw a crimp in your theory here, but why would the Shark do all that?" Tony asked. "I mean, I said he was a traitor all along, but why would he save Angel so many times and then go in and try to kill her?"

"Maybe he needed the kill to be blatantly blamed on the Vamloskaya so he could keep his undercover status with us and still appear loyal to them?" Chase answered matter-of-factly.

"Scotrovi did say that the Russians plan was to kill me first, then attack my family while they were in mourning," Angel added.

"Yeah, but he also alluded to the fact that the Vamloskaya wanted you alive so they could lure Giovanni and Salvatore out of hiding and kill them," Tony said.

"Maybe that was a back-up plan," Chase said.

"There's one more thing," Angel said. "This morning when I was on the ground next to Scotrovi, I saw a tear fall from his face." Angel felt her heart sink just thinking about it. "If was right after I told him he would be reunited with his family."

"Maybe he was crying because he was afraid to die?" Chase posed.

"He was crying at the mention of his family. I know it." Angel persisted. "Grown men don't cry over wives and daughters that don't really exist. He was telling us the truth."

"Son of a ..." Andrew caught himself before he finished the phrase.

"Is all of this enough to go on?" She looked at Tony.

"You sold me, Babe."

"Chase?"

"I'm on board."

"Andrew?" He didn't answer. "Andrew?" Angel called out.

"I should have seen this," he mumbled.

"When you're done with your pity party, we could use your help in the revolution over here," Tony quipped. "We ALL should have picked up on it, Ace."

"I especially should have," Chase snorted. "I'm the gun expert. I should have noticed it right away, that night; the minute we heard gun fire."

"You were too busy being claustrophobic," Angel joked and Chase gawked at her.

Tony patted his shoulder. "She just threw you under the bus."

282

"We need to get to this meeting," Angel said. "Tell everyone to be on the look out for the Shark. We'll give this information to Giovanni as soon as the meeting is over."

"He has access to this building," Chase added, "so we all need to have our eyes and ears open."

"And our weapons loaded," Tony said, checking the clip on his .45 and shoving it back in his pants.

Angel ran to her bathroom to freshen her lipstick and give herself a last minute once over in the mirror. Chase waited for Angel by the front door. "Damn," he blurted when she walked toward him. "You are one hot-ass Mafia mamma."

She grinned. "And you look like one bad-ass bodyguard."

"Right on," he gloated, adjusting the gun stuck in the front of his pants. "You like?" He asked, looking downward.

"I hope you talking about the gun," Angel smirked and Chase laughed out loud.

"I was, unless there's something else down there you wanna check out," he raised his eyebrows up and down and grinned ear to ear.

"Let me see your weapon," Angel rolled her eyes.

"Which one?" He said, inhaling and puffing out his chest. Angel gave herself a mental head slap. *You walked right into that one.*

She held out her hand. "Your gun, please?' He pulled it from his waistband and handed it to her. "Is this what I think it is?" She looked closely.

"A mint condition Pistol Makarova," Chase gloated. "One fine-ass Russian baby, right there."

"Where'd you get it?"

"The Shark. It was one of the guns he removed from the shooters at Tetterbaum's. He said that I should have it because I was one of the few people who would appreciate it." Chase snorted. "That's some sweet ass irony right there. I just might bring him down with one of his own guns."

"Let's see if you can keep it in your pants during the meeting," Angel teased.

"If I had a dollar for every woman that's said that."

When they stepped off the elevator and into the secret meeting room, Angel could feel the power hanging thick in the air. It was the distinct scent of arrogance and aroma of authority. The Bosses mingled and made small-talk while their bodyguards stood staunchly stationed throughout the room. The Underbosses were also present, which was unusual for a regular meeting; but everyone knew this was not a regular meeting since mere hours ago the media had announced the killing of Mob Boss, Vincent Galante. The press claimed that a business deal with the Russian Bratva had gone bad and resulted in Galante being gunned down. The scene was set just as Andrew said it would be. As they all began taking their seats around the large, round mahogany table,

Angel scanned the room. Boglevich stood as a bodyguard behind Giovanni. Chase stood as Angel's bodyguard. Tony and Andrew stood behind their fathers and the Snake stood behind Salvatore, as his stand-in bodyguard.

The men stood out of respect until Angel took her seat and then they all lowered themselves into their chairs. She sat with Giovanni to her right and Salvatore to her left. Next to Salvatore sat Carlo Cullato and his Underboss, then Charlie Andriachinni and his Underboss, then the Galante Underboss and next to Giovanni sat Joseph Venturini and his Underboss. After a brief introduction, Giovanni handed the floor to Angel.

She took a deep breath and folded her hands on the table in front of her. "Gentlemen, I would like to take this opportunity to share with you some exciting news. We have scored a victory today, not only by stopping the Vamloskaya from gaining control of our city; but from gaining control of any city. Even as we speak, Salvatore's men are disassembling the Vamloskaya's attempted take over in Sicily." There was a general look of confusion around the table as Angel motioned to Boglevich, who carried over a black briefcase and set it on the table in front of Angel.

"This is the briefcase Vincent Galante retrieved from the Vamloskaya jet this morning and placed inside his limousine just before he was killed," Angel explained

The Galante Underboss leapt to his feet and slammed his palms onto the table. "That is a lie. How do you know this?" He demanded.

"I know this because I was there and I watched him," Angel answered flatly. A low rumbling broke out around the table and Angel held her palm up to indicate they should stop talking. "Anyone who needs additional proof of my statement can meet with Chase after the meeting and view the surveillance video feed. It will confirm everything I tell you here this evening." The Galante Underboss sank back into his seat.

Angel opened the briefcase and handed each Boss a manila file folder, labeled with his family name. "Inside these folders are the Vamloskaya's plans for Chicago as a whole and for our bogatas individually."

More gasps and rumblings filled the air as the Bosses sifted through their respective files.

"As you can see, gentlemen, this information is invaluable," Angel closed the briefcase. "I would like to point out the list of Vamloskaya members in each folder. These are the names of the undercover Bratva within our own organizations, sent to infiltrate and gain information to be used against us."

"This cannot be," Joseph Venturini mumbled as he read the list of names.

"What are these organizations listed at the top?" Charlie Andriachini asked.

"They are terrorist organizations, supported inadvertently by our families," Angel answered.

"We do not support terrorists," Cullato blurted, angrily.

"Directly, no, you don't," Angel explained. "But if you have undercover Bratva members within your organization, they have been utilizing your resources to benefit terrorist activity." She took a breath and exhaled. "And they've been doing it for a greater part of the past ten years."

"This is an outrage," the Galante Underboss spewed. "These documents are fabricated lies that YOU have made up to gain power here in Chicago."

Angel stared at him. "The blood in my veins is all the power I need. I have no reason to muddle it with fabrications, outright lies or unjust accusations." She motioned with her hand and two of Giovanni's men lifted the Galante Underboss from his seat and dragged him out of the meeting room.

His bodyguard laid down his gun, raised his hands and laced them atop his head. "Giovanni," he pleaded, "I know nothing of the Russian Bratva or any terrorist activity. I beg for mercy for my unknowing association with traitors." He dropped to his knees.

Giovanni looked to Angel and Angel looked down at the man. "What is your name?"

"Alexander Carbone," he moaned. "I have a wife and I'm about to become a father. Please..." his voice tapered off into quiet sobs.

"How long have you worked for the Galantes?" Angel asked.

"Three months, ma'am, and I swear I didn't know anything about the Russians."

Giovanni slid the Galante folder to Salvatore, who opened it and searched the list of names. He then closed the folder and shook his head at Giovanni, who passed the folder to Angel.

"Seems it is your lucky day, Alexander Carbone," Angel said. "As your name is not on this list, you are free to leave."

He looked up at Angel with bloodshot eyes and trembling hands. He dove forward and kissed her fingertips. "Grazie," he uttered repeatedly. "Grazie."

Angel looked to Chase. "Have one of Giovanni's men escort Alexander Carbone from the building and make sure he returns safely to his pregnant wife." She wanted to have someone escort Alexander Carbone home, to make sure that the Shark wasn't lurking outside, ready to kill more innocent people.

"May I see the Galante list?" Joseph Venturini asked and Giovanni passed it to him. He studied the list for several moments. "Near as I can tell, this is well over half of the Galante bogata."

"Poor leadership flows from the top down," Giovanni uttered.

"Do you want us to take care of it?" Charlie Andriachini asked.

"Si," Joseph Venturini added, "it would be our pleasure to clean his house."

Giovanni looked to Angel and it felt to her as if time stood still. Giovanni was publically defaulting the question to her, establishing her authority in Chicago and she knew what she had to do. She knew the smart thing and she knew the right thing, and they weren't the same. Angel's eyes carefully scanned each man at the table, and then returning her glare to Giovanni, she gave one nod of her head. With that nod she sentenced many men to death for their disloyalty. With that nod, she made widows out of wives and left children fatherless. It sickened her and deeply saddened her heart, but she knew the alternative. She had witnessed what the Vamloskaya could do if allowed to infiltrate. She understood now that the only way to protect their families was to destroy their enemies.

As Angel rose from her seat, each man stood out of respect. "You have your lists, gentlemen. I urge you to clean your houses. We will reconvene in two weeks with recommendations for a new head of the Galante bogata." Angel walked briskly across the room and out the door. She made a beeline for the Penthouse and her bathroom, where she promptly broke into sobs, shook uncontrollably and vomited. She had sent one man home to his pregnant wife and the rest to their graves.

Sophia sneaked into the bathroom, held Angel's hair and rubbed her back as she clung to the toilet and cried. "Let it all out," she whispered, "cry it all out." Sophia stroked Angel's hair. "Your father used to throw-up after many meetings. No one ever knew, of course, because he appeared so strong on the outside; but it broke his heart to have to order a hit."

"How did dad do it?" She asked.

Sophia took a deep breath and exhaled. "He did what needed to be done for the greater good." She took Angel's hand. "Your father had such a peaceful, beautiful heart; the same as you. He hated the killing and the violence, but he, too, realized that there are bad people out there and often only one way to stop them."

"I think about their families, their wives and children..." her voice faded with emotion.

"I know, my Angel," Sophia wrapped her arms around her. "But that is not your job. God has given you a particular family of your own and your job is to first meet their needs, then you can go out and save the world."

When Sophia had left, Angel walked out of her bathroom and was startled to see Andrew sitting on her bed. "You know my demon felines are right behind you," she teased.

"Yeah, we've been talking and decided to call a truce."

"Oh, really?" She sat down next to him.

"Uh-huh. The big black one isn't going to growl and hiss at me anymore and that brownish one promises not to moan and hide."

"And what did you promise them in return?"

"I told them I wouldn't shoot them," he put his hand on her knee and gave it a squeeze and she smiled. "I'm really proud of you," he said, leading the conversation from silly to serious. "I just now read your text from this morning..." his voice tapered off and Angel felt her face flush. In all the chaos she had forgotten about it. "Let's talk about that in a minute." He abruptly stood up and took a deep breath. "I'm resigning from the Police Force effective immediately."

"What?" Angel was completely shocked. "Why? You love being a cop."

He nodded. "Yeah, I do. I used to think I loved being a cop more than I loved anything else, but I don't feel that way anymore."

"I think you're being hasty in your decision." Angel studied him. "Are you sure you're not just disappointed because you didn't pick up on clues about the Shark, and you're feeling a temporary insecurity about your abilities as a cop?" Angel didn't want to overanalyze the situation, but she never thought she'd see the day that Andrew wanted to leave the Force.

Andrew leaned against her bedroom door and folded his arms over his chest. "It's true that I'm kicking myself for missing the signs that pointed to the Shark. There is no question I should have put two and two together." He nodded his head up and down. "It does make me doubt my abilities, but that's not the reason I'm resigning." He unfolded his arms and walked toward Angel, kneeling down in front of her and taking her hands in his. "See, Sweetheart, I missed the signs that pointed to the Shark because I was looking at something else. I didn't focus on my job as a cop because my focus was somewhere else." Angel's pulse quickened as Andrew looked intently in her eyes. "You know what I miss?" She shook her head no. "I miss watching you behind the bar." He smiled and his eyes sparkled, "I miss the way you hang your apron over the beer tap or hide your lip gloss in the register drawer. I miss seeing you every day." Angel felt her face flush. "So, I was thinking that I would go into business for myself, maybe as a private investigator, special fields op, some sort of police consultant, something like that." Angel nodded, wondering where he was going with this. "And in the interim, I was hoping you might need a damn good bartender at Tetterbaum's..." his voice trailed off as he raised his eyebrows, undoubtedly trying to read her expression and anticipate her answer.

"You're asking me for a job?" Angel raised her left eyebrow. "You think you're qualified to work for me?" She teased.

"I know I'm qualified," he grinned. "I trained you on bartending, remember?"

"You really want to do this?" Her question was deeper than Tetterbaum's and they both knew it. Quitting the police force meant he was removing one of the obstacles that made a potential relationship complicated. He was still a Venturini and she, a Maratinzano so their relationship would always be complicated; but removing the cop factor would make it more palatable.

"I've wanted to do this since the day we discovered Tetterbaum's tapes and my undercover work at the pub ended." He gently moved a piece of hair from her face. "So, will you hire me or do I have to beg?

She intertwined her fingers with his. "If you're doing this because you're worried about me and you want to protect me, you don't need to. I'm okay."

"I know you are. You're stronger than any woman I've ever met." He stroked the top of her hand with his thumb. "Of course I want to protect you but that isn't what this is about. It's about wanting to be with you because..." he stopped and pursed his lips together.

Angel studied his face. "Because?" She prompted and Andrew released her hands, rocked back on his heels and stood up.

He began to pace. "I was angry this morning when I found out what you'd done, and then I was scared to death when I looked down from the chopper and saw you standing there surrounded by bad people with guns." Angel could see him fighting emotion as he spoke. "But when I saw you get shot, Sweetheart, my heart almost came out of my chest." He shook his head and inhaled deeply. "When I saw you lying there on the ground, the only thing I could think of was..." he paused. " I love you." He looked at her. "I love you, more than I love anything in this world." Angel's pulse quickened as he knelt back down in front of her and took her hands in his. "I want to be with you at Tetterbaum's and I know it's complicated, but it's even more complicated trying to pretend that I don't feel what I feel."

Angel's heart melted. She knew that feeling all to well. It was hard to conceal the powerful attraction between them. Even when she was angry at him, she still felt this undeniable pull towards him.

"I want to start a new chapter away from the police force and I want it to be with you." He looked deeply into her eyes.

She didn't know what to say. Part of her never felt more in love, more elated to hear those words, but the other part feared they were making a mistake. She touched his face with the palm of her hand and spoke softly, "but you love being a cop."

"I did and then I met you and it all changed. You have made me see that I can do more in the private sector working to eliminate violence, than I can as Special Detective Venturini who often has to cover it up or clean it up." Angel wrapped her arms around his neck. "It won't be easy and I might miss being a cop, but right now I just want to be at the pub with you." She had never seen Andrew reveal his heart like this...completely open, completely vulnerable. "If it's too weird to hire me to work for you, then sell me half of Tetterbaum's and we can be business partners."

"What's the matter? Are you afraid to sleep with your boss?" She smiled and bit her lip. His eyes sparkled as he leaned in closer, with his lips almost touching hers, making her heart beat wildly and butterflies flutter in her stomach.

"I don't want to just sleep with my boss," he whispered. "I want to show her the depth of my love for her in ways only a real Italian lover can do." Desire flushed her body with warmth and he inched forward, leaning her back on the bed and crawling on top of her. "I want to make love to her and fulfill her every desire."

His lips enclosed on hers in an embrace of passion and an entanglement of heart, as she wrapped her arms around his neck and surrendered to his kiss.

A loud banging on the door brought their moment to an abrupt end, as Andrew scrambled up. "Yes?" Angel hollered through the door.

"Giovanni wants to see you, pronto," Chase said.

Angel opened the door. "Why? What's wrong?"

Chase shrugged. "I dunno, but he's all uptight about something."

Angel, Andrew and Chase rushed down to the meeting room and the moment she entered, Angel knew what Giovanni was upset about. Standing behind him were Milo and Manuel.

Olga and Sophia came walking through the door a few seconds behind Angel. "Hey, there's Moe and Curly," Olga blurted.

"Uh-oh," Sophia exhaled.

"Uh-oh is right," Giovanni huffed. "Lucia, I forbid you to use your taser on my men." He looked at Sophia. "I expect this sort of thing from her," he pointed at Olga, "but I thought you were more refined."

"I'm sorry," Sophia said.

"We're all sorry," Angel added.

"Not only did you taser them, tape them up and hold them prisoner, but they tell me you forgot to set them free," Giovanni's eyebrows raised way into his forehead.

"That's sort of my fault," Andrew said. "Chase and I took them to the bat cave and then, well, we got distracted with everything going on and I forgot they were there."

"The bat cave?" Giovanni narrowed his eyebrows down. "What is this bat cave?"

"It's his really cool-ass lair," Chase piped in.

"You have a lair?" Giovanni shot Andrew a skeptical glance that made Angel giggle. "Michelangela, this is no laughing matter."

"I'm sorry," she put her hands up to hide her smile.

Giovanni gave her a scolding stare. "Do you have something you would like to say to my men?"

Angel nodded. "Milo and Manuel, we are very sorry for what we did. We would normally never behave like this and I hope you will forgive each one of us." She paused and then added, "Just out of curiosity, how did you get free and get back here?"

"The Shark brought us," Milo answered matter-of-factly, and Angel's stomach went hollow, as everything suddenly dropped into that surreal realm of slow-motion.

Chase's face drained of color as he quickly grabbed his .45 and pointed it at Milo and Manuel. "How'd the Shark know where to find your asses?" Chase yelled.

Milo and Manuel's eyeballs looked like they were going to pop right out of their head. "I don't know," Milo blurted.

"Yeah, he just showed up," Manuel added. "He said Andrew sent him."

Chase's eyes widened and he turned the gun on Andrew. "Did you send him?" Chase hollered. "Are you working with the Shark, man?" Angel turned toward Andrew, but he was already headed toward the elevator. Before he could get there, the elevator door opened and two men opened fire.

"Giovanni, get down!" Andrew hollered and Milo and Manuel instinctively dove on top of him, each taking a bullet in the chest. Chase pushed Sophia and Olga behind the mahogany bar and dove in front of them, firing off his .45 and taking down the shooter on the right; while Andrew dropped the shooter on the left.

Andrew grabbed the shooter's guns, put the PM in the back of his pants, and handed the Uzi pistol to Angel. He instructed Giovanni, Sophia and Olga to stay where they were, while he, Angel and Chase secured the floor. The good news was there was only one way onto the floor and that was through the elevator. Of course, the bad news was there was only one way off the floor and that was through the elevator. This made whoever came and went, an easy target.

Chase grabbed his cell and punched in the GPS code. "Tony is two floors up," he blurted.

"Warn him. Hurry!" Angel said. "Tell him the Shark is in the building and he needs to secure Salvatore."

"Right on."

The elevator dinged and Andrew and Angel took aim. As the doors opened, Angel beheld Stefano, covered in blood and gripping his stomach. He took two steps forward and fell face down. "Stefano!" Angel gasped and knelt by him.

"Sh...Sh...Shark," he stuttered and then he was gone.

Rage consumed Angel, leaving no room for tears. She screamed at the top of her lungs. "I will kill you! Show your face, you coward! I dare you and I will send you straight to hell!" Her teeth were clenched and she panted from the adrenaline.

"Stefano," Sophia cried from behind the bar and buried her face in her hands. "Not sweet Stefano."

Andrew grabbed his cell and called the police and then the Venturinis. Within minutes, they could see police cars, fire trucks and ambulances lining the street outside the

Towers and several teams of men entering the building.

Andrew glared at Chase. "Are you done accusing me now, because it's really starting to piss me off."

"Sorry man," Chase bounced his right knee back and forth. "I got a little crazy there."

Andrew shot him a glance that spoke volumes and Angel was certain that Chase wouldn't accuse Andrew of anything ever again.

"Here's the deal," Andrew explained. "None of the police have the code for this floor so they can't get to us here. Obviously the Shark knows the code, which means we are sitting ducks if we stay here. We've got to get to another floor so we can get Olga, Sophia, Salvatore and Giovanni to a secure location."

"Why can't we just stay here and take aim at the elevator?" Angel asked. "When it opens, we kill whoever is in it."

"What if it opens with a grenade in it?" Andrew shook his head. "I got a bad feeling about staying here."

Chase's eyes were wide. "Well, now I got a bad-ass feeling about staying here too. Why'd you have to go and mention grenades and shit?"

"We'll coordinate via phone with Tony, Boglevich, and the Snake. They can get some men to cover the elevator so we can get out."

Angel dialed Tony's phone. "Stay put, Babe," he answered, "I've got you on GPS and we've got a team coming to get you." She could hear gunshots through the phone and the call went dead.

"Andrew, Chase," Giovanni called out, "come, help me over here." He led them to the far wall, where a giant framed picture of New York City hung. "Behind this frame is a way for us to escape."

The frame was enormous and heavy, but the three of them were able to open it on its hinges just enough for everyone to crawl through. They closed it and Giovanni turned the deadbolt. "I designed it to lock from the inside," he said.

"Good thinking," Chase noted.

The stairwell was small, about the width of an average man, and very dark. They had to feel their way using the wall. "There is only one way into this stairwell and it leads to the Penthouse," Giovanni explained. "It will come out in Angel's bedroom, through the back floorboards of her closet."

"Another cool-ass secret passage," Chase beamed. "I love this shit."

Andrew's phone buzzed and it was Tony. "We can't get to the meeting room," Tony panted, "the Shark has us pinned on the Penthouse level." Andrew explained that they were on their way there to help.

The problem was that the Shark knew the building and he had an access card to go wherever he wanted. Anger boiled inside Angel. As they crawled out from the stairwell into her closet, Angel turned to Andrew and Tony. "I don't care what you have to do, I want the Shark dead."

"Got it, Babe," Tony said, checking the clip on his .45.

Andrew instructed the Snake to fly Giovanni, Salvatore, Olga and Sophia to safety.

"Please come with us," Sophia begged Angel.

"I can't," Angel said. "This is personal."

Sophia grabbed Angel. "I love you," she cried.

"I love you too, Mom. I promise I'll see you soon."

Sophia's face went blank. "That's what your father said."

Angel grabbed her mother's hand and squeezed. "I'm not dad and I'm not dying today."

Andrew lifted Sophia into the chopper and the Snake flew them away from the Towers and out of danger.

Chase fired up his computer and tapped into the surveillance cameras all throughout the Towers. "If he's still in the building, I'll find his ass," Chase said.

Tony peered over his shoulder. "Andrew, can you have your men flush him up toward us?"

Andrew got on his cell and a few minutes later they huddled in front of the computer and watched as Chase used the video feed to follow the Shark and his team of men up toward the Penthouse.

"How many men are we looking at? Andrew asked.

"Looks like the Shark's running point, with five on each side." Tony answered.

Andrew spoke into his cell to one of the cops, "we're picking up eleven men on video, now four floors below the penthouse."

"Roger that," the cop answered, "we'll get 'em to your floor and hold 'em there."

"Holy shit!" Chase blurted. "You see what he's carrying?"

Angel looked at the screen and her mouth went dry. She had looked down the barrel of that before and it wasn't any fun. "It's a grenade launcher," she gasped.

Andrew paced while he held his phone like a walkie talkie. "The Shark is carrying a grenade launcher. Repeat. Grenade Launcher. I need back-up to pursue and engage from the rear."

"We're approaching target now."

The Snake returned with the chopper, landed it on the rooftop patio and ran inside, carrying two M60 machine guns and five Kevlar vests. Chase's eyes bugged out of his head like a kid's in a candy store. "Where'd you get the sweet-ass M60s?"

"I got friends in low places," the Snake grinned, handing one of the guns to Chase.

"Righteous!" He blurted.

All of a sudden there was an outbreak of gun fire, heard from the hallway and through Andrew's phone. "They must be engaging from the rear," Tony said.

"Let's hope they're successful," Andrew mouthed.

Angel cringed at the sound of screaming and bullets ripping through bones and hitting walls. Her heart was racing as she slipped into the Kevlar vest and gripped the Uzi.

"Let's get into position," Andrew instructed and paused when a voice came through his phone.

"Six men down. They're wearing vests. We're pulling back. I repeat we're pulling back."

"That means all we've got to drop is the Shark plus four men," Andrew said. "Everybody ready?"

NO! She wanted to scream, as her insides trembled with fear; but on the outside, Angel nodded and took her position.

"They're gonna launch a grenade into the front door and it's gonna blow out this whole front section of the penthouse," Chase frantically warned.

"Roger that, Ace, that's why we're going to be in the back section," Tony barked.

The Snake added, "The explosion is going to make you think your head came off. It'll be loud and it'll hurt your ears and you won't be able to hear anything for several minutes afterwards. We'll need to use hand gestures to communicate."

"I got some hand gestures I'd like to show the Shark," Chase belted and Tony laughed.

"Tell you what, Ace, let's get him in here and while I drop him you can gesture to your heart's content," Tony said.

"Right on," Chase gave a thumbs up.

They all rushed down the hallway. The Snake stood to the left with the M60. Tony stood back by the kitchen with a .45 and a backup .38. Andrew stood to the right with an Uzi pistol and a backup .45. Angel was in the sitting room that led to her bedroom with an Uzi pistol and her 9mm tucked in her jeans. Chase looked at the computer before taking his position to the right of Tony. He took aim with the M60.

"They're going to launch at any second. Everyone get ready," Chase said.

Angel braced for impact, knowing the sound of the explosion would numb her ears. Her instructions were simple. Shoot the bad guys. The problem was she wasn't used to an Uzi pistol and she feared she might accidentally shoot her own men. Her heart raced and beat loudly in her ears.

"They're wearing vests," Andrew told her, "so when you shoot, keep shooting; and if you can, aim high or low."

"Hit the head and they're dead," Tony gave her a wink.

"Got it," Angel exhaled, trying to remind herself to breathe and be calm.

The grenade blew through the front door like it was made of toothpicks. Wood pieces flew everywhere and smoke filled the foyer. Not only did it destroy the front door and the foyer, but the impact exploded all the windows in the family room, showering the room with glass. Even though she wasn't in that room, Angel instinctively ducked and closed her eyes.

Two men appeared through the smoke-filled doorway and opened fire, but the Snake gunned them down and Tony put a bullet through their heads to make sure they were dead. No sense taking any chances. Two more men opened fire from further back in the hallway and Chase and the Snake unloaded the M60's in unison, dropping the men with ease. The hall grew quiet. Chase darted over to his computer and checked the surveillance video. "I'm not picking him up," he yelled, clicking keys and checking the feed.

"Find him!" Andrew hollered.

"I'm working on it," Chase yelled back.

The Snake and Tony kept their guns on the door, while Andrew and Angel joined Chase in the family room. Glass covered the furniture and carpeting, and the smoke billowed out onto the patio.

"Is there any movement anywhere?" Andrew asked Chase, squinting at the computer screen through the smoke.

"I've got nothing," Chase blurted. "It's like he just frickin' disappeared."

"That's part of his charm," Angel stated flatly, remembering when the Shark said it to her at the Barone place. Angel took a few steps toward the shattered windows. She could feel the glass crunching beneath her shoes, as she stepped onto the patio. All of a sudden the Shark's large hand gripped her neck from behind. Angel gasped and dropped the Uzi pistol, causing Andrew and Chase to whirl around.

"Lower your weapons or I crush her esophagus," he rasped in his low voice.

"Lower your weapons," Andrew yelled. Chase laid his gun on the table next to his computer. Andrew slowly set his on the floor. The Snake lowered his M60 but kept one eye on the front door, ready to grab it and fire if anyone appeared in the hall. Tony stood staunch with his .45 aimed at the Shark.

The Shark's grip tightened around her throat and Angel started to feel lightheaded as he blocked the air from reaching her lungs. "I said drop your weapon," he glared at Tony.

"How 'bout I drop you instead?" Tony uttered through gritted teeth.

The Shark bellowed out a deep laugh and raised Angel up to where her body was blocking a clean shot at his head. "Try it," the Shark taunted.

"Drop it!" Andrew yelled, but Tony didn't budge.

"If I drop it she's as good as dead and you know it," Tony held his aim steady.

"If he was going to kill her, he would have done it already," Andrew hollered at Tony. "Lower your weapon!"

"You can't negotiate with him," Tony shook his head.

Angel kicked her legs and her face started to turn purple as the Shark's hand tightened. Andrew hollered at Tony to drop his weapon and Chase slowly slid his hand to the back of his jeans and reached for the PM.

The Shark turned quickly and shot Chase in the thigh. Chase let out a yelp and fell over, gripping his leg and rolling on the floor.

Angel went limp beneath his grip as the Shark lifted his gun and took aim at Chase's head. Tony dropped his aim, pulled the trigger and shot the Shark in his left knee. The Shark let out what sounded like growl, dropping Angel into the broken glass and firing off a shot. The bullet soared into Andrew's chest, flipping him backwards over the arm chair. The Snake dove for his M60, sending a barrage of bullets into the Shark's torso and upper thighs. The Shark flew backwards, through the shattered windows and onto the patio. Catching himself against the patio wall, he went down on one knee, but quickly regained composure and lunged toward Angel. Tony dashed forward in pursuit, firing several rounds into his legs and planting a bullet through the back of the Shark's head. He fell face first into broken glass.

Tony scooped up Angel and carried her inside, while the Snake was helped Andrew up and off with his vest.

"Way to take your time there, Ace" Andrew barked at Tony.

"No shit," Chase moaned from the ground. "What the hell were you waiting for?"

"Excuse me for wanting to make sure it was a good shot," Tony grunted. "I only had one chance to save all your sorry asses."

Andrew grinned. "By the way, thanks, man. I owe you one."

"Actually, you owe me two, but who's counting."

Angel and Chase were loaded into ambulances and taken to the hospital while Andrew stayed behind to fill out police reports and meet with his Captain. There were countless bodies in the hallways, most were Vamloskaya but some, like Stefano, Milo and Manuel were good men who lost their lives.

"How many cops are down?" Andrew asked the Police Captain.

"Four wounded. Two dead." The Captain lit up a cigarette and scowled. "I want a full report on this, and none of that leaving out details to protect your family bullshit. I need to know what we're up against and why I've got dead Russians all over the goddamned city!"

"Yes sir," Andrew said.

"The Mayor is not gonna be happy," the Captain flicked his cigarette butt across the pavement. "I gotta go interrogate some poor schmuck we found handcuffed in one the rooms."

"Who?" Andrew's curiosity peaked.

"His ID says his name is Vincent Carlachi. Ring any bells with you?"

Andrew shook his head. "Not off the top of my head," he lied and watched as the Captain mumbled under his breath and huffed off.

When the police had cleared the building, Tony and the Snake picked up

Giovanni and Salvatore in the helicopter and flew them over the Towers to survey the damage. Giovanni didn't speak, but shook his head and tightened his jowls.

"Bratva!" Salvatore hissed.

When they arrived back at the hospital Giovanni instructed several men to return to the Towers and pack suitcases for himself, Olga, Sophia, Angel and Salvatore.

"Alas," he said to Salvatore, "we will need to acquire some rooms at a hotel for the next couple weeks until the Towers can be repaired."

Angel was examined and then sat in the emergency room, waiting for her release papers when Tony peeked through the curtain and sneaked in. He leaned against the bed where Angel sat. "It's nice to see your skin back to its normal color," he grinned.

"Yeah, funny what happens when you can't breathe," Angel said. "You want to see my necklace of Shark prints?"

He stood up and faced her and she extended her neck and opened her blouse to reveal a large hand print bruised into her flesh. Tony winced. "Sorry, Babe."

"Don't be sorry," she looked up at him and smiled. "You saved me life."

"Again," he teased.

"Though I heard you took your own sweet time," she smirked.

His mouth fell open. "Did Andrew say that? I swear, I save all your butts and he has the nerve to bust my balls about how long it took to do it."

Angel laughed. "I wasn't worried."

"That's because you were unconscious."

"No, before I was unconscious, when he first grabbed me." She looked into Tony's eyes. "I knew you'd save me."

He took her hands in his and gave her fingertips a squeeze. "I'm that predictable, eh?"

"No, I just knew you could make the shot. I remembered being with you and Stefano in the stairwell at the hospital, when Frank Vilachi had Kristen in a headlock; and you dropped him." Angel looked down, sadness and anger welling up as the memory of Stefano dying entered her mind. "You had that same look in your eye today so I knew you'd drop the Shark too."

Tony took his hand and lifted her chin. "I'd drop anyone to save you."

She stared up at him and a twinge of guilt stabbed her. She and Andrew had made some sort of unconventional, unspoken agreement to be together, at least she thought that's what they decided. Now, looking at Tony, the same old confusion rushed in. How could she choose between two men she loved equally, but in different ways? If she was going to try to build some kind of relationship with Andrew, she at least owed Tony an explanation.

She licked her lips and started to speak, but the sound didn't come out. It stopped in her throat and she realized she couldn't say it because she was suddenly petrified. She was afraid to tell him about her conversation with Andrew; afraid he'd leave and she'd lose him completely.

Angel stared blankly. The problem was she needed to face the truth and the truth was her heart wasn't ready to choose between them.

"Tony," she finally managed to say but before she could get the next word out, he slid his hands around her face and gently pulled her lips to meet his. Chills shot up the back of her neck and down her spine as the warmth of his kiss filled her.

When their lips parted and he released her face, she looked up and met his eyes. She knew there was no hiding the fact that his kiss affected her and that a part of her longed for him.

"Someday we need to talk about your text," he whispered, "and the fact that I'm dying to hold you in my arms and make love to you the way we used to." His lips were inches from hers as he spoke. "It feels like a lifetime ago." He brushed his lips lightly against hers. "But I'll wait until you're ready, Babe; as long as it takes."

Tony left the room and Angel thought her heart was going to pound right out of her chest. Her palms were sweaty, her face was flushed and she was angry at her own indecision. *How can I run a Mafia family, make life and death choices, and not be able to choose between two men?* She buried her face in her hands and sighed. Confused didn't begin to describe how she felt. *What am I going to tell Andrew?*

When she was finally released she peeked into Chase's room. "How come her ass gets to go home and I have to stay?" He complained to the nurse, who shrugged her shoulders and left the room. "C'mon," Chase pleaded, "get me out of here. I can't just lie here day and night and do nothing. I'll go freaking-ass crazy!"

Angel laughed. "I promise to come by tomorrow and bring your computer and any other equipment you want."

"Fine," he scowled.

She walked toward the door. "Who've you been making out with?" Chase called after her and Angel whipped around on her heels.

"What!" She exclaimed, her mind racing. *How could he have possibly known I kissed Tony? Did someone see us kiss and tell Chase? Does Andrew know?*

"You got hickeys all over your neck," Chase pointed. "Geeze, you look like you were really going at it."

Angel rolled her eyes. "Those are bruises from the Shark." Mental head slap. *Idiot!*

"Oooooh," Chase said. "I like my story better."

Of course you do, Angel thought, *it involves sex.*

On their way out of the hospital, Tony pulled Giovanni aside and told him about the Barone property. "It's vacant and has plenty of space for all of you. Olga would have a full kitchen to cook in and there's a cellar filled with good wine."

Angel overheard Tony's offer and joined the conversation. "What about the broken windows and glass?"

"I've already taken care of it," he gave her a sideways glance and wink. "I had guys out there fixing it right after it happened, Babe."

"Will it be safe? I mean, the Russians found us there once already." It was a valid question.

"They located us because of Scotrovi's tracking device. Besides, we wiped them out this morning, remember?" Tony made a teasing knock-knock gesture on her forehead and she smiled. He always knew how to make her laugh.

Angel wrapped her arm around Giovanni and leaned her head on his shoulder. "Well, I think the Barone fortress sounds like an offer we can't refuse," she joked.

"Very well," Giovanni said to Tony, "we accept your hospitality. Grazie."

CHAPTER 24

The Snake flew Giovanni, Salvatore, Sophia and Olga to the Barone fortress while Angel and Andrew drove the Tank and Tony and Boglevich followed in Tony's SUV. Andrew helped Angel climb up into the Tank and she immediately noticed the litter box and cat food bowls on the back seat. She stretched her neck to look into the very back of the SUV and saw Midnight and Mo curled up together. Angel shot Andrew a smile. "You picked up my cats?"

"I told you we made a deal. I wouldn't let them die if they stopped being demonic," he glanced at them in the rearview mirror. "Somehow I don't think they have any intention of holding up their end of the bargain."

They rode in silence for a moment and dread began to weigh heavily on Angel regarding the need to tell Andrew she was still torn between him and Tony. *Maybe if we can define our relationship better, I won't need to confess my confusion.* She sheepishly glanced over at him, then took a deep breath and let it out slowly. "I've been thinking about your resigning from the Police Force," she said, "and I think it's not such a good idea after all."

"Oh yeah?" Andrew kept his left hand on the wheel and reached over and held Angel's hand with his right. "Why not?"

"Well, if it wasn't for the police back-up today, we'd have lost against the Shark and his men. We might all be dead."

Andrew nodded. "True."

"I was just thinking that maybe we NEED you on the force?"

"Who's we?"

"Me, for one; and the rest of the families." She released his hand and fidgeted with her fingers. "You're a great cop and I just think you'll regret it if you leave now."

"So you think NOW isn't the right time?" He repeated, emphasizing the word now.

Angel swallowed. "I think maybe the decision is hasty and you should think about it a little longer." She wondered if Andrew was picking up on the fact that she wasn't only talking about his leaving the Force, but also implying that now wasn't the right time for an exclusive relationship.

"Yeah, I wondered if now was a bit premature." He sighed the way a person does when they're disappointed but not surprised, and then he reached over and took her hand, lifted it to his lips and lightly kissed her fingers. "You let me know when it's the right time."

"I'm sorry," she whispered.

He shot her a sideways glance, "don't ever apologize for being honest."

"I don't want to hurt you..." she started to speak and stopped when a broad smile filled his face.

"Sweetheart, I can handle anything as long as I know what I'm up against." He gave her hand a squeeze. "It's complicated right now, I get it; but I've got all the time in the world and I'm not going anywhere."

Olga made herself right at home in the Barone kitchen. "It serves that old Venito Barone right to have us invade his home and drink his wine," she said.

"You do remember Venito's dead, right?" Angel asked her.

"Humph! It still serves him right." Olga held her head high and gloated around the kitchen, preparing homemade pasta linguini, warm bread and wine. "The way I see it, all this stuff here belongs to us anyway," she waved a spatula in the air as she spoke. "He probably bought it with the piso that rightfully belonged to your father."

Angel hadn't looked at it that way, but Olga was probably right. *Now I don't feel bad at all about drinking the wine in the cellar,* she thought.

It felt good to sit and eat together as a family, though there wasn't a lot of talking at the table.

Angel assumed that everyone felt as exhausted and mentally drained as she did.

After the plates were cleared, Tony stepped out onto the patio with Angel. "I'm gonna go home, Babe, but I'll be back early in the morning to meet with Giovanni before he leaves town." He took her left hand in his and stroked the top of it gently with his thumb. "So, don't shoot me when you hear someone coming in."

Angel smiled. "I'm not the one you have to worry about. It's Olga and her taser you need to keep an eye on."

"You're not kidding. She's an animal with that thing." They both laughed and it felt good. Angel sat down on the curved rock wall that outlined the patio and looked out over the small lake. "You like it here, don't you?" Tony said.

"It's funny. It used to be my favorite place on earth."

"And now?" He sat down next to her.

"Now I have as many bad memories here as good ones, so they sort of cancel each other out." She shrugged her shoulders.

He moved closer. "You can't let the bad stuff over-ride the good stuff, Babe." He tenderly pulled her into his shoulder, planting a kiss on the top of her head. "I was thinking that maybe this place could be ours someday..."

Andrew stuck his head out the glass door and Angel instinctively sat up straight, lifting her head from Tony's shoulder. "Sorry to interrupt, man," Andrew said. "I just wanted to let you know Giovanni asked us to stay here tonight."

"Why, so he can have us killed," Tony joked and Angel elbowed him in the stomach.

"Ow," he winced.

"We're never speaking of that again," Angel scolded, and then turned her attention back to Andrew. "Why does he want you guys to stay?"

"He said he wants to meet with us first thing in the morning, before he heads for New York," Andrew explained. Tony and Andrew stared at each other and Angel felt suddenly awkward. "Are you gonna stay?" Andrew asked Tony.

"Are you, Ace?" Tony rebutted.

The corners of Andrew's mouth twitched, as if he were fighting a grin. "Well, I do have some files I need to look at, but I could do that here."

"Why don't you both stay?" Angel interjected and they smirked at each other as each one took a seat on the wall, next to Angel. *Back in the hot spot,* she sighed to herself, trying not to notice that they were both leaning into her.

"What files do you need to look at? Police stuff?" Angel asked.

"No, I have copies of the files from the briefcase Galante was carrying. Chase was going to run every name through the system, but since he's laid up I thought I'd just give them a once over."

"Are you looking for anything in particular?" Angel asked.

"Nope," Andrew exhaled, "just want to make sure nobody slips through the cracks."

"That's a first," Tony teased. "Learned your lesson from the Shark incident, did ya?"

Andrew raised an eyebrow at Tony. "You want to go there?"

Tony shrugged. "Not really. I'm too tired."

"Why don't you go to bed then," Andrew quipped.

"I will when you do," Tony grinned.

Angel did a mental eye roll. *Maybe having them both spend the night was not such a good idea.*

"My dad's already working his way down our list," Tony said, "and there are a lot of people on it. A lot more than I thought there'd be."

"Ours too," Andrew said, "but I guess that's to be expected with over ten years of infiltration."

"It's a shame. I trusted some of the guys on that list," Tony shrugged.

Angel looked up at the sky and tried to convince herself that the chaos was over and her muscles could relax. She knew it would take time, but something felt suddenly wrong.

"Can I see the Galante list?" Angel asked and Andrew retrieved the files from a box inside the door, and handed her the Galante file.

She skimmed the list and her uneasiness grew.

"What's up, Sweetheart?" Andrew asked.

Angel slowly rose to her feet. "Nothing. I was just noticing that the Galante Underboss is on the list and Alexander Carbone, the man with the pregnant wife, isn't."

"That's right, Babe. The people on the list are working with the Russians and the people not on the list are not." He shook his head teasingly. "List equals bad guys. No list equals good guys." Tony looked at Andrew. "Maybe she hit her head harder than we thought."

Angel scanned through several other family lists. "The Shark isn't on any of these lists."

"I noticed that too," Andrew said, "but I think his position was so precarious that no one really knew who he worked for."

Angel flipped to the Andriachinni file and skimmed the list of names. "Dane isn't on the list," she mumbled.

Tony looked over her shoulder. "Maybe the list was made after he was dead."

Angel's heart skipped a beat as her mind replayed the last sentence she heard Kristen utter. *We've got more surprises for you,* Kristen had said. "Omigod," Angel gasped, an all too familiar nauseating knot beginning to form.

"What's up, Babe?"

Angel could feel the color draining from her face. "The lists are reversed." Andrew and Tony stared at her and she felt as if time suddenly froze. "They reversed the names. These lists are people NOT working for the Russians. This is THEIR hit list, not ours."

Tony grabbed his family file. "No, Babe, look," he pointed. "I'm not on here, my dad's not on here, and we would definitely be on their hit list."

Andrew analyzed his family file. "Same here; none of my brothers or my father is listed."

Angel shook her head. "That's because that would make it obvious. The people on this list are the newly made members or the lower ranking cugines. The Vamloskaya knew if doubt were cast on them we would take them out without question. Besides, Scotrovi told us that they had special plans to wipe out all the Bosses, so they wouldn't need to put their names on the list. Everyone knows who they are."

"Holy ..." Andrew started and stopped.

"No way, man," Tony blurted, "that means we're ..."

Andrew interrupted him. "...massacring ourselves."

"Scotrovi told us they were using Galante to stir up trouble among the families and cause infighting, which he tried to do with your two families." Angel studied their faces to make sure they were tracking with her. "What if that was just the first step?" She began to pace. "What if their plan was to cause war between our families, then use Galante to give the lists to each Boss under the guise of cleaning our houses of all traitors; causing us to massacre ourselves, leaving our families weak ..."

"...and making an attack on the Bosses that much easier," Tony piped in.

"So there might still be an attack against the Bosses," Andrew mumbled.

Tony and Andrew both grabbed their phones from their pockets and immediately dialed. Angel went inside and explained to Salvatore and Giovanni what was occurring.

"They've got us killing our own people!" Salvatore yelled and shook his fists, while Giovanni hung his head. They made immediate phone calls to tell their men to stop every ordered hit.

"There is darkness upon us," Giovanni mumbled, rising from his chair and walking toward the hallway. "Gather your things, we are leaving immediately. It is not safe for us to stay here."

No one argued. No one even spoke. A sense of shock hung heavy in the air.

The Snake flew Giovanni, Salvatore, Sophia and Olga to the Marriott on Michigan Avenue, where they acquired the penthouse suite. He instructed Andrew and Tony to return to their families. Andrew took Midnight and Mo with him because cats weren't allowed at the Marriott.

While Sophia and Olga unpacked and settled in, Angel joined Giovanni on the couch that sat in front of large windows overlooking the city.

"I'm so sorry, grandfather," she whispered.

"It is not your doing, Michelangela." He took her hand and squeezed it. "It is your smarts that saved lives today. Just like your father." He gave her a wink. "When I leave in the morning I will leave Boglevich and the Snake here with you." He stood up and began to make his way across the room. Angel thought he looked like he was carrying the whole world on his shoulders. She couldn't remember a time when he looked so frail and weak.

"When will you come back?" She stood and followed him.

Giovanni turned to face her. "You do not need my presence here. "Siete pronto," he said and then translated. "You are ready to lead on your own."

Angel sighed. "I don't feel ready."

"Great leaders never do," he said, "because they are always striving to be better." Giovanni wrapped his arm around her and pulled her in close. "Siete pronto." He kissed her forehead.

"Grandfather," Angel paused and licked her lips. "I'm sorry for the hateful things I said to you."

"And I am sorry for my rage that almost killed your men." He exhaled slowly and loudly. "Your compassion and my anger are perhaps together the perfect balance or the deadliest of all combinations."

She wrapped her arms around him and gave him a tight hug. "Ti amo nonno."

"Ti amo, Michelangela; my beautiful, stubborn granddaughter in whom I am very pleased." He smiled and started toward the hall and then stopped abruptly. "I almost forgot to tell you. I have left a note for you detailing everything you need to know regarding access to accounts, businesses we own; a full overview of our finances and the names of our trusted attorneys, bankers and my Compare."

"You have a Compare?"

"Sì, and my Compare has me."
Giovanni raised his eyebrows playfully and patted her cheek. "Good night."

When Giovanni disappeared down the hallway, Angel stepped outside, onto the patio. She gazed up at the stars and let the sadness drip from her eyes. Despite the great news that Salvatore's men had taken down key players in the Vamloskaya organization in Sicily and thwarted terrorist plans, Angel's heart ached. Too many people had died because of the Vamloskaya. She couldn't help wondering if more innocent men were killed tonight because of those lists, nor stop wishing she had discovered the truth sooner. She gripped the railing on the patio. Anger and sadness consumed her as she thought about the men who died today. It wasn't right. Scotrovi was dead and Angel could only assume they had killed his wife and daughter as well. Though Salvatore promised his men would continue searching for Alonya and Zhanna, Angel knew their chances for survival were slim. Milo and Manuel died to protect Giovanni, which is the job of a good bodyguard; but disheartening nonetheless. Stefano died defending Angel, killing Kristen and trying to warn them of the Shark's attack. He would forever be a true hero in Angel's eyes. In the midst of the joy of victory was the agony of losing good men. Sadness shrouded her heart.

Sophia stepped outside and Olga followed, carrying a tray with three cups of coffee and Cannoli. "Merciful Heavens, what a lovely night," she gazed upward. "I brought us a snack. It's store bought Cannoli so it'll taste like creamy cardboard, but life always looks better with a snack." She set the tray on a small round table and they all sat and nibbled. "Now," Olga clapped her hands together. "I have an idea."

"Il mio Dio," Sophia exhaled. "You're ideas frighten me."

"What?" Olga threw up her hands. "What's wrong with my ideas?"

"They usually end up with people being zapped and me jumping atop a bidet." Sophia's voice elevated and the visual picture she painted made Angel giggle.

"She has a point there," Angel said.

"Humph!" Olga snorted. "This doesn't involve any twitching bodies, well, that is unless we meet with resistance to the idea. Then I might have to zap someone."

"What's your idea?" Angel asked.

"We never really had our girls' vacation. I mean, your mom and I were busy babysitting Moe and Curly, God rest their souls, while you were chasing down Russians," Olga explained. "So, I was thinking that we should go somewhere far away from all this stuff here…" Olga's voice tapered off and she raised her eyebrows high into her forehead. "I was thinking someplace you've never been," she pointed to Angel. "I haven't been there since I was a little girl and Sophia hasn't been back for a long time." A broad grin filled her face. "Are you following me?"

Sophia leaned in close. "You mean Sicily?"

"Bingo!" Olga blurted. "We have a winner."

"I don't know," Sophia bit her lip. "I haven't been home in forever."

"Better late than never," Olga took a bite of Cannoli. "Yep, it's creamy cardboard." She scrunched up her face. "Why are store bought desserts so disgusting?"

"You were saying?" Angel tried to steer Olga back on track, as she had obviously gotten distracted by the Cannoli.

"Yes, I was saying I think we should go." She slapped her hands together. "I bet there are LOTS of hot Italian men over there."

"I'm not looking for a man," Sophia and Angel blurted in unison.

"Merciful Heavens, of course YOU'RE not," Olga waved her hand at them. "You already have two Italian Stallions fighting over you," she said to Angel. "And you have a bad habit of winding up widowed," she said to Sophia and then added. "No offense and God rest their souls." She made the sign of the cross over her body. "I was talking about me. I could use me one fine Italian specimen."

Angel didn't know which was funnier, Olga's raging hormones or Sophia's expression of shock; either way, she burst out laughing and it felt good.

"So what do you say?" Olga leaned forward, "are you in? This has to be a team effort because we might have to convince Giovanni that Angel is depressed or suicidal and needs a GWO."

"I think you mean GNO," Angel corrected.

"She thinks I was born yesterday," Olga grunted to Sophia. "No, smarty pants, I don't mean GNO. Everyone knows GNO is a Girls Night Out and we need a GWO; a Girls Week Out."

Sophia grinned and Angel rolled her eyes.

"Don't be a bunch of stick-in-the-muds. Let's go live amongst the fine looking Italian males, where the wine runs free and the bidets are plentiful." Olga held up her coffee cup in toasting fashion.

"Here, here," Sophia clinked her cup with Olga's but Angel only raised hers slightly. She was mulling the idea around in her mind. *Maybe time away from Chicago, the bogatas, Andrew and Tony is exactly what I need. A new perspective. Maybe then I'll return with an unclouded vision of my life and an uncomplicated heart. Maybe then I will be able to put an end to the violence and all the killing.*

Angel slowly raised her cup higher, clinking it against Olga's and Sophia's. She didn't have all of the answers and most of the time she felt like she didn't have any of them; but one thing was certain, Mafia life was never boring. If you could survive it, you would know that blood is thicker than water, and that the love of family is always there to pull you through the darkest hours. If all else failed, there's Olga, proving that happiness can be found in life's simple treasures... like Tasers and bidets.

ABOUT THE AUTHOR

S.R.Claridge, nominated for the 2010 Molly Award, 2013 Pushcart Prize and awarded the 2011 Rocky Mountain Fiction Writers Pen Award, writes full-time and lives in Colorado. She loves autumn, moonlight and Grey Goose martinis with bleu cheese or jalapeno stuffed olives. She believes Friday nights are for indulging in Mexican food and margaritas and Sunday mornings warrant an extra-spicy Bloody Mary. Growing up in St. Louis, Missouri and earning her BA in Psychology from the University of Missouri, Columbia, S.R.Claridge is a mixture of mid-western family values and western wild nights. She loves Jesus, believes in the power of prayer, in the freedom of forgiveness and that life is a gift that should be enjoyed to the fullest. With a background in theatre, S.R.Claridge creates characters with dramatic flair and is known for her intense plot twists and engaging humor. S.R.Claridge would rather walk dangerously where there's a view than sit in idle safety and let life pass her by. Her spirited outlook comes shining through in her novels, as she takes readers to the edge of their seats with bone-chilling suspense.

AUTHOR ACCLAIM

"The Just Call Me Angel series is suspense at its best."
- RipeReviews

"A unique series from a one-of-a-kind author."
- APEX Reviews

"Riveting!"
- TrueBlueEbookReview

"One thrilling moment after another!"
- CanadaReviews

"A best-seller candidate indeed."
- BookWatchMagazine

BOOKS BY S.R.CLARIDGE

Tetterbaum's Truth *(book 1 in the Just Call Me Angel series)*
Traitors Among Us *(book 2 in the Just Call Me Angel series)*
Russian Uprising *(book 3 in the Just Call Me Angel series)*
Death Trap *(book 4 in the Just Call Me Angel series)*
Loose Ends (*book 5 in the Just Call Me Angel series*)
Divine Intervention *(book 6 in the Just Call Me Angel series)*
Petals of Blood *(short story; Pushcart Prize Nomination 2013)*
House of Lies (*Political cult suspense*)
No Easy Way *(debut novel; nominated for The Molly Award from the HODRW 2010)*
The Candy Shop *(Suspense Thriller)*